D0949849

THIEF'S MARK

CARLA NEGGERS

THORNDIKE PRESS
A part of Gale, a Cengage Company

Farmington Hills, Mich • San Francisco • New York • Waterville, Maine
Meriden, Conn • Mason, Ohio • Chicago

GALE
A Cengage Company

Thorndike Press® Large Print Basic.
The text of this Large Print edition is unabridged.
Other aspects of the book may vary from the original edition.
Set in 16 pt. Plantin.

LIBRARY OF CONGRESS CIP DATA ON FILE.
CATALOGUING IN PUBLICATION FOR THIS BOOK
IS AVAILABLE FROM THE LIBRARY OF CONGRESS.

ISBN-13: 978-1-4328-4076-1 (hardcover)
ISBN-10: 1-4328-4076-2 (hardcover)

33614080431025

Published in 2017 by arrangement with Harlequin Books, S. A.

Printed in the United States of America
1 2 3 4 5 6 7 21 20 19 18 17

To Henk and Christine
and our many good talks
on the veranda.

1

Dublin, Ireland

Colin Donovan eyed his wife of almost two weeks, a glass of champagne in front of her on their low table at the crowded, upscale bar at the landmark Shelbourne Hotel in the heart of Dublin. Since he knew Emma Sharpe as well as he did, he noticed the slight pull in her eyes that indicated tension. "Last night of our honeymoon," he said, leaning back in his comfortable stuffed chair.

She smiled. "We'll make the most of it."

He returned her smile. "We will. You look good, Emma. Rested, happy and rosy-cheeked."

"The rosy cheeks are due to the champagne."

"And the tension I see in those green eyes of yours?"

She picked up her champagne. "I'm in re-entry mode."

Colin got that. They would be back at their offices on the Boston waterfront in a few days. Right now, they could enjoy the views out the tall Shelbourne windows across to St. Stephen's Green as the long June day slowly wound down. Every seat at the polished bar and the tables was occupied with laughing shoppers with their Brown Thomas bags, tourists in sensible shoes and young office workers with loosened ties.

"Then there's Granddad," Emma added. "He's up to something."

Wendell Sharpe was always up to something but Colin knew he didn't need to tell Emma. "Speak of the devil," he said, nodding to the entrance off the lobby.

She followed his gaze, sipping her champagne as she watched her octogenarian grandfather, who lived in Dublin, make his way toward them in his rumpled khakis, sport coat and bow tie. He was semiretired, but no one believed he would ever fully give up his work as a private art detective. Not willingly, anyway. Meeting for drinks at the Shelbourne had been his idea.

He shuddered as he arrived at their table. "Could you two at least try to look less like FBI agents?"

"We *are* FBI agents, Granddad." Emma

set down her glass and rose, smiling as she and her grandfather embraced. "It's great to see you."

Colin got to his feet and he and Wendell shook hands. "Good to see you, Wendell."

"Welcome to Dublin. How was the honeymoon?" He grinned. "Don't answer." He pulled out a chair and sat with a heavy sigh. "I walked from my place. Beautiful day. When did you get in?"

"About an hour ago," Emma said. "We walked in the park and got here about twenty minutes ago. It's the last day of a perfect honeymoon."

"Your secret Irish honeymoon didn't stay secret for long, did it?"

Emma laughed. "It didn't stay secret at all."

"Everyone knows we're here," Colin added, glad to see some of Emma's earlier strain ease.

"You chose Ireland for Emma," Wendell said. "Tough to think of you as romantic."

"Not going there, Wendell."

"Are you making a stop in Dublin on FBI business?"

Emma shook her head, strands of her fair hair falling onto her forehead. She reached for her champagne and sat back with it. "We're here to see you, Granddad."

Colin picked up his Smithwick's. "What're you drinking, Wendell?"

"Sparkling water. I like to keep my head about me with you two."

A typical Wendell Sharpe exaggeration, but Colin ordered the water. He drank some of his beer and contained his impatience. He'd been on alert since Wendell had texted Emma two hours ago and suggested they meet at the Shelbourne instead of at his home a few blocks away.

The sparkling water arrived, and Wendell drained about a third of his glass before setting it on the table and taking a breath. "We're getting looks. I've lived in Dublin for fifteen years but I don't recognize a soul here. I'm an old man. It's got to be you two."

Colin made no comment. They weren't getting looks. It was a diversion tactic. No one near their table was paying attention to them much less sneaking looks at them. He and Emma were dressed comfortably but suitably for their surroundings, not in the hiking clothes they'd worn much of the past ten days in the Irish countryside.

"It's nice of you to invite us here, Grand-dad," Emma said casually. "Any particular reason for the change in plan?"

Wendell glanced around the elegant bar.

"I haven't been here in a while. I thought we should celebrate your marriage at a special place. I didn't make it to your wedding. Least I could do is buy you a drink." He settled back in his chair. "Glad you two didn't order expensive whiskey. I'm retired."

Emma gave him a skeptical look. "Semiretired at best."

Colin stayed out of this one. In the months he'd come to know Emma — as he'd fallen in love with her — he had learned to steer clear of meddling with or even trying to understand her deep-seated, often impenetrable relationship with her eccentric family. Wendell had launched Sharpe Fine Art Recovery sixty years ago in the front room of his home on the southern Maine coast. After his wife's death, he'd returned to the land of his birth and set up a Dublin office. When Colin had planned their Irish honeymoon, he'd included a night in Dublin for Emma to see her grandfather. Wendell had invited them to stay with him. It had seemed like a good way to start the reentry process back to their normal lives. Family, friends, their work with the FBI. No more boutique hotels, cute cottages and long walks in the Irish hills, at least not for a while.

"You two go back to work . . . when?" Wendell asked. "You're flying back to Boston tomorrow, right? They'll let you get home first, do a load of laundry, buy some milk and coffee?"

"We're flying to London tomorrow," Emma said. "We're taking advantage of being on this side of the Atlantic and meeting with a few people."

Wendell frowned. "So you're back to work *tomorrow*?"

"We'll return to Boston for the weekend and be at our desks on Monday."

"I thought Colin didn't have a desk."

"I don't," Colin interjected. "They let me nap on Emma's couch once in a while."

They being HIT, the small Boston-based team Emma had joined early last year and he'd been shoehorned into last fall. He wasn't a good fit, but for the past ten days, he'd had one focus and that was the woman on the other side of the table. It was Wednesday. They had an early flight to London. Emma would meet with her UK counterparts in art crimes, her area of expertise, and Colin would focus on . . . whatever Matt Yankowski, their FBI boss, wanted him to focus on. He and Yank would talk tomorrow. Colin had completed an undercover assignment before the wedding. Yank no doubt would be chewing on a new assignment.

Wendell took another big drink of his sparkling water. "I have a surprise for you. I'm treating you to a night here at the Shelbourne. Figured it's a better choice for the last night of a honeymoon than my guest room."

Emma folded her hands on her middle, eyeing her grandfather with a cool steadiness Colin had come to know and appreciate. "Thank you, Granddad, that's generous of you, but we'd have been happy in your guest room."

"You'll be happier here."

Emma unfolded her hands and touched a fingertip to the rim of her champagne glass, nothing casual about her move. "Are you sure this is a wedding present and you're not having your place painted, or you didn't suddenly discover mold in the walls? It's not a problem if it's inconvenient for you to put us up. We could find somewhere to stay. The Shelbourne is gorgeous, but having a drink with you here is a great wedding gift. We don't want you to go to any big expense."

Her grandfather looked around at the bustling bar. "Princess Grace stayed here back in the day. You've seen pictures of her. She was a beauty. Tragic end to her life." He shifted back to his guests. "This place

13

was built in 1824. I saw that when I booked your room. These walls ooze Irish history."

Wendell was engaging in pure, in-your-face evasiveness. No wonder he'd stuck to sparkling water. Colin snatched up his pint glass and nodded to Emma. "Do you want to get the truth out of him or do you want me to . . . or just forget it and pretend drinks and a night at the Shelbourne are a last-minute wedding gift?"

"They're a surprise wedding gift," Wendell said, unruffled. "They're not last-minute."

Emma sipped her champagne, returned the glass to the table and turned to her grandfather. "But Colin's right, isn't he, Granddad? You *are* hiding something."

Wendell leaned forward, plucked the slice of lemon out of his glass, squeezed it, then tossed it back in and took a drink. "You two missed your jobs while you were on your honeymoon, didn't you? You're rested and ready to pounce on an old man. I shouldn't have mentioned expensive whiskey and being retired. Put you on alert."

"When someone does something out of the blue, out of character, most people will notice," Emma said. "It doesn't take being an FBI agent."

"Helps, though."

Colin gritted his teeth. "Spit it out, Wen-

14

dell. Why don't you want us at your place?"

The old man locked eyes with his new grandson-in-law. "All right. I give up." He paused. "My place is a crime scene."

Emma stiffened visibly. Colin noticed a renewed strain in her Sharpe green eyes. "What kind of crime scene?" she asked quietly.

"Break-in. Someone slipped inside while I was out for a walk after lunch. I didn't have much time to think before you two arrived in town. Putting you up here was the easiest way to handle you until I could figure out what to do." He waved a bony hand. "One of the hazards of having FBI agents in the family."

"You didn't call the police," Colin said, making it a statement.

"No point. Nothing they can do." Wendell gave another sigh. "Damn, I'm getting old. Fifty years ago I wouldn't have spilled the beans this fast. *Ten* years ago. I should have just had you over to the house and handed you a broom to clean up the glass."

Emma's chin shot up. "Glass?"

"Guest-room window. That's how they got in. Do you have a car? Where are your bags? You can check in after your drink. I booked your room under Donovan. I assume you're using Sharpe professionally?"

15

"Unless you land in prison," Emma said. "Then I might reconsider."

"I wouldn't blame you."

"We turned in our rental when we arrived in Dublin and took a cab here. We left our bags with the bellman while we had drinks with you." Emma leaned toward Wendell and put a hand on his thin wrist. "Why don't we finish our drinks and then walk over to your place and have a look?"

"Check in and get settled first. I'll take a cab back to my place and meet you there. A one-way walk's my limit these days."

"You can call the gardai in the meantime," Colin added.

Wendell scowled at him but turned to Emma with a smile. "Take your time. I won't touch anything, but I'm not involving the gardai and the FBI has no jurisdiction here. Just so we're clear."

"Have you told anyone else about the break-in?" she asked.

"No, and I don't plan to. I didn't plan to tell you but Colin here had his thumbscrew look on and I caved." Wendell raised his glass. "Bottoms up, kids."

"Granddad could be overdramatizing and the break-in isn't a big deal," Emma said as she and Colin approached her grandfather's town house near Merrion Square. They'd decided to walk after checking in to the hotel. Wendell had staked them to an elegant, third-floor room with a view of St. Stephen's Green. "It's still possible we can have a good last night of our honeymoon."

"We will no matter what," Colin said.

She smiled. "You've turned into a romantic."

"The Ireland effect."

"Not being with me?"

He winked. "We'll see what happens when we get home."

Home was her tiny apartment in Boston and his house in his hometown of Rock Point, Maine. Now *their* apartment and house. She loved being married to him and had relished every second of their time together in Ireland. She looked at him now, her broad-shouldered, dark-haired undercover-agent husband with his ocean-gray eyes and sexy smile.

But her mind was on her grandfather. "I don't like the coincidence of a break-in and our arrival in Dublin," she said.

Colin gave a curt nod. "I don't, either. Do you think he has a suspect in mind?"

"I don't know. He's being slippery, that's for sure."

"I'm not touching that one."

"Best we stay on our toes when Granddad is in full obfuscation mode."

"Not regretting joining the family business instead of the FBI at the moment, are you?"

"Not at the moment, no. Not ever, actually." She sighed. "Granddad didn't look hurt or freaked out to you, did he?"

"No, but he never does."

True enough, she thought.

When they reached her grandfather's red-brick building, he pulled open the door before she could knock or ring the bell. "I suppose you want to go straight to the crime scene," he said. "Come on in."

Without waiting for an answer, he led them through the entry and front room back to a ground-floor bedroom. He moved aside, and Emma stood on the threshold, Colin to her left and a bit behind her. The room was small and square, with two twin beds, a nightstand, a dresser and photographs of Skellig Michael on the wall opposite the window, which looked onto a terrace at the back of the house. The only sign of a problem was a spiderweb of cracked glass emanating from a fist-size hole in the window.

"Bastard unlocked the window and came right in," her grandfather said behind them.

"Used a gnome statue on the terrace to break the glass. You remember it, Emma. It belonged to your grandmother. Otherwise I'd have left it in Maine. It's a homely little thing. Anyway, I think he went out through the back door. I don't know if it was a man. Could have been a woman."

Colin pointed at the bare tile floor in the bedroom. "No glass."

"I went ahead and swept it up. There wasn't much."

"You shouldn't have touched anything," Emma said.

"Yeah, I know. It would have been easier if I'd left the doors unlocked and he walked in and out again. Less of a mess to clean up and I might never have known anyone had been here. I'd never have looked if . . ." Wendell stopped abruptly. "Never mind. Doesn't matter now."

"If what, Granddad?" Emma asked.

He rubbed the back of his neck. "I spotted a piece of broken glass on the kitchen table when I got back from the pub. That's why I checked in here. The intruder must have taken the glass with him after he climbed through the window. If I'd been here and put up a fuss — well, you know. He could have threatened me or slit my throat."

Colin angled a look at him. "But you didn't see anyone?"

"No one in here or outside. I wasn't here when he broke in and I didn't get my throat slit. And," he added emphatically, "the glass could have been a practical consideration. A tool rather than a weapon, in case he needed to cut something."

Emma frowned. "Cut something?"

He motioned with one hand. "Come."

Emma felt Colin's tension as they followed her grandfather to his study, now his home office and where he spent most of his time. When the weather was dank and chilly, he'd have a fire going, but not today, given the lingering warm, dry June weather. It had rained only a few times during her and Colin's stay in Ireland, but the occasional lazy, drizzly day hadn't gone to waste.

"I turned over most of my physical files to Lucas when I shut down my outside office," her grandfather said. "He went through them when he was here last fall and took what he wanted back to Maine with him."

Lucas, Emma's older brother, had taken over the reins of Sharpe Fine Art Recovery and worked out of its offices in Heron's Cove, a picturesque village on the southern Maine coast. He'd just completed a massive revamp of the offices, located in the same

Victorian house where a young Portland security guard had launched his career as a private art detective. Six decades later, Wendell Sharpe was world-renowned, and Sharpe Fine Art Recovery was a thriving business, but still small in terms of staff. His only son — Emma and Lucas's father — had cut back on his role with the company after a fall on the ice had left him in chronic, often debilitating pain.

"Lucas is considering reopening a Dublin office now that I've retired." Wendell shrugged, waved a hand. "More-or-less retired, anyway. I work when he needs me or I land on something interesting on my own. The rest of my files are here." He tapped his right temple. "I told Lucas what he needs to know for the business. Everything else can go to the grave with me."

"The stuff you want to hide," Colin said.

Wendell snorted. "Damn right but not from the FBI. You and your lot wouldn't be interested. Neither would my family. Most of it's memories, ideas, suppositions, speculations, conspiracy theories . . . mistakes I've made, people whose reputations might be harmed unfairly because of their association with me. I'm an old man. I've done a lot."

Emma sat on the couch. She'd spent

21

countless hours here in her grandfather's study when she'd worked for him before she'd left Dublin for the FBI. She'd wanted to learn everything — about the business, art crimes, his contacts, his methods, his resources. She'd been a sponge. But she eyed him with measures of skepticism, anticipation, curiosity — the usual mix when she was dealing with her grandfather. "What do your files and memories have to do with the break-in?"

He hesitated. "Maybe I jumped the gun."

"Granddad, just tell us everything, okay? Don't make me pry it out of you."

"Rusty after your honeymoon?"

Colin took in an audible breath. "Quit stalling, Wendell."

"All right, all right. It's tricky timing, dealing with a break-in and having your FBI granddaughter and her FBI husband show up. It looks as if my intruder had a look around in here. He didn't toss the place, but there are signs." He pointed to a small, dark wood box on a shelf by the fireplace. "He got in there. It doesn't have a lock but there's no label saying what's inside. Never occurred to me anyone . . ." He didn't finish, instead plopping onto a chair across from Emma.

Colin remained on his feet. "What's in

22

the box, Wendell?"

He clearly didn't want to answer, but Emma knew. She sighed. "It contains the stone crosses our serial art thief sent Grand-dad after his heists."

"Oliver York," her grandfather said. "I don't mind saying his name out loud."

Emma noticed a muscle work in Colin's visibly tight jaw but he said nothing. For most of their Irish honeymoon, they'd managed to avoid talking about, thinking about or dealing with Oliver, a wealthy English-man with a tragic past. He was a self-taught expert in mythology, folklore and legends, a black belt in karate, a sheep farmer, a dash-ing Londoner with an apartment on St. James's Park and an international art thief. He'd launched his art-theft career on a bleak November night ten years ago when he'd slipped into a home in Declan's Cross, a small village on the south Irish coast. He'd walked off with paintings — including two prized Irish landscapes by Jack Butler Yeats — and an extraordinary sixteenth-century silver mantel cross. The police came up empty-handed in their investigation.

Six months later, after a small Amsterdam museum was relieved of a relatively un-known seventeenth-century Dutch land-scape, Wendell Sharpe received a package containing a brochure of the museum and a polished stone, about three inches in diameter, inscribed with a Celtic cross, a miniature version of the one stolen in Declan's Cross. More thefts followed in at least eight cities in England, Europe and the US. After each brazen heist, another package with another cross-inscribed stone arrived at Wendell Sharpe's Dublin home.

Last fall a murder in Boston put Emma and Colin in contact with an eccentric mythology consultant advising on a documentary — Oliver York, it turned out, working under an alias. He was their elusive art thief. Without question. That didn't mean he would ever face prosecution. He knew it, and they knew it. Over the winter, the stolen art — every piece except an unsigned landscape stolen on that first heist in Declan's Cross — had been returned to its owner, anonymously and intact. Oliver, in the meantime, had put his unique skills, knowledge and experience to work for British intelligence.

Given the unique relationship he and her grandfather had, Emma wasn't surprised to hear Oliver York's name, but she'd have preferred not to.

She shifted back to her grandfather. "Is anything else in the box?"

"A few photographs I took years ago in Declan's Cross."

"Would they explain to an intruder the significance of the stone crosses?"

Her grandfather shrugged. "Probably not by themselves. They'd be a clue, though. There's nothing specific in the box or anywhere else in here that connects the stones and the photographs to the thefts or to Oliver. Nothing's missing. The box lid was on crooked. That's the only reason I know the intruder got into it."

"Had the box been sealed?" Colin asked.

"No. Our perp didn't need to use his glass shard to cut through tape."

Emma forced herself to stay focused. Her grandfather was restless, fidgety. "You're sure the box was opened during the break-in?" she asked. "Could someone else have opened it on a different occasion and you didn't notice?"

"I'm positive," he said without hesitation. "And I didn't leave the lid on crooked and forget."

Colin's gaze steadied on her grandfather. "You have a soft spot for Oliver."

"He's an interesting character."

"You visited him at his farm in January. You stay in touch."

"So?"

Stubborn as well as fidgety and restless. Emma eased onto her feet. "Granddad, as you pointed out, Colin and I have no jurisdiction here. We're family. We want to help."

"I know you do." He uncrossed his legs and tapped his fingertips on his knees. "I didn't want to involve you. It's your honeymoon."

"Have you told Lucas about the break-in?" Emma asked him.

"No. No point. There's nothing he can do. He's in New York on business. With the time difference and everything — no point bothering him. I didn't tell your father, either. I can handle this situation on my own. I'm not five."

"You need to get the police in here, Wendell," Colin said.

He rose stiffly, with a small grunt, as if he was in pain. How much was a bit of an act Emma didn't know. Colin sucked in a breath — it was a sign, she knew, he was on his last thread of patience. She pointed toward the back of the house. "Did you go straight to the kitchen when you got in?"

Her grandfather nodded. "Yeah. Maybe I heard something. I don't know."

"Was the back door open or shut?" Colin asked.

"Partially open, like it hadn't been latched properly and the wind caught it. Then I saw the glass and went into the bedroom and saw the broken window. I figured whoever it was must have heard me coming in through the front door and bolted out the back door. Someone looking for cash, drugs — maybe just getting out of the rain."

Colin shook his head. "People don't break a window to get out of the rain."

Emma appreciated the back-and-forth between them. They were both strong, independent-minded men, each in his own way. Her grandfather grunted. "You know how to sweat a guy, Special Agent Donovan."

He grinned. "You're just out of practice. That was nothing. We'll see what the gardai want to do."

"Lock me up."

"Can't say I'd blame them but they probably won't. At least not tonight." Colin dug his phone out of his jacket. "Catch your breath, Wendell. I'll make the call."

Emma wasn't surprised when the gardai couldn't do much, given the delay and little physical evidence. At this point, it was unlikely they'd locate passersby who might have seen something. To complicate matters, the broken window opened onto a small, fenced terrace with a private gate — which her grandfather had left unlocked. Someone walking through an unlocked gate wasn't likely to draw attention.

Once the gardai left, he insisted she and Colin return to the Shelbourne. "Go," he said, opening the front door. "Enjoy yourselves. Room's paid for. It's too late to get a refund."

"I don't like leaving you here alone," Emma said. "You could always stay at the hotel, too."

"Three's a crowd anytime but on a honeymoon?" He shuddered. "No way."

She smiled. "I didn't mean in the same room."

Her grandfather grinned. "I bet you didn't. Relax. I'll be fine. If this guy wanted to harm me, he'd have jumped me when I came home instead of scooting out the back door."

"That doesn't make me feel better, Granddad."

"Lock up," Colin said. "Gate, windows, doors. We'll give you a hand."

"I don't need a hand. Go."

Emma hugged him, kissing his cheek. "Call Lucas and fill him in or I will. Thanks for our night at the Shelbourne. We'll stop by before we leave for London tomorrow."

He returned her hug, kissed her on the cheek. "Always good to see you, Emma." He turned to Colin. "You, too, Colin. Welcome to the family. We'll do better than a broken window next visit."

Once they reached the street, Colin glanced at Emma. "He'll have the whiskey before he locks up the place."

"No doubt. He's tired. He doesn't like to admit he's not forty anymore."

Colin slipped an arm around her. "We still have our fancy room for the night."

She leaned into his embrace. "That we do. I haven't heard from Oliver since he left us the champagne at Ashford Castle our first night here. Do you think the timing of the break-in with our arrival in Dublin is a coincidence?"

"I don't think anything that involves Oliver York and your grandfather is a coincidence."

They crossed a quiet street. "We can see Oliver while we're in England," Emma said.

"*You* can see Oliver."

"You'd let me go on my own?"

Teasing time. As if Colin "let" her do anything. He tightened his hold on her, drew her closer. "I don't know, I think I could get into a submissive Mrs. Donovan."

She laughed. "Oh, you think so?"

His deep blue eyes sparked with humor, and something else. "We can find out tonight."

They walked hand in hand past Merrion Square, one of Emma's favorite spots in Dublin, with its black iron fencing, lush greenery and soothing Georgian ambience. She'd spent countless hours there during her months working shoulder-to-shoulder with her grandfather, learning from him, enjoying his company, his experience, his brilliance as a private art detective and consultant. Everything she'd gleaned she'd put to use in her work with the FBI. The quiet, pristine square had been a pleasant spot to consider her past and her future. Her past had been a stint in a Maine convent. Her future was here, now, with Colin.

Her grandfather had accepted her decision to leave Sharpe Fine Art Recovery, if not enthusiastically at least with his good wishes. "You'll be Special Agent Emma Sharpe the next time I see you," he'd said with a grimace. "I'll never get used to it, but it's what everything you've done to date has prepared you to be. Go catch bad guys, Emma. Stop them. Lock them up. Keep us safe."

Colin tugged on her hand. "Lost in thought?" he asked.

She smiled. "Totally."

He pulled her closer. "It's a beautiful evening in Dublin."

It was, indeed. The warm weather and the prolonged daylight of June had brought the crowds out to the streets. Shops, pubs and restaurants were bursting, and people were flowing into St. Stephen's Green. Although tempted, they decided to skip a walk through the park and returned to the Shelbourne and their elegant room.

A plate of chocolate truffles and two glasses of whiskey were set out on a small table, with a note:

To Mr. and Mrs. Donovan,
  Enjoy the last night of your honeymoon.

Love,
Granddad

Colin lifted a whiskey glass and handed it to Emma. "Your grandfather is impossible, but he does have his charms."

"It was a spectacular ten days, wasn't it?"

"Yes. Spectacular."

She nodded to the note. "I like the sound of Mr. and Mrs. Donovan. I'll have an easier time in Rock Point as a Donovan."

"You think so?"

"Your brothers won't think you're manly if I go by Sharpe."

"That'd ruin my reputation for sure." He picked up the second glass. "I don't care what you call yourself, you know."

"I know. I'm learning to tease like a Donovan. I love being married to you whatever anyone calls me. We'll be home soon enough. Right now, we're on our honeymoon."

His gaze settled on her. "Yes, we are."

A warmth spread through her. She clinked her glass against his. *"Sláinte."*

Colin smiled. *"Sláinte,"* he said, and he set his glass and then hers back on the table.

2

"Just because something is old doesn't mean it's an antique of any quality," Oliver York said. "It could be rubbish."

Martin Hambly withheld his irritation. Henrietta Balfour, a local garden designer, was either preoccupied with her bucket of loam or ignoring Oliver, or perhaps both. Martin had hired her but Oliver was paying her. They were gathered outside the potting shed, located in a small, centuries-old dovecote on the southern edge of the York farm. The farm itself was located on the outskirts of the tiniest of Cotswold villages, a short drive to the busy market town of Stow-on-the-Wold. Martin had expected Oliver to stay another few days in London, but he'd returned last night. He would have thought a lazy morning was in order, but now here Oliver was, offering input in mat-

33

ters in which he'd never displayed any interest prior to ten minutes ago. For reasons Martin couldn't fathom, Oliver had decided to contribute his opinion of an old pot Henrietta had unearthed. She'd discovered it out back in a heap of discarded gardening materials, created when Oliver had converted part of the dovecote into a stone-cutting studio. At first, Martin had thought it just another of Oliver's solitary hobbies. Not quite the case.

Martin had worked for the Yorks for decades. He'd promised Nicholas and Priscilla York on their deathbeds he would never abandon their orphaned grandson, no matter how frustrating, annoying and outrageous Oliver could be.

Some days that promise was easier to keep than others.

Today wasn't one of those days.

Oliver had gone to London on his own last Friday and hadn't required Martin's assistance at the York home on St. James's Park. That could mean he'd been on a clandestine mission for MI5 or he'd discovered more stolen art he needed to return to the rightful owners — or he'd simply had a stack of books he'd wanted to read without Martin hovering about. They never discussed Oliver's decade as a brazen art thief or his current work with MI5. For that matter, his reading list was off-limits for discussion, too.

Old pots, however, he would apparently discuss.

"This pot belonged to your great-grandmother, Oliver," Martin said, fingering the slightly chipped terra-cotta pot. "It has *soul.* That's the point, not its monetary value."

"If you insist."

Oliver stood straight. He was in his late thirties and exceedingly fit, with wavy, tawny hair and the sort of looks that drew women to him, although he'd yet to marry or even have, as far as Martin knew, a long-term romantic relationship.

And Martin would know.

Oliver turned to their garden designer. "Henrietta?"

She raised her warm blue eyes to him. "Old rubbish with soul?"

Martin could have cheerfully dumped the pot on their heads. It was half-filled with soil — not the sterile kind from a bag, either. He'd personally dug loam from the hillside behind the dovecote. Henrietta had protested but he'd won that battle, if with the compromise that she could top off the pot with her preferred professional mix of soil.

Professional dirt. Martin had never heard of such a thing.

After years of neglecting the farm's gardens and overall landscaping, Oliver had taken Martin by surprise when he'd suggested they hire a garden designer and even provided Henrietta's name. She'd recently moved from London into a nearby cottage she'd inherited from Posey Balfour, her grandfather's never-married only sister and long a fixture in the village. Martin didn't like to think of himself as shallow, but he hadn't paid much attention to Henrietta in years and noticed at their first meeting about the gardens that she bore little resemblance to plain, gangly Posey, who'd died last summer in her midnineties. Henrietta was attractive with her mop of reddish-brown hair, her warm blue eyes and her pleasing curves. In her midthirties, she had a penchant for long, flowered skirts that she wore with a faded denim jacket or a battered waxed-cotton jacket and sturdy walking shoes. When conditions called for them, which they often did, she would don olive-green Wellingtons. How she managed her work in a skirt was beyond Martin, but she did occasionally pull on baggy pants, which also looked fine on her.

Perhaps Henrietta's presence explained Oliver's sudden acquiescence to professional help with the gardens and his early return from London. They'd known each other since they were small children, but she'd worked in London until recently and he'd . . . Well, Oliver had a variety of ways he kept himself busy.

Henrietta's extended visits to the Cotswolds had started when she was five or six, most often on her own. Her parents, born-and-bred Londoners, loathed Posey's "chocolate box" village. They'd steal away on exotic holidays, leaving Henrietta to amuse herself by helping her great-aunt with her gardens. Although she'd had no children of her own, Posey had doted on Henrietta, the only other female Balfour.

Martin had been heartened by Oliver's interest in his somewhat neglected landscaping but suspected it had more to do with his attractive garden designer. He and Henrietta had played together as children, creating an easy familiarity that still existed between them. Martin didn't want to read too much into his observations. Oliver could have ulterior motives. He often did. Martin had learned to be wary. He didn't like to be a suspicious sort but it came with keeping his promise to Nicholas and Priscilla.

At the same time, Martin had to acknowledge an undercurrent, warning him something about Henrietta Balfour's charming eccentricities was off — not faked so much as unpracticed. Perhaps her move to the Cotswolds from London and her radical career change explained the disconnect.

She dipped her gloved hands into the bag, set on the worn stone landing in front of the dovecote. "Sentimental value counts for something, don't you think, Oliver?"

The pair were familiar enough with each other they'd never bothered with "Mr. York" and "Ms. Balfour." Oliver didn't answer. Instead, without a word or so much as a grunt, he gave a curt wave, spun around and shot back out to the narrow lane that ran along the southern edge of the farm. It was a gray morning but it wasn't wet, although there was talk of rain later in the day.

Henrietta rolled back onto her heels and frowned, hands deep in the bag of soil. "He can be like that, can't he?"

Martin knew there was no point denying the obvious. "He can."

"The lads down the pub say he can be dashing and sweet, too."

Not in Martin's experience, but he let it

go. "What kind of flowers do you have in mind?"

"Depends where we decide to put the pot. It's a gem, isn't it? I do like the idea of having it out here."

"You love old rubbish, do you?"

She smiled, her eyes lighting up despite Oliver's rudeness. "Especially if it has sentimental value. Does Oliver remember his great-grandmother?"

"It's possible. She died when he was three."

"I don't remember, of course, her but you must."

Martin nodded. "I do. She was a lovely lady. She expanded the gardens here, although it was her daughter-in-law, Oliver's grandmother, who converted the dovecote into a potting shed."

"I remember Priscilla, of course. She and Aunt Posey were friends." Henrietta dumped two heaping handfuls of soil into the pot, atop what he'd dug from the hillside. "We're not going to discover Oliver bought this pot at a white-elephant sale and forgot about it, are we?"

"I'm sure we won't. I can vouch for it. I remember his great-grandmother planting flowers in this very pot."

"It's a forgotten family heirloom, then.

What kind of flowers were they, do you recall?"

Martin managed a genuine smile. "Dahlias. Peach-colored dahlias."

Henrietta smiled again, wispy curls escaping her hair clip. "Perfect. Consider it done."

Martin left her to her work. He didn't see Oliver, or anyone else for that matter, on the lane, part of one of the marked, public walking trails that crisscrossed the Cotswolds. He could hear Henrietta humming now that she was rid of both him and Oliver. Continuing simply to tend the gardens was no longer sufficient but the process of overhauling them would take time. Martin had seen her in recent years on her visits with her aunt, but he knew little about her life in London. She was friendly and amusing, but she didn't invite that kind of intimacy. Although charming and delightful in many ways, she was all about her work. These days discovering old pots was Henrietta Balfour's idea of excitement.

Martin walked up the lane toward the farmhouse. After a spell of warm, clear days, he appreciated the cloudy sky and looked forward to a shower. The gray weather brought out the smells of early summer and suited his mood. He hadn't missed joining

Oliver in London, but he had to admit to a certain uneasy restlessness. It wasn't like Oliver to go *this* long without getting into some kind of trouble. Even MI5 hadn't contacted him in weeks. Oliver hadn't acknowledged he was working with British intelligence — and he never would — but Martin knew better. There were subjects between them that were understood but never discussed and that was one of them.

A scream penetrated his brooding. He jumped, nearly tripping. His first thought was an accident involving one of the farm workers. Then he realized it was Ruthie Burns, Oliver's housekeeper. In another moment, he spotted her at the lane's intersection with a path up to the main house. She was running madly toward the dovecote, her arms pumping at ninety degrees at her sides as she picked up speed.

"Help! He's *dying.* Dear God. Help!"

Although not one of Martin's favorite people, Ruthie wasn't prone to hyperbole or overreacting. He felt a jolt of adrenaline. Did she mean Oliver? Was *he* the one who was dying?

Henrietta burst up the lane from the dovecote. "What's happened?" she asked, intense but steady. She'd removed her garden gloves and didn't seem impeded by her long skirt.

"I don't know yet," Martin said.

She pointed a slender, dirt-covered hand up the lane. "That's Ruthie, isn't it?"

Martin nodded. The stout housekeeper was in her sixties, a few years older than he was, and had worked for the Yorks almost as long as he had. He felt an unwelcome tightness in his throat but forced himself to maintain his poise and equilibrium. Hysteria wouldn't do anyone a bit of good.

Henrietta started toward Ruthie. "No," Martin said. "Stay here. I'll handle whatever's happened."

"Not alone, Martin. I'm going, too."

He took in her natural sense of command, her composure, her directness — and he knew. He'd been expecting them to emerge. Any suspicions he'd had about her had transformed to certainty.

Henrietta Balfour was MI5.

Martin shook off the thought. Who and what Henrietta was didn't matter now. They needed to get to Ruthie and find out what had her in a panic. He pushed forward but didn't break into a run. Henrietta eased next to him, clearly holding herself back from charging ahead. She was younger and fitter, but it wasn't just that. She hadn't hesitated. She'd relied on training, experience — perhaps just her nature but Martin doubted it. It was something more.

In thirty seconds, they intercepted Ruthie. She was breathless and red-faced, barely able to speak. Martin touched her arm. Accidents and crises weren't unheard of on the farm. She'd dealt with many of them herself over the years. "Ruthie," he said gently. "What's happened?"

"A man. I didn't get a good look at him. There's so much blood." Her eyes welled with tears. "It's awful, Martin. Just awful. I think he's dead."

"Where's Oliver?" he asked, trying to stem her panic as well as to get information.

"He's there. He was trying to help him. The man who was bleeding. I don't know what happened."

"Have you called for an ambulance?" Henrietta asked.

Ruthie looked stricken, as if she'd done something wrong. "No, no — I didn't. Oliver, I thought he . . . No."

"Call 999 at once, in case Mr. York hasn't had a chance to ring them," Martin said.

"I have my mobile . . ." Ruthie mumbled.

"Shut the door first and lock it," Henrietta said. "Then make the call."

Ruthie gulped in air. "You don't think . . . Surely it's an accident."

"We want to be on the safe side," Martin said softly.

"Of course." Sweat mixed with drizzle and streamed down the older woman's temples. "You two take care."

"We will," Henrietta said.

Ruthie sniffled and lurched forward, picking up her pace as she ran toward the dovecote.

Henrietta turned to Martin, who knew he had to look both annoyed and shocked. "I'm good in an emergency," she said, then gestured toward the house. "Shall we?"

Given her uncompromising manner, Martin didn't consider arguing with her to stay with Ruthie and let him go alone. He didn't want to waste time on what he knew in advance would prove to be a futile effort. She started off, and he fell in behind her.

Skirt or no skirt, Henrietta could move. As they charged up the private drive that curved to the main entrance at the side of the gracious stone house, Martin was pushing hard in an effort to keep up with her quick pace. The drive ended at a parking area surrounded by mature hedges, trees and flowerbeds. She glided onto the flagstone walk. He huffed and puffed a step behind her, his sense of dread mounting.

Violence had devastated the Yorks thirty years ago, but it had occurred in London — never had violence touched the York farm.

But Martin warned himself against leaping ahead. He didn't know what had happened.

Henrietta slowed her pace and thrust out an arm, as if he were a five-year-old about to jump into traffic. He saw the door standing wide-open. His first thought was that Oliver must have grabbed Alfred, his wire-fox-terrier puppy, for an urgent walk. Wouldn't *that* be a welcome change? Martin cared for him when Oliver was away, but had dropped him at the house before heading down to meet Henrietta to discuss dirt and flowerpots.

"There," she said, pointing at the entrance.

Martin lowered his gaze as if by the sheer force of her pointed finger. It took a half beat for him to grasp what he was seeing.

A man lay sprawled facedown on the stone landing in front of the threshold. Blood had pooled around him on the pavement.

Henrietta cursed under her breath. "I hope Ruthie's called the police." She lowered her hand. "Do you know this man?"

Martin pretended not to hear her. *Did* he know him? *No. It can't be.* His knees wobbled, but he forced himself to focus. "I should check for a pulse."

"He's gone, Martin."

There wasn't a note of doubt in her tone. He blinked at her. "Dead?"

She gave a grim nod. "I'll check to be absolutely certain, unless you'd rather —"

"No. Please. Go."

She hadn't waited for his answer, regardless, and was already stepping forward, circling the pool of blood. She bent from the waist, touched two fingers to the man's carotid artery and stood straight, stepping back, shaking her head. "Dead. No question. We need to wait for the police."

"Oliver . . ." Martin stifled an urge to vomit, shock and what he took to be the smell of blood taking their toll. "Ruthie said Oliver was here. He was helping . . ."

"Well, he's not here now. There's no sign he administered first aid. The man's upper arm was cut. I didn't get a good look at the wound, but with this much blood, he must have nicked his brachial artery. He'd have had only minutes to get help. Oliver must have been too late."

"How do you know these things?" Martin asked, gaping at her.

"What?" As if everyone knew. She waved a hand. "BBC."

"I should check inside. Maybe Oliver is ringing the police."

She shook her head, firm, knowledgeable. "I don't think so, Martin. Look. His car isn't here."

Martin glanced behind him at the empty spot along the hedges. Oliver had left his Rolls-Royce there last night, instead of parking it in the garage. "Oliver mentioned last night he wanted to go out today." Martin heard how distant his voice sounded — his tone one of shock, disbelief — but at least the nausea had passed. "I noticed when I went down to meet you at the potting shed."

"Did he say where he planned to go?"

"No, he didn't. I'm not sure he had a plan."

Henrietta adjusted her skirt, which had gone askew in the charge up to the house. "Why would he run?" she asked, her tone neutral.

Martin didn't answer. It was a loaded question, anyway.

She peered at the dead man. "I haven't seen him before that I can recall. Have you?"

The woman was relentless. MI5 wasn't far-fetched at all. "I don't think . . . at least I'm not certain . . ." Martin stopped himself. He didn't need to speculate and didn't want to lie, but he hated stumbling around for what to say, no matter the provocation. Time to get hold of himself. "I can't say for certain I've seen him before. We get a lot of walkers on the south lane this time of year. I seldom pay attention to them."

"All right, then."

He heard the skepticism in Henrietta's tone but let it be. He glanced at the dead man, hoping to take in more details of his appearance, but he felt another surge of nausea and turned his head quickly, if too late. He'd seen enough. Much of the man's blood had emptied onto the landing and oozed onto the pavement. What a dreadful sight it must have been when he was alive, his heart pumping arterial blood. Martin hadn't noticed blood on Ruthie, but Oliver, if he'd been helping this man, surely he would have been sprayed with blood.

Martin felt the bottom of his shoe stick to the pavement. He looked down and saw he'd stepped in a smear of blood himself. Ruthie hadn't exaggerated. There was a great deal of blood. He felt bile rise in his throat. "Someone else could have taken the car," he said, forcing himself to keep his wits about him. "There are several routes on and off the property. One of the workers or a walker might have seen the car leaving and might even be able to identify the driver. Ruthie was in a panic. She could have been mistaken and it wasn't even Oliver she saw."

"Perhaps," Henrietta said.

She was humoring him. Martin felt a surge of irritation but knew it wouldn't help. She was right. Of course Ruthie wasn't mistaken. "My point is we don't have enough information to draw any conclusions." He stared at the open door. "I shouldn't wait. I need to search the house —"

"No, Martin. The police will be here shortly. They'll check the house. They'll deal with any possible intruders or additional casualties. We'll only muck things up sticking in our noses now."

Her self-assurance, decisiveness and brisk efficiency snapped Martin out of his stupor of shock and worry. If not oblivious to the blood and death at their feet, Henrietta was remarkably focused and steady. No panic, no wild speculation, no fear.

He turned to her with a cool look. "You speak with authority for a garden designer."

She gave the smallest of smiles. "One learns to be decisive when planning gardens."

No doubt true, but he was now convinced she was MI5. Her grandfather, Posey's older brother, Freddy, had been a legend with Her Majesty's Security Service. Henrietta obviously took after him — except for the heavy smoking and penchant for opera.

"Come." She pointed toward the edge of the driveway, where the hedges grew tall. They were an item on the long list of garden-related tasks, but Martin saw she was pointing at a stone bench that had occupied the spot in front of the hedges for decades. "Let's have a seat there, shall we? The police will be here in a matter of minutes."

Martin followed her to the bench but he didn't sit. She did, crossing one leg over the other, skirt only slightly askew. He peered at the dead man, attempting to absorb the details of his appearance, his attire, his injuries. They were a jumble. He was reeling, fighting a sense of urgency that had purpose but no direction. "Is anyone in the house?" he shouted. "Do you need assistance?"

Henrietta frowned at him, but he ignored her. He remembered his solemn promise to Priscilla York he would look after her only grandson. She'd known it would be difficult. "Oliver has his ways, Martin. Don't be too hard on yourself when he goes astray, as he surely will."

He steadied himself, taking in the pungent scent of the evergreen hedges. He calmed himself and peered again at what he could see of the man sprawled at the door — what *was* clear and not out of his view or blurred by fear, shock, adrenaline and horror.

The man looked to be in his fifties.

The right age.

Martin allowed himself a moment to listen to birds singing in the trees behind him, but he couldn't do it. He felt himself being transported to the past, against his will . . . to the arrival of the police and the unfathomable news that Charles and Deborah York were dead — murdered in their London home — and their young son was missing. At that moment, his own life had been forever changed. He'd been here on the farm. He'd wanted to run, as he did now.

He'd located Nicholas and Priscilla and sat vigil with them through those tense, grief-filled days, every second seared into his memory. Eight-year-old Oliver had escaped from the Scottish ruin where the two men who'd killed his parents had taken him, with the hope of earning a hefty ransom in exchange for the boy's safe return to his family. A priest out for an early morning walk had come upon him and taken him to safety. Young Oliver identified the killers and kidnappers as Davy Driscoll and Bart Norcross, two men in their midtwenties who had done groundskeeping and a variety of odd jobs in London for Charles and Priscilla. They'd worked on a contract basis and had quit a short time before the murders.

Physical and circumstantial evidence confirmed the boy's eyewitness account.

For their part, Driscoll and Norcross disappeared as if into thin air.

Until today.

Martin raked his hands through his grayed hair. He was aware of Henrietta silently watching him from the bench, but he didn't care. He could be letting his emotions get the best of him. He could be wrong and it wasn't Davy Driscoll lying dead before him.

He didn't need to panic or go off halfcocked. He hadn't known either killer well. They were wanted men. With no credible sightings of them and no leads, *surely* they'd altered their appearance and adopted new identities.

The face of the dead man, the line of his jaw, his slight build, his age . . .

Was he Davy Driscoll?

Martin sighed heavily. He was certain it was.

Almost.

He wondered how the dead man had

sustained his fatal injuries. A knife wound? A gunshot? Martin hadn't heard gunfire and assumed no one else had, either. He shuddered. Never mind the shock that had seized him — he made no pretense of expertise in violent death, whether accidental, self-inflicted or the work of another.

He could hear approaching police cars. The York farm had always been a refuge, not just for Oliver, but for him, too — for all those who loved the land, its history and the family. The violence done to Charles and Deborah and their young son had occurred in London, not here.

"Alfred . . ." Martin bit back fear. "He was here when I left the house."

"Oliver didn't bring him to the potting shed. He probably returned Alfred to your cottage before he came down."

It had to be the case. The puppy would have been out the open door, yapping at their feet by now, and he was trained to stay close and wouldn't have gone far. Martin shut his eyes. "Oliver," he whispered, "where the devil are you?"

"Good question," Henrietta said.

He opened his eyes and turned to her. "You weren't supposed to hear that."

"I know."

She didn't look ruffled by his gruffness.

53

She seemed sincerely troubled by the day's events, but if she *was* MI5, she'd be able to fake sincerity. "Oliver isn't a killer," Martin said.

Henrietta turned by a tall, cracked stone urn. Her eyes had an unexpected, genuine warmth to them. "Of course he isn't."

3

London, Heathrow Airport

Emma eased toward an empty carousel, away from the throngs in Heathrow's crowded baggage claim. She hadn't expected a call. It was an unknown caller. She almost let it go to voice mail but instead answered with a simple hello, without using her name.

"Dear Emma. Where are you?"

She recognized Oliver York's voice and slowed her pace. "Heathrow. Did you get my voice mail?"

"This morning. Yes. You and Colin want to see me. Why?"

"We'll come to you. Are you in London or at your farm?"

"I didn't do it."

Emma went still. His voice was ragged, barely a whisper. This wasn't the irreverent, relentlessly good-natured Oliver York she knew. "Do what, Oliver?"

"I didn't kill that man. I tried to help him. I don't know if it was murder, suicide, an accident. I don't know anything. Tell the police. They're looking for me."

"Oliver, talk to me. Where are you?"

"I'm going dark. I trust you. Trust me. Colin and I will never be friends now." His attempt to return to his natural cheekiness fell flat. "I hope you two had a fabulous honeymoon."

"I can't help you if you go dark," Emma said. "We'll come to you."

He was gone.

She slid her phone into her tote bag and rejoined Colin at their baggage carousel. He'd collected their bags, hers a wheeled case, his a duffel he had slung over his shoulder. They'd packed more than they would have for a typical business trip. They'd put together the meetings at the last minute but were dressed professionally in clothes that had seen them through nights out in Ireland.

She told him about Oliver's call. "He's in trouble, Colin."

"Damn right he is. I just got a call from my MI5 contact. Oliver took off from his farm this morning and left behind a dead body."

"Who?"

"They don't know yet. It was a quick call. He wants our help. He'll pave the way for us to talk to the detectives." Colin hoisted his bag higher on his shoulder. "Looks as if we're renting a car and driving to the Cotswolds instead of taking the train into London."

Emma absorbed the change in plan. She didn't know Colin's MI5 contact, just that they'd met during his first undercover mission five years ago. She raised the handle on her bag. Matt Yankowski, their boss in Boston, would want to know she and Colin had landed in the middle of a British death investigation involving Oliver York. "We need to check in with Yank."

"Have at it."

"It's your MI5 contact."

"It's your art thief on the lam and your grandfather whose house was broken into. If we walked into a bunch of arms traffickers, I'd make the call. I'll rent the car." He dipped a hand into her jacket pocket and withdrew her phone, then folded her fingers around it and winked. "Tell Yank I said hi."

"All right. It does make sense that I make the call. I'll check with my brother at the same time to see if he knows anything about the break-in."

Colin took the lead as they switched their

route and started toward the car rental kiosks. Emma unlocked her phone and hit Yank's cell phone number. It was early in Boston but Yank picked up on the first ring. "I just had a call from MI5. They know you're in London and called Oliver York this morning, asked if you have an idea where to find him. Imagine that."

"We don't know where he is. Do they know the identity of the dead man?"

"Not yet. Where's your grandfather?"

"I haven't been in touch with him since we left Dublin. We stopped to see him on the way to the airport. He was having tea on the terrace."

"Has Oliver been in touch with him?"

"Not that I'm aware of."

"Will he now that he's on the run? Those two have an unusual friendship."

"Anything is possible," Emma said.

"Keep me posted. I'll see what we can do on our end."

Yank disconnected without further comment. A short conversation. Emma pictured him at his Back Bay apartment with his wife, Lucy, a clinical psychologist who'd opened up a knitting shop on Newbury Street after balking at moving from their home and her work in northern Virginia. As unorthodox and risky as his brainchild,

58

HIT, was, Yank was a straight arrow. Late forties, chiseled good looks, crisp suits and dedicated to the FBI. He'd known what he was getting into when he'd gone after her — an ex-nun and a Sharpe — to join the FBI and then to become a part of his unique team.

She dialed an art-crimes detective she knew at Scotland Yard, and he put her in touch with the detective chief investigator leading the inquiry into the death at Oliver York's farm. He listened attentively and instructed her and Colin to come straight to the farm when they arrived in the village.

The calls to her grandfather and her older brother, Lucas, who ran Sharpe Fine Art Recovery, were easier. Neither answered. She left voice mails and caught up with Colin. He had the paperwork finished for their rental car. They'd be on the road to the Cotswolds in no time.

"How'd it go?" he asked her. "Did Yank ask if we had a good time on our honeymoon?"

"He did not. I wish we'd run into arms traffickers. They're more straightforward than Oliver York."

"But nowhere near as charming."

A few minutes later, they were on the road,

heading west to the rolling hills and classic honey-stone villages of the picturesque Cotswolds. Colin was doing the driving. Emma was preoccupied, thinking about Oliver's call. "You know this has something to do with the break-in at Granddad's."

"What do you want to do?"

"I left him a voice mail. I left Lucas a voice mail, too. I'll try Granddad again."

She was almost surprised when he answered. "Emma," he said. "You're in London?"

"Just landed. What are you up to?"

"Contemplating finding a hardware store to fix my broken window."

That didn't sound suspicious, and there was nothing suspicious about his tone. "Has Oliver York been in touch by any chance?"

"No." A pause. "Why?"

"Something's happened. I'm not sure what I can tell you at this point. Let me know or let the gardai know if Oliver gets in touch. And keep your doors locked."

"Don't talk to strangers and drink my milk. Got it."

"Granddad . . ."

"It's okay. I can tell whatever's going on is bad."

"I just want you to stay safe."

"Always," he said.

Colin glanced at her after she'd hung up. "First day back on the job," he said.

She stared out the window at the busy motorway. "It's going to be a long one."

4

Near Stow-on-the-Wold, the Cotswolds,
England

Henrietta walked home after the police
finished with her. They'd blocked off en-
trances onto the York property, including
the lane that ran past the dovecote potting
shed and was part of a waymarked trail.
Walkers out for the day, unaware of the
events that morning, would have to take a
detour, at least until the scene was cleared.
Henrietta had witnessed deaths and seen
corpses in her previous life but never one
involving a childhood playmate as a witness
— a man as enigmatic, frustrating, larcenous, tortured and sexy as Oliver York.

He was maddening, and he was the reason
she had quit MI5.

That was the short answer, at least.

She continued along a dry wall, constructed God knew when, of the region's
ubiquitous yellow limestone. Oolitic Juras-

sic limestone, it was called. She'd thought she'd needed to know that as a garden designer, but no one had yet to ask. She wasn't concerned about running into a mad killer. The police hadn't been, either. She'd take care, of course, but whatever had happened behind her at the York farm, it hadn't been random.

She crossed a bridge over the same shallow stream that ran behind the York dovecote. The paved lane would eventually take her into the village, but she needn't go that far — never mind the temptation to. It'd been a day. She'd love nothing better than to spend the rest of it at the pub.

Instead she turned onto a narrow lane, lined with more honey-stone walls, and came to what was still known as the Balfour farm. Her great-grandparents had purchased it in 1909 as a country home and working sheep farm. They'd proceeded to have three children — Freddy, Posey and Anthony — and had left the entire property to Freddy, the eldest Balfour and only surviving son, Anthony having died young. Freddy had promptly turned over most of the acreage to tenant farmers. He'd spent holidays — not *every* holiday — at the house and let friends and colleagues use it for getaways, but he'd never had a great affinity for the Cotswolds or country life. Surprisingly, he'd moved to the farm after he lost his wife to a stroke. Widowed, his only son busy with his own life in London, Freddy had enjoyed several good years before he developed lung cancer and died in his Cotswolds sitting room at age seventy-seven. Henrietta had been only five, but she remembered him, her chain-smoking grandfather with the kind eyes. She hadn't known then, of course, that Freddy Balfour was an MI5 legend and British hero. That had come later.

Posey Balfour had fallen in love with the Cotswolds as a young girl and couldn't imagine living anywhere else. The family had carved out a lot for her, and she'd built her own home, where she'd stayed, content, for the next seventy years. Henrietta's father had sold the rest of the original farm after Freddy's death. As far as she knew her dad had never considered keeping it.

She came to her great-aunt's house.

My house now.

She was relieved to see only her Mini and not Oliver's Rolls-Royce in the drive.

A silly thought, that he might have come here.

"Blast it, Oliver, where *are* you?"

Normally she would drive to work in order

to haul tools, pots, seedlings, bags of soil and supplies — her Mini amazed her with its hauling capacity — but that morning she'd walked. She'd been working at the York farm for two weeks straight and had everything she needed there. The day had started with sunshine, but she enjoyed walking even in less-than-lovely weather.

She felt tense as she unlocked her front door. After twelve years with MI5, she liked to think objectivity and emotional distance had become natural for her. She'd managed in the midst of the crisis, with Ruthie Burns in a state and Martin Hambly about to have a stroke, but now, on her own, she was anything but objective and distant. It wasn't that she was out of practice. She'd only left MI5 in March. It was that today involved people she'd known her entire life. Friends, neighbors, villagers.

Oliver.

She fumbled with the door lock. His fault, damn him.

She got the door open and felt her tension ease the moment she crossed the threshold. Posey had died in her sleep of general organ failure at ninety-four and left the house to Henrietta and small inheritances to Henrietta's father and his cousin, Anthony's only son.

Posey would have relished a mysterious death in the village, provided it wasn't too gruesome and involved someone who'd had it coming. Henrietta had yet to figure out what to do with her great-aunt's daunting collection of cozy mysteries. They lined the study shelves and filled more than one cupboard.

She went back to the kitchen and filled the kettle with water and set it to boil. In addition to the kitchen, the house consisted of a sitting room, study and powder room on the ground floor, and, upstairs, two slanted-ceiling, dormered bedrooms and a bathroom. Posey had had the house built to her standard. She'd decided on new construction rather than selling the lot and buying an existing house. She would never have had the patience to fuss with anything listed or mildly historic that would require her to follow rules and regulations and entertain unsolicited opinions from villagers. "I didn't want my house to be the subject of postcards, tourist photographs or chocolate boxes," she'd told Henrietta more than once.

Posey hadn't cleared out a single possession before her death. Henrietta knew she needed to get on with sorting what didn't suit her. Sell it, give it away, toss it. It seemed like a daunting process at the moment. Of course, it wasn't. Surveillance and penetration of a violent cell bent on mass murder were daunting. Deciding what to do with Aunt Posey's stacks of murder mysteries was emotionally challenging but hardly the same.

As she waited for the kettle to boil, Henrietta gazed out the kitchen window at the glorious June blossoms. As plain as the house was, the gardens were incredible. They were Posey's creation and had been her greatest joy. Pink foxglove, cobalt-blue delphinium, white daisies, artfully placed grasses — Henrietta let the burst of color soothe her. In the months since her great-aunt's death, she had maintained the gardens, at least to a degree, without touching their essential structure. The rose trellis needed replacing. Most of the perennials needed thinning and a good chop. She'd get to it all one of these days.

How far would Oliver get in his Rolls-Royce? It wasn't an inconspicuous vehicle.

Henrietta shook off the intrusive thought but she couldn't ignore a tug of emotion. She'd felt it before — this unexpected, unwilling attraction to Oliver. They'd known each other since childhood and she hadn't felt anything remotely romantic toward him until last Christmas. She'd tried to blame winter for her sudden, uncomfortable feelings — the short days, the gray, the damp — and when that hadn't worked, she'd tried to blame grief and nostalgia given Posey's recent death. She'd looked up Oliver in London after the new year and joined him for a drink at Claridge's, his favorite spot, thinking that would do the trick. He'd be back to being the Oliver who'd always been there — dashing, good-looking, solitary, a man coping with unspeakable tragedy, but not anyone she could imagine sleeping with.

But that hadn't happened.

Henrietta wasn't sure what to call how she felt. She'd been out of touch with anything resembling a romantic life or romantic feelings for so long, how was she supposed to know? She wasn't in love with him, she kept telling herself. Oliver was irresistibly fascinating, with his knowledge of mythology, folklore and legends, and his unusual lifestyle. Given his expertise in karate and tai chi, he was fit and capable.

Sexy, in fact. That was the truth of it.

Maybe what she felt was simple lust. Maybe she just wanted to sleep with him and once she did, that'd be that.

"The man's a bloody thief," she said aloud, getting the teapot off an open shelf.

It was hers, although Posey had left a half-dozen teapots. She needed a few things of her own in her new life.

In a way, learning Oliver was a serial art thief had somehow permitted her to indulge in these fantasies about him. His eccentricities and solitary ways kept people at bay. They didn't ask questions about the true nature of his hobbies and travels.

Henrietta envisioned him slipping past security guards, disabling alarms, carrying off valuable works of art without breaking into a nervous sweat. Each of his heists had required detailed planning and careful execution. The man was brazen, brilliant, wily.

She sniffed. "He's still a thief."

One of his covers was his occasional work as a film-and-television mythology consultant, under his assumed identity of frumpy Oliver Fairbairn. He'd fly off to Hollywood and chat with writers, producers, actors.

Not an easy man to figure out, her one-time childhood playmate.

Henrietta couldn't let her fascination with him lead her astray, but perhaps it was too late and it already had. She'd just come upon a dead body at his door, hadn't she?

Her unsettling attraction to him wasn't the only factor in her departure from MI5, but coupled with recent frustrations on the job, it had helped her to understand that twelve years in domestic intelligence had been enough. She wanted more from her life, or at least something else, even if she wasn't sure what that was. Right now she needed to get a grip on herself. Oliver York was a thief, if a charming and sexy thief, who'd shown no interest in her whatsoever beyond their childhood bond, and he'd just taken off from the scene of a suspected homicide.

Any thought of a relationship with him was delusional.

For all his quirks and misdeeds, however, Henrietta couldn't see Oliver as a murderer.

She rummaged in a near-empty bag for two slices of bread. Tea and a cheese-and-pickle sandwich weren't a pint but they were what she needed right now. She'd reorganized the kitchen a few weeks ago to suit her. Slowly but surely, she was making the house her own. It needed remodeling but that would come in due course. She'd been focused on establishing her garden-design business.

She was slathering on Branston pickles when her phone vibrated on the table. She swooped it up and sighed when she saw it was Martin Hambly. She'd wanted it to be . . . who? Oliver? MI5? It didn't bear considering.

She answered. "Hello, Martin," she said.

"How are you doing?"

It wasn't why he'd called. She could hear it in his voice. "I'm fine, thank you."

"Good."

She frowned, on her feet, silent phone at her ear. "Has something happened?" she asked finally.

"No, no — sorry. I'm distracted. Two FBI agents are on the way. The police want us to talk to them."

Now this was interesting. "Are these Oliver's FBI-agent friends?"

"Emma Sharpe and Colin Donovan, yes, but 'friends' is perhaps too strong. I didn't realize you knew about them."

"Everyone in the village knows about them, Martin."

"I see." He sounded resigned to the fact, if not pleased. "They might be able to help us find Oliver. They arrived at Heathrow this morning."

"Excellent. I can show them our vintage flowerpot."

"Henrietta?"

"Sorry. No problem. I'll have a bite and be along."

"Thank you. I'll let them know when they arrive."

She rang off, finding herself torn between wanting to meddle in the death investigation and wanting to grab sheers and prune something — anything — in Aunt Posey's garden.

Classic fight-or-flight.

She finished making her lunch and took it outside to the terrace. She settled at a metal table and chairs. They'd been Posey's. Henrietta hadn't had a garden in London. There were cushions, but she was always forgetting to take them in when it rained, or out when it didn't rain. The seat wasn't as cold as it had been that morning, when she'd had breakfast outdoors, before leaving for the York farm.

She tried to focus on a clump of cheerful Shasta daisies. Posey had been a master gardener and might have raised her eyebrows at Henrietta calling herself a garden designer. On her many visits since childhood, she'd soaked up her great-aunt's gardening wisdom and expertise. On all matters, not just her house, Posey had preferred to consider only her own opinions. She'd inherited enough money from her parents to get by if she lived frugally — which came naturally to her — and had supplemented her income with the occasional magazine and newspaper article on gardening. As opinionated as she was, Posey had been relatively open-minded when it came to gardening. She had a simple philosophy: "Plant what you like where it will grow." Everything else, she said, would follow and sort itself.

Henrietta ate her sandwich, hardly noticing its taste. Her plans for the day had been thoroughly messed up. She was in no hurry to meet with the FBI agents. Would they know she was ex-MI5? She was certain Martin suspected that she'd been sent by MI5, perhaps, to keep an eye on Oliver. The truth was considerably more complicated.

Well, not *that* much more complicated. She'd quit MI5 in March, moved to the Cotswolds and put out her shingle as a garden designer. Half her former colleagues believed she'd been sacked, but it wasn't true, at least technically. One day she'd realized she'd had her fill and put in her papers. The "one day" had followed a bad run-in with a senior intelligence officer and a seriously inexplicable longing to call Oliver and talk to him about it. She'd realized she needed to move on.

"Focus," she said aloud. "Don't let your mind wander."

Her new job was enhanced by a wandering mind. It gave her something to do while finding old flowerpots as she had that morning.

She poured more tea, taking care to note its heat, its scent, its splash in her cup. She found the ritual reassuring, a way to stay fully present and to step out of the whirlwind of the dead man at the York farm and Oliver's disappearance.

She drank a few more sips of tea and gave up. Her mind wasn't on tea or flowers. She was can-do by nature, and she wanted to pace, jump up, *do* something — clean, wash, throw things, anything that wasn't sitting, keeping her cool. She'd been cool and decisive that morning but that was different. That was real. It wasn't debating whether to have biscuits with her tea or to wander in the garden.

The humidity was building ahead of the rain. It worked its dark magic and frizzed up her hair. She could feel it.

She pounced when her phone vibrated next to her. "Hello —"

"Tell the FBI agents everything. They know who you are. I told them."

"And you are?"

But the man on the other end of the connection was gone. It didn't matter. She

74

knew who it was. MI5, in the form of Jeremy Pearson. The same uncompromising senior officer who'd given her such a hard time in March.

Now it was time to wander in Aunt Posey's gardens.

"Henrietta!" Cassie Kershaw, who owned the original Balfour farm with her husband, waved by the iron gate in the stone wall that divided their two properties. "Are you all right? I just heard what happened."

"Hang on," Henrietta said. "I'll come to you."

She extricated herself from examining a crumbling rose trellis and took a well-trodden footpath through the back gate. Cassie stepped aside, tucking strands of her fine, pale hair behind her ear as if to help calm herself. "My God, Henrietta, what a day. *Are* you all right? Did you just get back from the York farm? I've been worried about you."

"I'm fine," Henrietta said. "I wasn't hurt. I spoke with the police and came back here for lunch. You've probably heard more details than I have."

"Gossip, not details."

Gossip about an unexplained, bloody death was inevitable, but Henrietta had discovered that people in Oliver's small Cotswold village seldom gossiped about his family tragedy. She didn't believe they considered it a forbidden subject as much as one well in the past and none of their business. Oliver had been on his own since the back-to-back deaths of his grandparents when he was in his late teens. Henrietta had accompanied Posey to their funerals. She remembered how sad and yet self-contained he'd looked at the cemetery service, the wind catching his tawny hair as he'd stood in front of his parents' graves. He'd kissed her cheek and told her he was glad she was there, but it had felt mechanical and rote, an upper-class young man remembering his manners. He'd promptly dropped out of Oxford, dividing his time between London and the farm — and eventually his illicit travels to steal art.

In the years since, he could play the dashing, aristocratic Englishman when it suited him, but for the most part he'd kept to himself, particularly when he was at his farm. Henrietta had never been under the impression villagers judged him for his solitary ways. They left him alone, since it was what he wanted.

Or *had* wanted. Bit by bit since last fall, he'd been lifting himself out of his self-imposed isolation, venturing to the pub, having visitors, now that his secret career as an art thief had come to an end.

Something, of course, Henrietta couldn't discuss with Cassie or anyone else in the village. "There's not much I can tell you," she said.

"You walked home?"

"I didn't have my car. Someone would have dropped me home, but it felt good to walk after such an intense couple of hours."

"What a fright. Just awful."

Henrietta noticed a pair of bright pink work gloves in a wheelbarrow next to a compost bin off to Cassie's right. She looked in her element, dressed in a baggy flannel shirt, baggy jeans and muddy Wellies. She was American, but she and Henrietta were related through a circuitous connection to the Balfours. Henrietta had introduced her to Eugene Kershaw, an unhappy Oxford solicitor now a deliriously happy farmer. He and Cassie were the parents of two young boys. Eugene's grandparents had purchased the Balfour farm from Henrietta's father shortly after her grandfather's death. It'd been their dream to own a Cotswold farm, but they'd never managed to make much of a go of it. Eugene's parents were Oxford professors and had no interest in taking on a thriving farm, much less a struggling one.

By the time Eugene and Cassie took over, the property had been seriously neglected and getting it back in shape was proving to be considerably more work at far more expense than either had anticipated. The risk and effort were paying off, and now they were drawing a sufficient income that allowed Eugene to quit his outside work. Both he and Cassie worked at the farm full-time. Henrietta had never heard them complain about the vagaries of farm life. They'd helped spread the word about her garden-design business when she'd made her career change. This was the life Cassie and Eugene wanted to live, how they wanted to raise their sons.

"I've been in the compost pile, as you can see," Cassie said. "Eugene and the boys love mucking about in compost more than I do, but it does feel good to work up a sweat. We only just heard about the mishap out at the York farm. The police came round to ask if we'd seen anyone about. We hadn't, of course. The death — It was a mishap, wasn't it?"

"I honestly don't know," Henrietta said truthfully. "I'm still trying to absorb everything."

"But you're not one to panic," Cassie observed, making it sound almost like a criticism.

"Dealing with plants will do that." Henrietta left it there. She wasn't accustomed to family and friends living close by, seeing people she'd known for years — since childhood, in many cases — on a regular basis. She'd maintained a very different existence in London. "One imagines all sorts of dramatic scenarios to cope with the parts of the work that are pure drudgery. Plucking weeds gets boring after thirty seconds. I've imagined myself in so many dangerous situations, it was second nature to deal with a real one." None of which was an outright lie. "I had Martin's example. The man is unflappable."

Cassie relaxed slightly. "I can imagine. He strikes me as the epitome of 'keep calm and carry on.' Do you know the man who was killed?"

Henrietta shook her head. "I never saw him before that I can recall. If the police know, they haven't told me. Where's Eugene?"

"He's just back from the post office. I think he's in the cottage we're renovating. I've been so distracted since the police were here. They were gracious and professional, but you know how it is." Cassie stopped abruptly and pointed at Henrietta's forearm. "Is that *blood*?"

Henrietta glanced at her sleeve. It was blood, indeed. She hadn't noticed until now. Neither Martin nor the police had mentioned it, but she'd had on her jacket. She must have got blood on her sleeve when she'd checked the dead man's pulse. She lowered her arm, discreetly angling the blood smear from Cassie's view. "Martin and I tried to help, but we were too late. There was nothing we could do."

"How dreadful. Maybe you should have stayed in the potting shed with the housekeeper."

"How did you know about Ruthie?"

Henrietta winced at her quick question — her MI5 past bubbling up — but Cassie didn't seem to notice. "Nigel Burns," she said.

Nigel was the older of Ruthie's two adult sons, a mechanic who often worked on the equipment at the York farm. Lately he was helping renovate a traditional stone-and-timber cottage on the Kershaw farm. It predated the farmhouse. At one point, Posey had considered it for her home, but Henrietta doubted that thought had lasted long. The low ceilings alone would have done in Posey. The cottage was located just down the stone wall, amid trees that bordered a stream and a field, green with spring grass. Cassie's parents planned to retire later in the year and move into the renovated cottage.

"Ruthie did well today," Henrietta said. "She's old-fashioned, dedicated, a thorn in Martin's side and part of the furnishings as far as Oliver's concerned, but she's reliable. I appreciate her — I promise you I do — but if I ever get as proprietary about gardens as she does about muddy footprints and spots on water glasses, I expect you to elbow me in the ribs."

Cassie nodded warmly, some color returning to her cheeks. "Consider it done."

"Today wasn't easy for her," Henrietta added guiltily.

"I'm sure it wasn't. You're gaining quite a reputation throughout the Cotswolds, you know."

"A reputation for what?"

"Garden design and a cheerful demeanor."

Henrietta sighed. "A cheerful Henrietta Balfour. That would shock some people."

"Life among flowers and winding paths will do that even to a jaded Londoner like yourself." Cassie paused, studying her friend. They'd known each other for almost a decade but they'd never really spent much time together. "I'm glad you found a career that suits you, but you don't fool me, Henrietta. You're bored. The pace of a garden designer and a Cotswold life is different from what you were used to in London."

"True enough."

And more so than Cassie knew or likely would ever know, but Henrietta couldn't explain she'd entered Her Majesty's Security Service fresh out of university, trained and worked as an operator in the field, specializing in surveillance, and then moved up the ranks to an office in Thames House. There'd never been any job in a London financial office. She was happy not to explain, either. Best to put those years behind her.

"I'm a Balfour, Cassie. Gardening's in the blood." So was MI5, but Henrietta kept that point to herself. "Bored or not, I could do without what happened today. My only interest at the York farm involves annuals, perennials, herbaceous borders —"

"You can stop there," Cassie said with a welcome laugh. "I definitely do not have the Balfour gardening gene. Eugene and I are amazed at the landscaping here, though. It's perfect for us to build on. People say your grandfather puttered in the flowerbeds after he left MI5, right up until his death. That's heartening somehow. He'd have been proud of you today, don't you think?"

"I hope so."

The lighthearted moment dissipated and Cassie turned serious again. "And Oliver York? Did he really take off?"

"I only saw him at the dovecote," Henrietta said. "He left a short while before Martin and I found the body."

"Just awful. Truly. Eugene and I ran into Oliver at the pub last week. He was on his own but he sat at the bar and chatted with people. He doesn't mingle often. We tend to notice when he does. He's quite the character, isn't he? Good-looking and a bit mysterious."

Henrietta pushed up her sleeves, hiding the blood. "I haven't really thought about it," she said casually.

"Haven't you?" Cassie reached for her gloves. "You don't have to answer. It'll keep. This isn't the time to discuss such things. I know you're intrepid and all that, but finding a dead man must be a shock. Do you have any idea what happened . . . how this man died? It had to be an accident, however terrible, don't you think? He didn't attack Oliver, did he? Oliver didn't kill him in self-defense?"

"I don't know any more than you do, Cassie. The police told me best to leave the investigation to them and get back to my plans for the day."

Cassie stared at the worn gloves, bits of compost debris and dirt stuck to the fingers. "Can you at least tell me if they suspect murder? I have two small boys . . ."

"The police haven't said."

"I've been trying not to freak out. Eugene says even if it was murder, it's got nothing to do with us. We aren't targets. We always keep an eye on the boys. Still, I'm keeping them close to home until we hear more. My parents don't know yet. They're so looking forward to retiring to the peaceful Cotswolds. If this man's death was murder . . ." Cassie shook her head. "No. I'm not going to think that way. It's a York thing, whatever it is, and nothing to do with us." She frowned, cocking her head to one side. "Are you sure you're all right, Henrietta? How can you be so calm?"

"I'm afraid I'm still in shock." She licked her lips. "I'm sure it will hit me later."

"Yes. I imagine so. Be careful, won't you? And come to dinner tonight. You won't want to be alone."

Actually, Henrietta *did* want to be alone.

She couldn't imagine being sociable after today, but Cassie and Eugene loved to entertain. Henrietta had invited them over for wine and olives on the terrace one evening but had whisked them to the pub for dinner. She knew how to cook. She just didn't like to.

"Don't forget we can provide you all the compost you can use," Cassie said, then sputtered into laughter. "For gardens, I mean, not for dinner."

Henrietta managed a smile. "Thank you."

Cassie grabbed her garden gloves. "I found a painting in the cottage the other day. It was tucked in the back of a small closet that I doubt had been opened in years. I've been meaning to ask you about it. I'll show you at dinner. It'll be a pleasant diversion after this morning."

Henrietta was in no hurry to return to the York farm and chat with the FBI. "Why don't I take a look now?"

As they reached the cottage, Tony Balfour came out the front door. Cassie jumped — she was in easy-to-startle mode — but Henrietta was pleased to see him. He was her father's first cousin, the only child of Freddy and Posey's middle sibling, Anthony, who'd died tragically when Tony was

85

a baby. He'd retired in April after a career as a landscaper at various public gardens throughout England. He was living in the Kershaw cottage temporarily, in exchange for overseeing the renovations, a perfect arrangement as he figured out what was next for him. Henrietta suspected gardening was perhaps a stronger Balfour family tradition than intelligence work. Divorced with no children, he hadn't decided where to settle in retirement. He was in excellent shape and still muscular from decades of physical work, but he was clearly ready to go at his own pace and do other things.

"Henrietta, love," Tony said, taking her by the hand and kissing her on the cheek. He was dressed in his work clothes, and she could smell plaster dust on him but saw no sign of it on his gray, paint-stained hoody. He stood back. "I heard the news. What on earth happened?"

"It wasn't the morning I had in mind, but I've rallied."

"Thank heavens you weren't hurt. You weren't, were you?"

"Not at all. No one was, except the man who died."

Tony nodded, his expression a mix of grimness and curiosity. "We've lived quiet lives compared to Oliver York, haven't we?"

"Henrietta's going to take a look at the painting we discovered," Cassie said.

"Great idea. It's priceless in its own way. I'm sorry I'm in a rush. I need to pick up a few things at the hardware store." He shifted again to Henrietta. "Phone me if the adrenaline wears off and you want to talk. Once a worker cut his arm and the resulting mess . . ." He made a face and held up a hand. "Never mind. It wasn't a fatal accident but you don't need to have that picture dancing around in your head."

"I imagine not," Henrietta said. "Thank you."

"I'll see you later, then."

He headed up the path toward the Kershaw house. Henrietta had never seen anyone quite so happy to retire. Tony heartily approved of her career change and had assured her Posey would have, too. Of course, he believed she'd worked in a dull London office job.

Henrietta followed Casey into the cottage. The front room was cleared of any furniture while the plastering was being redone. Tony did most of the work, but he'd bring in professionals when needed or grab Nigel Burns or Eugene for easier jobs that needed more than one pair of hands. Since the cottage had once belonged to the Balfours,

Henrietta was madly curious about the renovations but tried not to be too nosy.

Eugene emerged from the kitchen. "I was just in the village," he said. "Everyone's shocked at the news of the death at the York farm. I suppose it's natural for our minds to jump to violence rather than an unfortunate accident. Oliver bolting doesn't help, but one can understand why he might, under the circumstances. After what he went through as a boy, who wouldn't?"

"Best to let the police sort this, Eugene," Henrietta said.

"Yes, of course. You're right." He smiled. "You're sensible like your aunt, Henrietta."

"Posey was thrilled when you decided to take on the farm."

"A late bloomer, I believe she called me."

Eugene was nine years older than Cassie, a bit grayer and balder these days but in good shape from his farm work and as amiable as ever. He and Cassie had clicked the moment Henrietta had introduced them to each other, the only instance she'd successfully played matchmaker — not that she'd meant to play matchmaker. It was an accident, really. She'd looked up Cassie on a trip to Boston given their family connection, and they'd hit it off. Cassie had come to the Cotswolds to visit and Henrietta had shown her out to the old Balfour farm. Eugene had been there, cutting the grass after work. They'd ended up at the pub together and eight months later, Cassie and Eugene were married at the village church.

Henrietta had known Eugene since her visits with her aunt as a child. Her parents would drop her off in the Cotswolds for weeks while they binged on opera or scooted to Paris without her. Eugene and his younger sister, who now ran a restaurant in Oxford, had spent holidays with their grandparents on the former Balfour farm. For as far back as Henrietta could remember, Eugene had expressed his desire to revive the farm. He'd loved to talk about horses, Cotswold sheep, dairy cows and grain fields. Henrietta couldn't say it'd ever been her ambition to move into Aunt Posey's house full-time, but she did love the place. It had seemed like a practical, workable option when she'd quit MI5. Flowers, herbs, shrubs, pots, cutting and watering regimes. Simpler than uncovering schemes to commit mass murder.

She turned her attention to the matter at hand. "Well, what do we have?"

Cassie went into the kitchen and came out with a mounted canvas. She set it on the floor and leaned it against the wall, standing aside so that Henrietta could see it was an oil painting of a scene of a mountain and a lake. It wasn't in the class of paintings Oliver York had stolen, but it was charming.

"It's wonderful, isn't it?" Cassie beamed. "A bit amateurish, I know, but I love its sensibility. It's Queen's View in the southern Scottish Highlands. It's supposedly named for Queen Victoria, after she visited in 1866. I looked it up after I found the painting. That's Loch Tummel and the Tay Forest. Eugene and I drove up there for a few days before we had children. Have you ever been, Henrietta?"

She nodded. "I went a few years ago with a churl of an ex-boyfriend."

Cassie grinned at her. "One day I want to hear all the details of your life before you moved back here. I know so little about it." She turned back to the painting. "It's not signed, and there's nothing on the back to indicate who painted it. We were wondering if you have any idea."

"I've never seen it before," Henrietta said, certain.

"Did your grandfather paint?"

"Freddy? Good heavens, no. Well, I doubt he did — I was very young when he died. My father has never mentioned Freddy painted. Posey didn't, either, when she was alive. I remember him smoking cigarettes and rambling in the garden."

"What about Posey?" Cassie asked. "Could she have painted it?"

"I can't imagine she did. I never saw her paint, and I haven't discovered any old canvases or supplies and such since I moved into her house."

Cassie frowned. "Hmm. A mystery. Could it have been your grandmother . . . Freddy's wife?"

"No one ever mentioned she painted, but I really don't know," Henrietta said. "I don't remember her at all. She died when I was a baby. A shame you didn't find it when Posey was still alive. Does Tony have any memory of it?"

Eugene shook his head. "I asked him. He said he didn't know but he wasn't a good one to ask. He was only a tot when his mother moved to the US with him. I suppose his father could have painted it, but he was a tortured soul — I can't believe he'd have produced something this sweet."

"Anthony's been dead for sixty years, too," Cassie added. "This cottage was pretty much in ruin then. Freddy had it restored but it's been decades since anyone's really used it. It's a good thing Tony isn't particular. Anyway, I suppose someone could have discovered the painting somewhere else and tucked it in the closet and forgot about it."

Eugene squatted down for a closer look at the painting. "You can almost feel the sun on the loch."

"I really do love it," Cassie said. "If Anthony painted it, maybe Freddy or Posey found it after his death and couldn't bear to keep it but couldn't bear to throw away it away, either."

"That would make sense." Eugene rose, his eyes still on the captivating scene. "It's not discussed but everyone knows Anthony Balfour died of alcoholism. Well. That's not a cheerful subject any day but especially today, given what happened this morning."

"And it's such a cheerful painting," Cassie said with a sigh. "Well, I don't care who painted it, really. I was just curious. Freddy Balfour's housekeeper could have bought it at a yard sale and a ten-year-old painted it, and it wouldn't matter — I love it. I'm going to frame it and hang it in here when we're done with renovations. I'm sure Mum and Dad will love it, too."

Henrietta followed Cassie and Eugene out of the cottage. Cassie explained she'd invited Henrietta to dinner. Eugene seemed to be as keen on the idea. "The boys always love to see you," he said cheerfully. "They got into nettle the other day. You can explain it to them."

"Every country girl and boy needs to understand nettle," Henrietta said. "I learned the hard way myself when I decided to investigate the field across the stream on one of my visits with Aunt Posey. It's like the nettle was lying in wait for me."

"It's brutal stuff," Eugene said, grinning at her. "I remember that day. Both your legs were covered in welts. Didn't Oliver rescue you?"

"He thinks he did. He was twelve and I was nine." Henrietta grinned. "It was the worst."

Eugene said he'd see her later and returned to the cottage, but as Henrietta started back to the gate, she noticed worry return to Cassie's face. "Let us know if you hear any news about the investigation, won't you?" She motioned vaguely toward the compost pile. "I'll get back to work before it rains."

Henrietta went back through the gate. As she brought her lunch dishes to the kitchen, she contemplated polite ways to get out of dinner. She wanted to go. She *should* go. Be with friends after a difficult day. At the same time, she didn't want to go.

The definition of ambivalent.

She'd shower and go see what the FBI agents wanted.

5

A rail-thin man in his fifties introduced himself as Detective Inspector Peter Lowe and took Emma and Colin through what he knew so far. The body had been removed, but the forensics team was still working on the immediate scene. "We haven't identified the deceased yet," Lowe said as they stood on the edge of the taped-off area around the side entrance. "He didn't have a wallet or phone on him. We don't know how he got onto the property. We haven't found a vehicle. He could have walked. We're checking the village."

"What shape's the house in?" Colin asked.

"Untouched as far as we can tell so far. All the blood is right here. He didn't go far once he was wounded."

"How was he wounded, do you know?"

The DI shook his head. "He wasn't shot. We know that much. The artery was in bad shape. It appears to have been cut with an extremely sharp instrument. There's no guarantee it was a survivable injury even with applied pressure and timely medical intervention." Lowe's eyes narrowed on Emma. "Now, Special Agent Sharpe, tell me about your call from Mr. York."

Emma did so, repeating Oliver's words verbatim. It wasn't as if there'd been many to remember. The DI twisted his mouth to one side, taking in the information. He and the investigative team had been professional and courteous, but it was clear they didn't appreciate two FBI agents turning up, even with MI5 having paved the way — through whatever means, direct or indirect. Emma understood their reluctance. She and Colin had a personal and professional history with Oliver that could help, but it also complicated matters. The personal history irked Colin but Oliver deliberately exaggerated their relationship. Despite his attempts to forge a friendship, Emma considered her relationship with their unrepentant art thief entirely within her role with the FBI.

"And this break-in at your grandfather's house in Dublin?" the DI asked. "Relevant?"

"I don't know," Emma said. "The Irish police are investigating."

Lowe nodded. "We'll speak with them."

Colin watched two members of the forensic team finishing up by a stone bench across the driveway from the entrance. "How close are you to identifying the deceased?"

"Not close enough. We'll know when we know. I don't guess, Special Agent Donovan."

"Duly noted. Thanks for your time."

They left the DI to his work and walked down to the dovecote, taking the same route DI Lowe had described Ruthie Burns had taken from the house to alert Martin Hambly and Henrietta Balfour. The gray weather only seemed to make the sloping fields look greener, a contrast to the grim events earlier in the day. Emma had been here in February on FBI business, winter in the Cotswolds different but still beautiful.

"I smell roses," she said.

Colin shook his head. "Not me."

"What do you smell?"

"Sheep."

She smiled, appreciating the light moment. She watched a lamb prance in the grass on her right, near the fence. She could imagine whiling away an afternoon out here, enjoying the views of bucolic fields, listening to sheep baaing. She doubted Oliver made much of an income off the farm, but she knew it met expenses. Her grandfather had given her that information when he'd visited in January.

A police car was just down the lane past the dovecote, an officer at the wheel. Emma was familiar with the dovecote, built to house pigeons at a time when they were a pricey, sought-after delicacy. Pigeons had fallen out of favor on the dinner plate, and now only a comparatively few dovecotes remained. The York dovecote was on the smaller side as dovecotes went, but it was well-suited to its modern purpose as a potting shed. Ruthie Burns was out front, frowning at the mess Emma assumed Henrietta and Martin had left behind — bags of potting soil and composted manure, a bucket of what appeared to be freshly dug loam, an array of garden tools and a cracked terracotta pot. It was as if the ordinary work of the day would resume at any moment.

The DI had let them know Ruthie wasn't doing well emotionally, but she'd agreed to talk with them. "Please, ask whatever questions you'd like," she said even before Emma could greet her. "I'd be happy to answer them. DI Lowe said I should." She paused, her eyes red and puffy from tears, her skin ashen from the shock of the morning. "You and Special Agent Donovan are Oliver's friends."

Emma didn't voice any objection to the housekeeper's characterization of her and Colin's relationship with her missing boss. Now wasn't the time, and she saw that Colin agreed. "We want to help if we can," she said.

"I understand. I'm sorry you're not here under better circumstances."

"I am, too."

"Mr. York didn't know you were coming?"

"We called this morning and left a voice mail. I don't know if he received it."

"You called on his mobile?"

Emma nodded. "Yes."

Ruthie bit her lower lip, crossed her arms tight on her chest and lowered them again. "I don't know what to do with myself — stay here, go home, be alone, be with people. I can't make sense of today." She spoke more to herself than to Emma. "I keep seeing the blood — so much blood — and Mr. York, desperately trying to help. You hear about such things but never expect to see something like it yourself."

Ruthie pointed up the lane to a thickset man shambling toward the dovecote. "That's my son, Nigel. He's a mechanic."

"Was he here this morning?" Emma asked.

"He was, yes. He was at the barn, working on one of the tractors."

Nigel reached the dovecote, coming up the rudimentary flagstone path to the entrance. He rubbed the back of his hand across his jaw and its two-day stubble of beard, mostly dark but splotched with gray. No sign of gray in his thick, fair, curly hair. He looked to be in his early forties, a solidly built man in oil-smeared work clothes. He addressed his mother. "Police said I should come down here and tell the FBI agents what I saw this morning. That all right with you, Mum?"

"Of course. Do what the police say."

Colin sat on a bench next to the front door, a gesture, Emma suspected, to make him look less intimidating. "You were here on the farm this morning, Nigel?"

"Yes, I got here about eight o'clock. I was working on the old tractor down at the barn." He shoved his hands in his pockets, clearly awkward and uncomfortable in his role as witness. "I came to tell you Mr. York is gone." Nigel reddened to his ears. "Not dead. I don't mean that. He left in his car a few minutes before the police got here. No more than that. I saw him myself."

"Do you mean you saw the car or that you saw Oliver?" Colin asked.

"I saw them both," Nigel said without hesitating. "Mr. York was driving. I didn't see anyone with him."

Ruthie twisted her hands together, as if she needed to release tension before she hit someone. "Are you sure it was Mr. York?"

"I am. No question."

Colin put a foot on the rim of a bucket of dirt. "Where exactly did you see the car?"

Nigel pointed a thick, callused finger down the lane, in the direction of the barn, which wasn't visible from the dovecote. "The west gate. He drove past the barn. It's on this lane."

"It meets up with the main road to Chipping Norton," Ruthie added. "The public route continues across the road through a hay field but it's strictly a walking trail. It can't handle a vehicle."

"I didn't see which way Mr. York went once he reached the road," Nigel said. "Even if I'd thought to look, I wouldn't have been able to see from where I stood."

Emma considered his response. "And where was that?"

"I told you —" Nigel stopped, took in a breath. "In front of the barn door facing the lane. I was up on the tractor, heard the car and took a look, since it's odd to have the Rolls-Royce down there."

Colin toed a small pile of spilled soil. "You recognized the Rolls-Royce by the sound of its engine? Before you saw it?"

"I did. Always've had an ear for an engine. I told the police."

"They were all right with it," Ruthie said.

Colin's eyes narrowed slightly, and Emma knew he, too, had heard the note of defiance in Nigel's tone and the protectiveness in Ruthie's. "How did Mr. York look to you?" she asked.

Nigel picked up an open bag of soil that had fallen on its side and stood it upright against the dovecote. "Same as always," he said, stepping back. "Only unusual thing was seeing him driving down by the barn. He didn't look as if he'd been hurt or was bloody or in pain, anything like that. You know. Given what happened up at the house."

"And the dead man?" Colin asked. "Did you see him?"

"I didn't see anyone else, sorry. I got to the farm at ten and went to work. I drove. I know you'll be asking. I live in the workers' rooms at the pub. I do some work there, too. It's temporary. My ex lives in the village with our two kids." Nigel again shoved his hands into the pockets of his work jacket. "I'm saving for a place of my own. I've worked for the Yorks on and off since I was in my teens. Mr. Hambly can vouch for me. So can my mum, but, y'know —" He grinned at her. "She's my mum." He shrugged his big shoulders. "That's it."

It was clear he'd finished his story. "Thank you, Nigel," Ruthie said. "If you think of anything else, you'll notify the police straight away."

"I will. They said I can go home but I can stay if you need me."

"No, I'll be all right. I'll head home soon. It's been a rough day, and I've no idea when the police will finish. Go on home."

"I'll come by and stay with you. I don't want you home alone." Nigel shifted to Emma. "I remember you from this winter. The man who died — he's not one of yours, is he?"

"No, he's not," she said. "Any idea who he is, Nigel?"

"Not a clue. It was just a day like any other until I saw the Rolls-Royce and then my mum texted me after she called 999." He gave an apologetic look. "Sorry I couldn't do more to help."

"It'll be all right, Nigel," Ruthie said.

He left without comment and started back up the lane toward the barn. His mother turned to Emma, gesturing vaguely toward her son. "I'll go now, too. You ring me if you need anything else."

"Of course," Emma said. "Thank you."

Ruthie Burns nodded grimly, then hurried after her son. "You'd think he was twelve," Colin said.

Emma didn't disagree. "It's been a rough day. Brings out a mother's protective instincts, maybe."

"My mother was never that protective. She sure as hell won't be when my brothers and I hit our forties."

"There are four of you. She'd have worn herself out being protective."

Martin Hambly walked up from the police car, where he'd been chatting with the officer, obviously killing time until Ruthie and Nigel left. "Were they any help? I imagine not much. The officer told me Nigel saw Oliver go toward the west gate in his car. What terrible witnesses we are. I feel as if I missed a thousand important clues that by now are beyond my grasp. To think . . ." He glanced at the half-filled terra-cotta pot. "To think the day started with the delightful memories this old flowerpot brings. Henrietta found it this morning. She'll be along soon. Would you two like to sit down while you wait for her? You can take the bench. There's not much room inside, but we can go in if you'd like."

Emma shook her head and noticed Colin

didn't make a move for the bench, either.

Martin walked to the edge of the grass and looked at the green, sheep-dotted pasture that sloped up to the elegant farmhouse. "I hate that the police and their forensic teams have been crawling through the place. By now they must know more about what happened here this morning than I do."

"Do you have any idea where Oliver might be?" Emma asked.

He turned to her, the strain in his face unmistakable. "None, I'm afraid."

Colin studied him. "Would you tell us if you did?"

Martin shrugged. "Depends, doesn't it?" He nodded to the bucket next to Emma. "I dug that dirt myself this morning," he said absently.

"Here?" she asked.

"In back." He pointed vaguely behind him. "I was preoccupied with other matters this morning. Ordinary matters. Now . . ." He paused. "The police have cleared the body, but you've spoken with them."

His tone was laden with suspicion and doubts, but he didn't go further. Emma wouldn't be surprised if he guessed that MI5 had paved the way for her and Colin to be here. She pointed at the bucket. "It looks like good dirt."

"That's what I told Henrietta. She and Oliver have known each other since they were children."

"They're friends?"

"I wouldn't go that far. The Balfours have deep roots in the village but Henrietta only moved here a few months ago. She and Oliver aren't always here at the same time. He's not . . . well, you know. He doesn't often seek the company of others. Henrietta lived in London until March, but as I understand it, she and Oliver only saw each other there once or twice."

"Was she a garden designer in London?" Emma asked.

"She worked in a financial office."

Martin inhaled and let out his breath slowly, shutting his eyes, as if he was meditating. Emma remembered when he'd greeted her, Colin and Matt Yankowski last fall at Oliver's Mayfair London apartment. From the moment Martin had opened the door to three FBI agents, he'd kept a professional distance, never admitting or denying what he knew or suspected about Oliver's secret life as a thief. Emma was convinced it was a lot, if not everything.

"We look forward to talking with Ms. Balfour," Emma said. "Are you concerned Oliver was hurt or kidnapped this morning?"

"No," Martin said without hesitation. "I can't explain why. I'm just not. The police haven't found anything to indicate he was injured or taken against his will. And with the car gone . . ." He didn't finish, the ending to the sentence obvious. With the Rolls-Royce gone, it looked as if Oliver had taken off voluntarily and deliberately before the police had arrived. "The police have little to go on at the moment," Martin added finally. "The house isn't alarmed. There's no video of the incident. Only Ruthie and Oliver seem to have been at the house when it happened."

With a burst of energy, Martin started tidying up the area in front of the dovecote, grabbing garden tools and setting them inside by the worktable. He left the door open and came out and grabbed the bags of soil. Emma decided it was best not to offer to help. Given his employer's ways, Martin was accustomed to running the show at the farm, and probably in London, too. He would want to be useful in some small way and reassert a sense of control.

"How long were you down here before Oliver arrived?" she asked.

"Here at the potting shed? Forty minutes." Martin spoke with certainty as he stood in

107

front of the dovecote door. He tapped his watch. "I happened to look at the time. Oliver stayed perhaps ten minutes."

"And the gardener — Henrietta Balfour? Was she here when you arrived?"

"No. I got here first. She'd been out back yesterday and wanted to show me the flowerpot she'd found. We carried it around front. I went out back again to dig loam from the hillside while she gathered her potting supplies. Then Oliver came down from the house." Martin paused. "And Henrietta's a garden designer, not a gardener. She'll tell you herself."

"I see," Emma said.

Colin peered through a small window into the dovecote. "Did Oliver say whether he'd come straight from the house?"

"No, he didn't, not specifically, but where else would he have come from?"

"Pasture, barn, another outbuilding, one of the cottages."

Martin held up a hand. "Point taken." He grabbed the rest of the tools and set them inside. He shut the door behind him, but not tightly, and dusted off his hands. "That's done, then."

"How long after Oliver left here did Ruthie Burns alert you?" Emma asked.

"Five minutes or so. I didn't check my

watch but it wasn't more than that. Henrietta might know." He sounded stronger, and his color was better. "I assume she's walking here. She didn't have her car this morning and the police didn't discourage her from walking home. They haven't said they're investigating the death as a homicide. It could be a terrible accident, couldn't it?" He sighed. "I know. Not for you to say."

Colin returned to the bench, stretching out his thick legs. "The police will have a better idea of what happened once they have autopsy results. They'll figure it out."

"We've had nasty accidents on the farm," Martin said. "Years ago a worker lost a finger. I can't see how an accident this bloody and catastrophic could happen so close to the house. The police didn't find blood inside the house, at least that I'm aware of. It can't be just one of those things for a man to incur a cut that causes him to bleed to death."

"Oliver could have found him outside after he'd been cut, when it was too late to put pressure on the wound to do any good," Colin said. "A cut brachial artery can be repaired."

"Death isn't inevitable?"

"It is if you don't stop the bleeding and get help fast. I'm not a doctor and I can't say what happened this morning."

Martin perked up. "Oliver is trained in martial arts. He might have known what to do in such a situation but was simply too late. If the man attacked him, Oliver's martial arts training would have kicked in. He'd have defended himself, but not . . ." Martin went pale. "Not in such a grisly fashion."

Emma plucked a dried lobelia leaf from a pot and tossed it into the grass. "Do you have any idea when and where the injury to this man occurred?"

Martin shook his head, squinting as if he was envisioning the scene. "I didn't see a weapon — a sharp instrument or anything like that — but the cut must have occurred close to where Henrietta and I found him. I would think it happened moments before Ruthie, before Oliver . . ." Martin jerked his chin up. "You don't think *I* killed this man, do you?"

"Take us through your morning, if you would," Emma said gently. "From when you woke up until the police arrived."

"Please sit, Agent Sharpe," he said. "You two make me nervous enough as it is."

Emma smiled and complied, sitting next to Colin on the bench. He crossed his ankles and gave a slight smile, in a deliberate effort, she suspected, to look less threatening. Martin needed to relax and focus on the details of his morning, not on his audience.

"I rose at five," he said, remaining on his feet but sounding calmer. "It was earlier than usual because Alfred was pestering me. He's Oliver's wire fox terrier, although I do most of the caring and training. He's a puppy and needed a walk. I don't let him loose to wander wherever he chooses. I put him on his lead and took him out behind the cottage. He did his business and we came back in and I made tea and toast."

"Does Alfred always stay with you?" Colin asked.

Martin hesitated a fraction of a second, but enough. "No, he doesn't. When Oliver is here, Alfred stays with him at the house. It's good for them both. They need to get to know each other. I expected that would be the case today, with Oliver back from London."

Emma shaded her eyes with her hand, the sun breaking through the clouds if only for the moment. "Why didn't you accompany Oliver to London?"

"He wanted me to stay with Alfred and oversee the landscaping. He said he didn't trust Henrietta not to start chopping everything in sight."

"How long was he away?"

"He left Friday and returned last night. He's been spending more time here on the farm of late. He hates to miss June in the Cotswolds. I can understand that. It's especially beautiful here this time of year. Well, not today, obviously. It started beautifully, but . . ." Martin trailed off, looking tired and ashen again.

"What were Oliver's plans once he was back here?" Emma asked.

Martin sniffed. "You don't think he'd tell me, do you? He might have had plans, he might not have. He pretends to operate on whims, but we know better than that, don't we?" He flushed purple, held up a hand. "I don't mean whims that might concern the FBI. I mean whims like sending you sheepskins. I was going to sit him down tomorrow and go over the calendar for the summer. Pin him down as much as possible."

"After your tea and toast this morning," Colin said. "Then what?"

Martin seemed relieved at the redirect. "I got dressed and went up to the house. Ruthie wasn't there. She arrived at seven and left again at eight to run into the village for a few things."

"By car?" Emma asked.

He nodded. "She returned at ten. She went in through the kitchen and then came upon Oliver and the injured man outside the entry. I only learned this after she spoke with the police. She said the injured man was bleeding profusely but she didn't think he was dead yet. She could tell he was in dire condition. Dying, in fact, but I'm getting ahead of myself. After I arrived at the house I fussed about a bit and then walked down here to meet Henrietta."

Colin leaned back against the bench. "With Alfred?"

"No. I left him at the house." Martin went still, his brow furrowed as he stared down at a cracked flowerpot. "I didn't think of this before now. I went to my cottage after the police finished their interview with me, and Alfred was there."

Emma felt Colin straighten ever so slightly next to her. "Do you know how he got there?" she asked quietly.

"I don't, no," Martin said. "I didn't think anything of it. Oliver could have popped him into the cottage before he walked down here to talk pots with Henrietta and me. He has no patience if Alfred is hopping about, but I would think it more likely he'd have come down with Alfred and handed him off to me. Alfred must have got loose and

Ruthie or one of the workers found him wandering in the garden and put him in my cottage. Do you suppose a killer — if there was a killer — could have done it? To keep Alfred from barking? He can be temperamental but he's not a biter. And why not just kill him?"

"We can speculate but best you amend your statement to the police," Colin said. "They'll want to know about Alfred."

"Of course. At once."

Colin got to his feet. "When you met Henrietta Balfour this morning, how did she strike you?"

"As I said, she'd been out back, unearthing the old pot. She was quite pleased with herself when she brought it around front. Muddy hands, a smudge of mud on her cheek, hair hanging in her face, big smile. Typical Henrietta Balfour as far as I could see."

"When did she start work here?" Colin asked.

"A few weeks ago. She's new to garden design but she came highly recommended by the Kershaws, a local family. Oliver doesn't like change but the gardens are past needing professional help. I thought to take things slowly and let him get used to the changes, but he's been quite keen. He wasn't as excited about the pot she discovered, although it's a family heirloom. It belonged to his grandfather's mother. I remember her well." Martin squared his shoulders, his skin more flushed than ashen now. "I've said too much. I don't want to waste your time. The rest you know."

Emma thanked him. "I know it's been a difficult day."

"Oliver didn't kill that man," Martin said with conviction. "I promise you he didn't."

Colin looked up at the clouds. "How well did you know Davy Driscoll and Bart Norcross?"

Martin gave no indication he was taken aback, irritated or even surprised at the sudden mention of the two men accused of killing Oliver's parents and kidnapping him as a boy. "We met a few times." A note of expectation had crept into his tone, as if he'd been waiting for their names to crop up. "I didn't hire them. Deborah York — Oliver's mother — did. They didn't work here at the farm."

"London, then?"

"Almost entirely." Martin glanced at the field across from the dovecote, sheep grazing, oblivious to the events around them. "The active manhunt went on for weeks. The police had their names. We thought they'd find and arrest them, but they never did."

"The dead man this morning," Colin said. "One of this pair?"

Martin steadied his gaze on him. "Why do you ask?"

Colin glanced at Emma and she answered. "It might help explain Oliver's reaction. He called me after he fled. He didn't give any details about what happened or where he was."

"I can't say for certain who the dead man is." Martin's voice was subdued. "I didn't get a good look at his face and it's been . . ." He stopped himself.

"And it's been thirty years," Colin said, finishing for him.

"All right, then." Martin cleared his throat, squared his shoulders. Any hesitation vanished. "I'll tell you. If the man I saw dead this morning wasn't Davy Driscoll, it was his long-lost twin brother or a dead ringer."

"That must have been a shock," Emma said quietly. "Would Oliver have recognized him?"

Martin tilted his head back, eyeing her with sudden coolness. "There's no way for me to know the answer to that question, Special Agent Sharpe."

In the US, she and Colin might have pushed the point, but they had a different role here. "I'm sorry for what you're going through," Emma said.

"Thank you." He had a slight catch to his voice, but the coolness had gone as quickly as it had come about. "I'm sorry for everyone. This is a bloody mess is what it is."

"Oliver needs to come in," Colin said, blunt. "If you're in contact with him or know how to reach him, tell him that. Don't mince words."

"I'm not in contact with him. I wish I were. I wish I had more I could tell you that would be of help." Martin gave a vague wave. "I should get back to the house. I'll finish cleaning up here later. I hope we meet again under better circumstances. You'll head on to London after you speak with Henrietta?"

"We'll see," Emma said. "Take care, Martin."

"I will. Yes. Thank you." He hesitated, as if he meant to ask a question or make a comment, but he nodded down the lane toward the police car. "I'll go on and tell the police about Alfred. Henrietta should be along soon. I'll leave you to speak with her."

Colin watched Martin head down the lane

until he was out of earshot. "This situation is finally hitting him. Shock's wearing off. Hambly's your stiff-upper-lip sort, but I bet he thought Oliver hid in the bushes and would turn up by lunchtime. Oliver's put him through his paces for a long time."

"There's a big difference between stealing a painting and killing a man." Emma eased next to Colin. The breeze had died down, and now she only smelled the dirt Martin had stirred up during his tidying. "Oliver's art thefts were an emotional outlet for him, a way to cope with the trauma he'd experienced. It was an inappropriate outlet —"

"And illegal."

"No question," Emma said. "I've always believed when it comes to his parents' deaths and his own kidnapping Oliver's more interested in answers and justice than personal revenge."

"That was before he found himself face-to-face with one of his boyhood tormentors. We need confirmation the dead man is Davy Driscoll. It's a good bet, whether or not Oliver recognized him. Ten-to-one DI Lowe suspects it's Driscoll but he won't say too much until he has confirmation." Colin shifted his gaze to Emma, his blue-gray eyes more gray against the English landscape. "How're you doing?"

"I miss Ashford Castle." She gave him with a quick smile, hoping it reached her eyes. "The first night of our honeymoon."

"It was a good night."

"Yes, it was."

6

Emma wanted to take a look behind the dovecote, so Colin went with her. He didn't know if interviewing witnesses was getting them anywhere, but presumably Henrietta Balfour was next. She could be interesting. He stayed on the strip of grass between the back of the dovecote and a wooded hillside that descended to a stream, barely visible through the dense foliage. Emma was inspecting disturbed ground a few yards away, likely where Martin Hambly had dug his bucket of fresh loam. Henrietta had found her vintage flowerpot in the heap of junk by the back wall. She and Martin wouldn't necessarily have seen or heard someone walking past the front of the dovecote. Even if they'd run into the man they'd later found dead, it would have been reasonable for them to assume he was a walker on the way-marked trail.

It would have been a feat for either of

them to sneak up to the house, attack the now deceased and then slip back to the dovecote to discuss flowerpots with Oliver York. To work, such a scenario would have required a significant delay between the cut and the man's death. Someone — including possibly the dead man himself — would have had to apply pressure to the wound long enough for Oliver to get back to the house from the dovecote.

Fairly implausible and perhaps not technically, medically or humanly possible. Colin didn't even know for certain the deceased had been attacked. He and Emma might not get the final determination ahead of the public. He'd been in similar positions as DI Lowe when he'd been with the Maine marine patrol. He tended to be tight-lipped by nature but some investigations called for trust and sharing. He couldn't say this one did, especially given his and Emma's relationship with their fugitive. If Colin was in charge, he'd probably tell them to turn around and go back to London, MI5 or no MI5.

Colin had promised to keep crusty Jeremy Pearson — his MI5 contact — in the loop, but he'd gotten the mildest of warnings in return. "That's okay," Pearson had said. "I'll know what you two are up to."

"Henrietta Balfour?"

"Don't be fooled because she's planting flowers these days."

"I'm never fooled by people who plant flowers."

Pearson hadn't laughed.

Colin gathered that Henrietta was a garden designer for the same reasons he sometimes flirted with becoming a tour-boat operator — it was a way to avoid or cope with the stress of the job, burnout, decompression. He hadn't quit to take tourists out on the Atlantic to see puffins, seals, whales and Arctic terns. Henrietta Balfour had quit MI5 to design gardens.

A woman he assumed was the ex-MI5 officer came around the dovecote. "You must be Special Agent Donovan," she said, approaching him as she tucked windblown red-brown curls behind her ear with one hand and lifted the hem of her maxi skirt with the other. "Henrietta Balfour. I understand you and Special Agent Sharpe want to talk to me."

"We would, thanks." Colin took in her muddy, somewhat disheveled state. She had on a dark green rain jacket over her top and skirt. He wasn't sure anything matched. He had to admit she wasn't what he'd expected. "I spoke to a mutual friend earlier. He says you'll be straight with me and give complete answers to my questions."

"Mmm. Yes."

"Do you want to speak with him yourself?"

She shook her head. "He called me before I left the house. We have a history. I got the message loud and clear. Since when is the FBI investigating a UK crime?"

"We're not. We're assisting."

"Is that what you call it? I know about you two. You're Oliver's FBI-agent friends."

Colin gritted his teeth at being referred to as one of Oliver York's friends. "Would you like to talk here or would you prefer to go somewhere else?"

"Here is perfect." She breathed deeply, as if the smell of the lush greenery was just what she needed, and then looked up at the sky before shifting to him with a slight smile. "The rain's holding off but we've had such a stretch of beautiful weather, I won't complain when it downpours. We could use the rain. Honestly, Special Agent Donovan, I don't know how I can help you. I'm a simple garden designer these days. I told the police everything I saw."

A cagey remark since *saw* wasn't quite *know* and Henrietta, an experienced intelligence officer, would know the difference.

Colin let it go. "Where have you been since you finished with the police?"

"I had tea and a sandwich at home, met friends, cleaned the kitchen, took a shower and walked here. I wasn't in a hurry. Now, what can I do for you? You must already know the basics. Martin Hambly and I found a man dead on Oliver York's doorstep."

"Go through your story with me if you would." Colin paused, not sure yet what to make of her. "And tell me why you're here."

"I'm here because you want to talk to me."

"Ms. Balfour."

She gave him a cool look. "You mean tell you why an ex-MI5 officer is now a garden designer and Oliver is a client. I suppose now isn't the time to get cheeky with you, is it?"

"Not for me to say."

"Of course it isn't but you've managed to make your point, anyway, haven't you? I'm not the sort to break into a sweat, but I'm out of practice and your rugged, kick-ass American manner is breaking me into quite the sweat."

"Could be you walked faster than you thought," Colin said mildly.

She gave him a grudging smile. "Could be. I didn't kill that man, if that's what you're trying not to ask me, seeing how you have no jurisdiction here, but that you want to know, seeing how you *are* an FBI agent."

"Ms. Balfour, if I have something to ask, I'll ask. Answering is up to you."

Her eyes narrowed, and he saw she was on her game — alert, deliberate, calculating. "All right, then. Fair enough. This morning I was mucking about here in the potting shed with Martin. Then Oliver arrived for a few minutes, gave us his opinion on a vintage flowerpot I'd discovered back here and left. Not long after that, Ruthie Burns, the housekeeper, alerted us to an emergency at the house involving Oliver and a dying man. I had her ring the police and Martin and I went to see what we could do. By then it was too late. The man was dead and Oliver was gone."

"Did you recognize the dead man?"

"No, but I think Martin might have. There was a great deal of blood. There's not much question his brachial artery was cut. I shouldn't be surprised, should I, Special Agent Donovan, if you have personal experience with cutting arteries? My own experience is theoretical. I've never actually seen an arterial bleed-out before. I did help stop one a while back, before it could spurt blood."

"An injured colleague?"

"In fact, no. A suspect. Not that it matters." She seemed to just notice a spot of mud on her skirt, by her right hip, then flicked it off and zeroed in on Colin again. "Presumably you, Special Agent Sharpe and I are all on the same side. We want to find Oliver and we want to know what happened today that resulted in that man's death. Who he is, why he died, how."

Colin considered her crisp account and decided she wasn't unaffected by the morning's events. "No argument from me," he said.

"But you're not satisfied. You want all the details." She sighed, glancing down toward the stream. "I had such different plans for today. I wonder if the man who died did, too, or if the day went exactly as he'd planned. And Oliver." She turned to Colin, a warmth to her eyes but also an intensity that suggested her MI5 past. "You had different plans for today, too, I'm sure. I understand you're on your honeymoon."

"Were."

"Yes. Well, then. I've given you the basics, but why don't I repeat exactly what I told the police? Then you can ask any questions."

"Whatever suits you."

"Mmm, yes. No doubt."

126

She ditched the sarcasm and gave him the details of the morning in a professional manner, with the specificity Colin would expect from someone with her background. He didn't notice any obvious discrepancies between her and Martin Hambly's versions.

"Who hired you to do the York gardens?" Colin asked when she finished.

If she was surprised by his question, she didn't show it. "Martin Hambly, with Oliver's approval. My grandfather and my great-aunt were friends with the elder Yorks."

"Could Oliver have gotten out of here without Martin's assistance?"

"Oliver managed to steal paintings in at least eight cities across the globe without Martin's assistance."

"That's the assumption," Colin said. "Did you recommend MI5 get in touch with Oliver?"

"How is that relevant?"

"I don't know that it is."

"My aunt died last year and left me her house. I'd been in and out of the village a lot, and I decided to make a career change."

"Tired of being an intelligence officer or were you helped along in your career change?"

"You mean was I sacked? No, I wasn't. I

could have been, thanks to our mutual friend, if that matters."

Colin shrugged. "It doesn't to me. You didn't answer my question about Oliver but we can let that go. Any guess how long between the cut to the artery and unconsciousness and death?"

"It's impossible for me to say. It was a grievous wound, obviously. It's possible but not certain pressure would have made a difference or he'd have survived if he'd received medical attention sooner."

Colin motioned to the dovecote-turned-potting-shed. "Do you get restless digging up old flowerpots, Ms. Balfour?"

"Henrietta. Please." His question didn't seem to bother her. "I've always loved gardening. My aunt's death and then the last months of my previous career helped me to see I was more suited to gardening than to intelligence work. Perhaps a tough FBI agent such as yourself wouldn't understand. It's been a dark day, Colin. I'm entitled to let off a bit of steam. And it's all right if I call you Colin, isn't it?"

"Sure thing, Henrietta."

"To answer your earlier question, I have no doubt Oliver managed to get away without help. Absolutely. He's a solitary creature and I suspect he had a plan in place for years for a quick exit should the need arise."

"I've no doubt, either," Colin said, appreciating her directness.

"We're in agreement? Excellent. I have no idea where Oliver is. I have no relationship with him besides impressing upon him the importance of a proper pruning regimen."

"But you did put MI5 onto him."

She shoved her hands into her jacket pockets. "It's not as simple as that. We knew about him after you and Emma — I hope it's all right to call her Emma — unveiled him as a serial art thief. I suggested we could benefit from his particular expertise, contacts and outright brazenness. Since I quit to do garden design, I don't know what happened with my suggestion."

"Would you tell me if you did?"

"Yes."

Colin suspected she was telling the truth. "The police?"

"They aren't FBI agents with high-level MI5 friends."

"I understand you and Oliver grew up together."

"I grew up in London but I visited my aunt often. Oliver's three years older than I, and we did see each other growing up, and since. If you're asking if I'm sleeping with him —"

"I'm not but you can tell me if you want," Colin said, his tone neutral.

"Right." As if she knew what he was thinking. "Did our 'mutual friend' put you up to this line of questions? Because it's ridiculous. Oliver is as solitary as they come. He doesn't have relationships."

"No one put me up to anything, Henrietta."

She pulled a bit of dried leaf out of her hair and cast it into the grass. "Oliver and Martin could be friends, I suppose. Martin can be formal and old-fashioned, but so can Oliver in his own peculiar way. At root, though, theirs is an employer-employee relationship. It's not what I would call a true friendship."

"A lonely existence for them both?"

"Perhaps, to an outside eye. Martin's driven by an uncompromising sense of duty to the Yorks. Oliver's a survivor." She gave her curls a shake, as if she wasn't sure if more leaves might fall out. "What about you and Emma? Is your relationship with Oliver a true friendship?"

Colin shook his head. "Not going there, Henrietta."

A light breeze blew curls into her face but she didn't brush them aside, instead keeping her gaze steady on him. "Oliver says your hometown is a gloomy fishing village on the southern Maine coast, not far from Heron's Cove, where Sharpe Fine Art Recovery has its central offices. Oliver likes Heron's Cove. Right so far?"

"Right so far, except my hometown isn't gloomy." Colin grinned. "It's not always gloomy, anyway."

There was a spark of humor in her eyes. "I suppose even struggling Maine fishing villages have their charms. It's not as cute as Heron's Cove, though, is it?"

"Few places are."

"This area is famous for its twee honey-stone villages."

Emma joined them from her spot by the digging. Colin introduced her. She'd been within decent if not great earshot but wouldn't want to interrupt an interview or distract them. She and Henrietta shook hands.

"Pleased to meet you, Emma," Henrietta said, then turned again to him. "I've never been to Maine. Perhaps one day."

"I'm sure you'd love it." Emma rubbed her fingertips on the old stone of the dove-cote, next to the pile of junk where Henrietta had found the vintage flowerpot. "Did you meet my grandfather when he visited

Oliver in January?"

"No, I didn't."

"Do you know if he and Oliver have been in touch recently?"

Henrietta frowned. "No idea. Why?"

Emma told her about the break-in at Wendell's place in Dublin.

"Oh, well, now, that's interesting," Henrietta said. "Good your grandfather wasn't hurt, but the break-in can't be a coincidence, can it? I understand he and Oliver have formed an odd friendship."

Odd was the word Colin would use, too, but he said nothing.

"We don't know if the break-in and the events this morning are connected," Emma said.

Colin noticed she hadn't told Henrietta about the call from Oliver. In her place, Colin would have made the same decision and let DI Lowe decide what to tell them.

Henrietta zipped her jacket, signaling she was wrapping up. "I'm feeling a touch of survivor's euphoria, I think. Just seeing a man minutes after he bled to death will do the trick, whether or not he was attacked. As I explained, I'd never seen him prior to finding him this morning. Martin was incredibly composed, did I tell you? He went into a bit of a stupor for a moment but he pulled himself together." She patted her hips, obviously signaling she was done. "Well, then. Anything else?"

Colin shook his head. "Thanks for speaking with us."

"You're welcome." She pointed vaguely toward the main road. "Don't hesitate to get in touch if you have further questions or any thoughts you'd like to share. Let's hope Oliver simply panicked and will surface by nightfall."

Oliver York hadn't become a successful international art thief and eluded authorities for a decade by panicking, but Colin didn't offer Henrietta his opinion. She said goodbye and eased around to the front of the dovecote, her gait and demeanor normal, if not as perky as it probably had been when she'd arrived at the York farm that morning.

"What do you make of her?" Emma asked, peeking into a compost bin.

"She's a pro," Colin said. "She wasn't unaffected by coming upon a bloody corpse, but it didn't shake her to her core."

"Her training kicked in."

"I've never met an MI5 agent turned English gardener."

"What do you think the police know about her?"

Colin shrugged. "They won't tell us. I wouldn't, in their shoes."

Emma moved toward him, away from the back wall of the dovecote. "Oliver will be less valuable to MI5 and MI6 the more distance he puts between himself and his past."

"The longer he goes without sneaking around the world stealing art, the better. It's time he led a quiet life. Even after MI5's finished with him, he'll never be prosecuted for his thefts."

"Returning the art undamaged helped. Do you suppose he kept it here on the farm? A moot point now." She peered down through the trees toward the stream. Birds twittered nearby. "It's a pretty place. I wonder where we'd all be now if Oliver had returned the stolen artwork before we figured out he's our serial thief."

"It took identifying him to get him to return the art," Colin said.

"Maybe. Probably." Emma shifted, the dappled light on her face darkening, deepening the green of her eyes. "I don't think Oliver's thieving past is behind what happened today."

"It's not a good day, Emma. Oliver needs to show himself."

She didn't respond. She didn't need to.

They returned to the front of the dove-cote. Henrietta Balfour hadn't stuck around. Other than the police officer, Colin didn't see anyone else. He studied his bride as she stared up the lane toward the York house. "What's on your mind, Emma?"

She turned to him and nodded toward the dovecote door. "I want to take a look in Oliver's stonework studio."

"Doesn't he keep it locked?"

"Yes, but I know where he keeps the key."

7

They didn't need a key. The door to Oliver's stone-cutting studio was unlocked. The key, an ordinary skeleton key, was hanging on a hook, out of sight on the wall above the potting table. Emma left it there. "Going through an unlocked door is easier to explain than going through a locked one," she said. "Oliver told me he gave up stone-cutting. He said he lost interest."

"Do you believe him?" Colin asked.

"I believe he's not doing any stone-cutting here. Whether he's given it up entirely, I don't know. I think so, though."

But thinking so wasn't enough, she knew.

She and Colin entered the studio, a small room on the west side of the dovecote. This was where Oliver had polished and inscribed a series of small, polished stones with Celtic crosses and symbols honoring Saint Declan. He'd taunted her grandfather with them for years, and eventually her and Lucas, too.

Now, though, most of the tools of Oliver's stone-cutting "hobby" were packed into crates stacked against the wall, ready for sale, donation or storage. Saws, heat guns, polishing wheels, different kinds of glue, various hammers and chisels. The rough wood workbench was cleaned off. Emma didn't see any stones, sketches or tracings that might have hinted at what had gone on here. A row of small chisels in a variety of sizes and shapes remained on a magnetic strip, perhaps awaiting special packaging — she had no idea.

Colin ran his fingers across the top of the workbench. "No point locking up with nothing to hide. Lock the outside door and call it a day. No need to bother with the studio door. Wouldn't matter now if Henrietta Balfour, Martin or one of the farm workers got in here. Nothing to see."

Emma nodded in agreement. Privacy and discretion were no longer an issue for Oliver and his secret work here. The once-incriminating studio was now tidy and sterile.

"You wonder how a troubled English boy ends up fascinated by an early Irish saint," Colin said. "Did his interest prompt him to choose the O'Byrne house for his first theft, or did that theft prompt his interest in Saint

Declan? One of your chicken-and-egg questions."

"You do have a way of cutting to the chase," Emma said with a smile. "The silver cross he stole and the crosses on the headland where he hid that night depict Saint Declan. By then Oliver was already an expert in pagan Celtic and early Celtic Christian history, myths, legends and folklore."

"He named his consulting business Left Hand Enterprises after an Irish proverb."

"Lamh chle Ultain id ughaidh," Emma said. "My Irish pronunciation isn't great but close enough."

"It means 'the left hand of Ultan against evil and danger.' " Colin winked at her. "I remember. Ultan was a disciple of Saint Declan who raised his left hand against Nordic invaders and stopped their attack on the Irish coast.

"He kept the people safe," Emma said.

"An ancient Batman."

Colin liked to compare Oliver York and Martin Hambly to Batman and his trusted aide, Alfred. Amused, cheeky as ever, Oliver had chosen Alfred as the name for his wire-fox-terrier puppy. But the analogy fit with the stories about Saint Declan's healing miracles and Ultan's standing up against attacks on the innocent. Unraveling the meaning of Left Hand Enterprises had been a pivotal clue in identifying Oliver as the serial art thief who'd launched his career in Saint Declan country on the south Irish coast.

"I wonder what hobby Oliver will move on to next. Gardening, maybe." Emma noticed a gap in the line of small tools above the workbench. "It looks as if one is missing, doesn't it?"

Colin shrugged. "Could be a tool that broke and never got replaced or an intentional gap."

"Oliver is an expert in martial arts. He wouldn't necessarily need a weapon to kill someone, but it would be difficult for someone to kill him without one. If he was attacked this morning, he had a right to defend himself." She touched the empty space, trying to picture what tool had been there. "I know I'm stating the obvious."

"Sometimes it bears stating."

"We can ask Martin if there's a tool missing. I wouldn't be surprised if he's inventoried every chisel, knife, pair of pliers and glue gun in this place."

They left the studio and went outside. A slight breeze stirred, but Emma couldn't smell any roses. Colin headed to the police officer and let him know about the gap in the line of chisels. The officer could decide whether to notify DI Lowe.

When Colin returned to the dovecote, Martin Hambly was walking toward them from the farmhouse. He waved, signaling he wanted to speak with them. "I was in such a state I didn't think to offer to help you find a place to stay," he said as he joined them. "Oliver would invite you to stay at the house if he were here. The police say they'll have the crime scene cleared soon. The bloodstains . . ." He cleared his throat.

"We'll get to that."

"Thanks, Martin," Colin said, "but we're not staying at Oliver's house."

"At least let me offer you a bottle of his best Scotch. He'd want that."

Emma gave him a reassuring smile. "We'll be fine, thanks."

He nodded. "Understood. The police had me take a look around inside the house. I saw nothing unusual, no indication Oliver left in a hurry, packed a bag, washed off blood. There's no blood in the house, in fact. Not so much as a drop."

"That probably means Oliver went straight to his car without going inside," Emma said. "Might he keep a packed bag in the trunk or tucked in a safe spot away from the house?"

Martin shook his head, his growing fatigue and exasperation evident. "I have no idea. I wouldn't be surprised if he does, though." He motioned toward the house. "I should check on Ruthie and Nigel, and Henrietta. It's been an upsetting day. If there's anything I can do for you two, please don't hesitate to give me a ring."

"A tool seems to be missing from Oliver's stone-cutting studio," Colin said. "Do you know anything about that?"

Martin's chin snapped up. "What?"

Emma explained what she and Colin had discovered in the studio. "We noticed it wasn't locked," she added.

"We haven't locked the studio for weeks," Martin said. "We just lock the outside door. Oliver's particular about his tools. There were no gaps the last time I was in there. That was about five o'clock yesterday afternoon. I didn't check this morning. I doubt Henrietta did, either."

"If there is a tool missing," Colin said, "could it be sharp?"

Martin nodded, gulped in a breath. "Those particular tools are all extremely sharp."

Sharp enough to cut an artery, then.

Emma knew she didn't need to articulate that point. It hung in the air between them, understood if not proof a tool was missing, never mind responsible for the fatal cut.

She and Colin went with Martin back into the studio. He nodded immediately when he checked the row of small tools. "A chisel is missing. I can see it now. It's slender and lightweight, about twenty centimeters long with a flat blade."

"It would fit into a palm or a jacket pocket, then," Colin said.

Martin gave a grim nod. "I've never touched any of these small tools and certainly not that particular one."

"So we won't find your fingerprints on it." Colin glanced at the packed crates and boxes. "You're positive Oliver didn't come in here this morning?"

"Positive," Martin said. "He didn't enter the dovecote at all when he met Henrietta and me here this morning. I have no way of knowing if he'd come down prior to that, but I also have no reason to suspect he did."

Emma leaned against the workbench and crossed her arms on her chest. "Did Henrietta go inside the dovecote?"

"Yes, of course, as did I, but we didn't come in here to the studio." Martin rubbed the back of his neck. He was clearly agitated.

"We left the outside door unlocked while we were out back for a bit. I suppose someone could have slipped inside then — looking for a gardening tool, perhaps — and discovered the stone-cutting tools."

Colin eased into the studio doorway. "Dusk comes late this time of year. Did Oliver go out after he returned from London, maybe to get some air or walk the dog?"

"Not that I'm aware of," Martin said. "I had Alfred with me at my cottage and took him to the house to see Oliver. I still had Alfred's crate, so he didn't stay. Terriers prefer one master. I want it to be Oliver, but we're working on that."

"The police will want to talk to you about the missing chisel," Colin said.

"Yes, of course. I'll wait here for them." He glanced around the packed-up studio. "Oliver has decided to let this room be reincorporated into the dovecote's main purpose as a potting shed. Henrietta will put it to good use, no doubt, now he's redoing the landscaping and adding more flowerbeds and flowerpots and who knows what. He's finally seen the wisdom of why his grandmother converted this building into a potting shed in the first place."

Emma and Colin thanked him and headed back outside. The air was cooler, but she

143

could feel the humidity that spelled impending rain. Colin stood next to her. "Who stole the chisel out of the quaint Cotswold potting shed?" He sucked in a breath. "Hell."

"Not our usual case, I know," Emma said. "The chisel might not even matter. Oliver could have grabbed it to cut open a package and forgot to put it back. If he didn't take it, maybe it disappeared a while ago or he accidentally threw it away."

"Or someone took it," Colin said.

"Right. Or someone took it. Killer, witness, our dead man, an accomplice who wanted to cover up what happened and didn't have much time to think."

"If Martin's right and this man is Davy Driscoll, Oliver could have recognized him — or thought he recognized him — and snapped."

Emma frowned. "Do you think that's likely?"

Colin didn't answer at once. "Oliver doesn't snap," he said finally. "He's self-disciplined and well-trained. He'd never have pulled off a ten-year string of high-profile heists if he couldn't cope with surprises."

Emma nodded in agreement. "He buried his emotions after his ordeal as a boy. His studies, his thefts, his solitary life, his dual

144

identities — they all helped him keep his feelings stuffed deep. If they exploded to the surface this morning, it's hard to predict what he'll do." She digested her own words. "We need to find him."

"It's better if he surfaces on his own."

"Yes."

DI Lowe arrived but he didn't go straight into the dovecote to see Martin. "Mr. York's Rolls-Royce has been found in Stow-on-the-Wold in a church car park. A wallet and phone were on the front seat. They belong to a man named Reed Warren. We're almost certain he's Davy Driscoll. You know that name, don't you, Agents Sharpe and Donovan?"

Emma answered. "Yes, we do."

"This isn't just a courtesy update," Colin said.

The detective inspector turned to him. "That's right, it isn't. Reed Warren's phone contains text messages between him and a Father Finian Bracken. I believe you know him."

Emma recognized Colin's look. Bridled aggravation. "Yes," he said. "We know him."

DI Lowe clearly had already known the answer. "Stick around," he said. "I'll talk to Martin Hambly. You two be where I can find you."

8

Heron's Cove, Maine

As much as Finian Bracken longed for fish chowder and tea — even the terrible tea at Hurley's on Rock Point harbor — he found himself pulling his BMW into the car park next to Sharpe Fine Art Recovery in Heron's Cove. The day had started foggy, dreary and bleak, which matched his mood, but now the sun was shining, glistening on the tidal river in front of him as he got out of his car. His BMW was his most conspicuous indulgence as a parish priest. He'd bought it with funds he'd earned as a whiskey man back home in Ireland, before seminary and the priesthood.

A lifetime ago, those days seemed now.

He was a fish out of water in Maine. A fish out of water in the priesthood, too. He'd lost his wife and their two small daughters eight years ago in a sailing accident. Shattered, drinking too much, he'd spent months in a stupor of self-recrimination, despair and unfathomable grief, until finally he'd received a call to a different life. He'd entered seminary and had begun the long, exacting process to become a priest. He'd expected to serve a parish in his home country of Ireland, but a chance meeting with a priest planning a year-long sabbatical had landed him in the struggling village of Rock Point, Maine. He'd met Colin Donovan on his first day in Maine last June, and they'd become friends. Now Father Callaghan had decided not to resume his duties at St. Patrick's Holy Roman Catholic Church, and Finian was staying. For how long was anyone's guess.

Heron's Cove was quainter and more upscale than Rock Point, but both offered a charm he had come to recognize and appreciate as pure coastal Maine. Next to the car park was the gray-shingled Victorian house that served as the main offices for Sharpe Fine Art Recovery, a small, highly respected family business. During his year in Maine, Finian had come to know the Sharpes, including Dublin-based Wendell Sharpe.

He wasn't here to see the Sharpes. He was here to see a guest at the inn next to the Sharpe offices.

Finian hesitated, his tentativeness a signal, perhaps, he wasn't as fully committed to his mission in Heron's Cove as he'd been when he'd started out from the rectory twenty minutes ago. It was understandable, he supposed. Not once since he'd left Bracken Distillers and entered the priesthood had he envisioned his new vocation sending him to check on a killer.

A man he had good reason to suspect was a killer, anyway.

"I did a terrible thing in my youth, Father Bracken. A terrible thing."

Those had been the man's words on Tuesday morning in Finian's office. He'd identified himself as Reed Warren, but Finian knew that wasn't his real name. Although never explicitly stated, Finian was convinced Reed Warren's real name was Davy Driscoll, and he was one of the two men who'd killed Oliver York's parents and kidnapped him as a boy. Finian had no proof and the man hadn't confessed to those unspeakable crimes, but it was understood between them those were the facts of the matter.

It was high tide, and Finian could feel the chill of the sea, past the narrow channel to his left, where the Atlantic and the Heron River met. With the arrival of spring and warm weather, boats of every kind — sailing, motor, yacht, lobster, marine patrol, kayak — sailed through the channel, to and from private and public moorings. He'd never had a passion for boats. His first attempt at a boating holiday had ended in tragedy. Sally and little Kathleen and Mary had boarded ahead of him. He'd had work to finish up at the whiskey distillery he owned with his twin brother, Declan, and had looked forward to meeting them. As they'd sailed up the west Irish coast, a rogue wave had capsized their boat, and they'd drowned. His beloved wife and their two daughters, gone to God in a flash.

Now he had this new life on the southern Maine coast. FBI agents. Murder and mayhem. International criminals. And romance, he thought. Not for himself, of course. Colin had found a woman in Emma as strong-minded in her own way as he was — and she a man who didn't run from the complexities of her family and her past. Finian had performed their wedding service almost two weeks ago. He had good reason to expect two of Colin's three brothers to announce their engagements soon, too.

Right now, however, Finian had other matters on his mind, namely the killer who'd knocked on his office door two days ago.

He glanced at his phone in his hand and reread the last text message on the screen. You won't tell anyone about our talk, will you?

He'd received the text at 2:00 a.m. but hadn't read it until seven — noon in Ireland, where, presumably, Emma and Colin were enjoying whatever remained of their honeymoon. Finian didn't know their exact schedule and hadn't heard from them since their wedding. Properly so.

As far as he knew, Reed Warren was still in Heron's Cove. "I'll probably be at the inn next to the Sharpe offices for a few days," he'd told Finian. "I'll think about what you said."

Finian had urged him to surrender himself to authorities and take things from there, one step at a time. He'd offered to go with him to the Rock Point police. "Don't wait," he'd said. "We can go now. They'll know what to do."

"Hold on, Father. Let's not get ahead of ourselves."

Finian had realized then the man before him — in his late fifties, in failing health if not dying — hadn't come to the church seeking to confront the grave sins he had committed. He'd come seeking information

150

and an easy way out. His words describing his yearning for the healing of his soul through contrition and amends had been little more than lies and manipulation. Whatever his inner turmoil, it hadn't brought him to Finian.

Reed Warren had wanted to know about Oliver York, Emma Sharpe and Colin Donovan.

"You're friends with them, aren't you, Father Bracken?"

Finian hadn't answered the question. He'd sent Reed Warren on his way and hadn't heard from him until the text that morning.

He glanced at the text he'd sent in reply, after his morning prayers. I haven't spoken to anyone but you should. Where are you?

He saw that Reed Warren hadn't yet responded.

The sea breeze stiffened. Finian slipped his phone into an inner pocket in his black jacket. Perhaps coming to Heron's Cove hadn't been one of his finer ideas but he'd had to do something. He'd been troubled by this man's visit since Tuesday. With the text, *not* acting had struck him as an untenable proposition. He half expected his would-be penitent to bolt out of the inn and race to one of the parked cars, but he didn't.

He walked across soft grass and stepped onto a deck at the inn that overlooked the river and sea. At one of the sprinkling of tables, an elderly couple sat across from each other, reading separate sections of the newspaper. They glanced up but paid little mind to the Catholic priest entering the inn through a glass door.

Finian walked down a short hall, past a large aquarium with a range of small fish darting in the clear turquoise water. The inn's decor was contemporary but the colors were traditional Maine seacoast — turquoise, sea green, crisp white. He had dined at the restaurant a few times, on his own and with his sister when she'd visited in May. Never with his FBI-agent friends, or with anyone from Rock Point.

He stopped at the reception desk and spoke to a young woman who told him Reed Warren had checked out of the inn on Tuesday around lunchtime. That was after he'd visited Finian in Rock Point. He thanked the receptionist and went back out to the deck. The elderly couple had gone, leaving behind their newspaper, held down by their coffee mugs. He appreciated the wind. Maybe it would help clear his head. Where had Reed Warren been when he'd sent his texts? Had he returned to England?

Finian could see him rapping his knuckles on his office door two days ago. "Father Bracken? My name's Reed Warren. You don't know me. I don't belong to this parish. I want to make a confession. Please hear me out, Father. I'm Catholic, and I'm dying."

Warren had been in clear distress, but he'd also been lying and insincere, as another few minutes of conversation had revealed. Dying? Doubtful. Catholic? No. Seeking absolution — on some level, perhaps, but on his terms, without genuine contrition.

A sacramental confession was between the penitent and God. The priest was forbidden to hold the details of a confession in his memory — to actively try to remember what had been said. Even a partial confession — one started and stopped for any reason — was privileged.

But what was his conversation with Reed Warren?

A man in a gray suit stepped onto the deck. It took a moment but Finian recognized Sam Padgett, one of Emma and Colin's colleagues in Boston. Recently of Texas, he had short-clipped dark hair, dark eyes, a strong, fit physique and a no-nonsense manner that was evident as he greeted Finian. "Father Bracken. Interesting to see you here."

"Special Agent Padgett. What brings you to Maine?"

"I'd like to talk to you, Father." He gestured to an empty table. "Have a seat."

Finian looked out at the river. Two kayakers were coming through the channel on the incoming tide. They raised their paddles out of the water, riding on a swell. The sun was bright, sparkling on the wind-whipped waves.

He turned to Padgett. "What's happened?"

The FBI agent pulled out a chair and stood aside. Finian got the message and sat. Padgett took a seat across from him, but he didn't relax. "Tell me about you and Reed Warren, Father."

Finian considered the directive. "I can't," he said finally.

Padgett acknowledged the statement with a neutral nod. "Let's do this another way, then. I'll tell you about him. He was found dead this morning in England, on the doorstep of Oliver York's country home. He bled to death due to a cut brachial artery. Police are investigating. They have his phone. I'm here because Reed Warren texted you, Father. Those texts aren't privileged."

"What time did he die?"

Padgett's dark eyes settled on Finian. "He was already dead when you sent your second text."

"Oliver?"

"Missing."

"I'm deeply sorry to hear this news, Special Agent Padgett."

"Reed Warren flew to Boston on Saturday. He stopped at the Sharpe Fine Art Recovery offices here in Heron's Cove on Monday afternoon. He saw Lucas Sharpe. Lucas was on his way to New York and didn't have much time. Mr. Warren didn't have an appointment and hadn't called ahead. He said it was a spur-of-the-moment visit and wanted to know more about their work in art recovery. Lucas gave him over to his assistant, who provided him with basic materials. He left after a few minutes."

"Was this an unusual visit?"

"As Lucas put it, unusual but not completely weird. The Sharpes might have a different definition of weird than the rest of us, but interesting, don't you think? Why did Reed Warren want to talk to you, Father Bracken?"

"I can't talk to you about him, Agent Padgett."

"Did he come to you to make a confession?"

"I can't discuss confessions."

The FBI agent sighed. "Can someone who isn't a parishioner walk into your office and make a confession?"

"Under certain circumstances."

"If he's dying?"

Finian nodded. "That's one." He looked out at the kayakers. They were riding the tide onto the riverfront, its beach covered in small, sea-polished stones.

"I don't know yet if Reed Warren was dying before his artery was cut," Padgett said. "Would that make a difference? If he told you he had a terminal disease and he didn't?"

"Hypothetically, no, not necessarily."

"What are you doing in Heron's Cove, Father?"

Padgett merely had to speak with the receptionist to find out. Finian shifted his gaze from the kayakers back to the FBI agent. "I was doing a wellness check on Reed Warren. His text this morning concerned me. He stopped at the church on Tuesday shortly after ten. Two women were there and saw him. Your colleague Colin Donovan's mother, Rosemary, and Franny Maroney. I don't know what they overheard but they will remember Mr. Warren, I've no doubt. I don't think he spoke with them."

"This man's real name wasn't Reed Warren, Father." Padgett's look was steady, steely. "It's Davy Driscoll. Do you know who that is?"

"Yes, I do," Finian said.

Padgett withdrew his phone and showed Finian a photo, a head shot of the man who'd come to his office on Tuesday. "Recognize him?"

"That's the man who told me he was Reed Warren."

"I want to know everything about his visit with you."

Although a priest, a whiskey man and Irish, in the past year Finian had come to have an understanding of FBI agents and their law-enforcement role, their thinking, their training. "I've told you what I can."

"All of it's information you know I have or can get without you." He sat back in his chair, alert, in control. "Your texts and coming here to check on him suggest your conversation with Reed Warren wasn't strictly a sacramental confession, don't they, Father? I'm guessing we're in kind of a gray area."

It was a straightforward question but Finian didn't answer. It didn't matter if a confession had been partial, insincere or cut short by priest or penitent for any reason. He wasn't permitted to reveal to the FBI or anyone else what he and any penitent discussed. Privilege also applied outside confession, in his role as a pastoral counselor.

"All right," Padgett said. "Let's move on. Have you heard from Oliver York?"

Finian shook his head. "No. Did he see this man die?"

"Davy Driscoll died in Oliver's arms, Father."

Finian had come to know Oliver since they'd met in Boston in November, when they'd both got caught up in a murder investigation. "I visited Oliver in February. I stayed at his home in the Cotswolds. To think . . ." He didn't continue. "I'm sorry. This must have been a terrible shock for him. To see one of the men who killed his parents after all these years — do you know if Oliver recognized him?"

"I don't know. I would expect so, though, based on his reaction. Did Reed Warren — Davy Driscoll — give you any indication he or anyone else was in danger?" Padgett leaned forward, placing his elbows on the table and folding his hands as he kept his gaze on Finian. "Father Bracken, did this man say he or someone else planned to harm anyone? Did he make any threats? Was he afraid for his life? Did he tell you he'd committed a crime? Did you encourage him to turn himself in? You get the idea. One man is dead. Another man is missing. We need answers."

"Those are all valid questions," Finian said calmly.

"You thought he was still in Maine. That's why you're here."

"As a point of information, a priest can warn authorities about imminent danger he's heard in confession provided he go into specifics. He can't in any way reveal the source of his information."

"Since you didn't warn anyone, I'll take that to mean Driscoll didn't make or reveal any threats to you."

"You can draw whatever conclusions you like, Agent Padgett. That's not up to me."

Padgett leaned back in his chair and looked out at the kayakers, out of their boats now and pulling off their life vests. "Wendell Sharpe's home in Dublin was broken into yesterday. Did you know that, Father?"

He shook his head. "Is Wendell all right?"

"As far as I know. When did you speak with him last?"

"When he was in Heron's Cove in May.

We discussed Emma and Colin's wedding. He'd expected to stay in Maine through the wedding, but he couldn't do it. The memories. The changes. Dublin is home for him now."

"That wasn't a privileged conversation, Father?"

He smiled. "No, it wasn't or I wouldn't have mentioned it. He told everyone."

"All right." Padgett pushed back his chair and stood. "You know how to reach me if you decide you can reveal more about your conversation with Davy Driscoll, aka Reed Warren. Or call Colin or Emma. But don't get involved in this investigation. Understood? You have a bit of a reputation. Go back to Rock Point and have clam chowder and blueberry pie."

"Thank you, Special Agent Padgett. Good luck with your investigation."

There was a hint of humor in his dark eyes. "I'll need it. I'm going to talk to Colin's mother. She has four sons. Not one of them's going to like it." He grinned, clearly unintimidated. "Take care, Father."

After Padgett left, Finian ambled across the car park, and decided chowder and pie sounded good. It wasn't too early for whiskey, either. Not, he thought, after a grilling by the FBI.

9

Declan's Cross, Ireland

Oliver York punched in Finian Bracken's number on the mobile phone he'd borrowed from the proprietress of the O'Byrne House Hotel in the heart of the south Irish coastal village of Declan's Cross. The borrowing was without Kitty O'Byrne's knowledge, but it wasn't stealing since he would return the phone as soon as he finished his call.

"Hello, Father Bracken."

There was a sharp intake of breath on the other end of the connection. "Oliver. The police are looking for you. Turn yourself in at once. Why are you calling on Kitty's phone?"

"I don't have my phone with me."

"You left it behind or discarded it not wanting to risk the police tracking you."

"There's that, yes."

"But you *are* in Declan's Cross?"

Oliver looked up at the boutique hotel,

framed against ominously churning gray clouds. The long June daylight would work in his favor. He could hear the boisterous laughter of a man, an Irishman, one of the hotel guests gathered in the lounge. The O'Byrne House had changed since Oliver's first clandestine visit a decade ago. Kitty, the elder of the two nieces of the previous owner, John O'Byrne, had converted the rambling old house into what was now a thriving hotel. She was engaged to a garda detective, but he would likely be in Dublin, where he was based. At any rate, Sean Murphy was the least of Oliver's worries at the moment. He knew he'd taken a chance in coming here, but today — the past ten years — had been filled with chances.

He'd had to leave England. He'd had to get away from the dead man, the blood, the rush of memories and questions.

He'd had to come here, to Declan's Cross.

He couldn't fully explain, and right now he didn't have to.

He ignored Finian's question. "I saw the texts between you and Reed Warren. That's not his real name. His real name is Davy Driscoll. He was one of the two men who killed my parents. One of my kidnappers. But I think you know that, and I think you know he died in my arms this morning. Why

162

did he come to you, Finian?"

"I can't talk to you about this man, Oliver."

It was not an unexpected answer from his Irish-priest friend. "I don't remember everything about that night. It's as if some of it's wrapped in gauze. I remember Davy's face. He was scared. He carried me to their getaway van. He and Bart Norcross debated killing me and dumping my body in an alley or on the side of the motorway. Davy didn't do the driving. I was in back with him. Norcross drove." Oliver paused, no sound at all — not even a breath — coming from the other end of the connection. "I've always been certain they killed my parents. Driscoll and Norcross."

"You were a traumatized boy but you were able to identify them."

"What if I got it wrong?" Oliver said in a half whisper. "Is that why he came to you? Davy? Did he tell you he and Norcross didn't kill my parents?"

Finian didn't answer immediately, as if he was taking great care to consider his response. "Some people draw a sense of power from manipulating others to get what they want," he said finally. "That's a general statement. It's not specific to any particular person."

163

"Why would a man who knew he was dying lie to me?"

"Why wouldn't he lie?" Finian asked quietly.

"A dying man who doesn't care about eternal damnation or doesn't believe in it could lie and manipulate to get something he wanted. Satisfaction, vengeance, something tangible for another person." Oliver heard how hollow his voice sounded. "Maybe a stab at cheating God. Lie to get eternal salvation instead of eternal damnation. Do Catholics believe in eternal damnation, Finian?"

"We believe in God's transforming and unconditional love. Oliver, please —"

"If an amoral, unprincipled man — or woman — lies and manipulates to get what he wants, even if he's not alive to see the results, it's mission accomplished. He gets what he wants." Oliver swallowed, aware he was still reeling from his ordeal that morning. "What did Davy Driscoll want? What was his purpose in coming to the farm?"

"Oliver . . ."

"I know. You can't tell me. I assume it's a question of priestly privilege. Or do you have a Donovan breathing down your neck? I assume our mutual friends Colin and Emma are in my twee Cotswold village by

164

now. Another FBI agent? Sam Padgett? Matt Yankowski? I'll guess Padgett." Oliver didn't wait for Finian's response. "Did Reed Warren tell you that wasn't his real name? Did he tell you he'd been on the run for thirty years for murder and kidnapping?"

"Oliver, I can't . . ." Finian took in another sharp breath. "I urge you to turn yourself in to the gardai, or phone Emma and Colin next and ask them what you should do."

"Did this man confess to murdering my parents?" Oliver kept his voice steady, cool. "Is that why you're ignoring my questions? Did he tell you about Bart Norcross — where he is, what he's been doing all these years?"

Finian sighed softly. "Are you safe, my friend?"

"Yes. For now. What do you know, Finian? I had to scrub Davy Driscoll's blood off me in a public toilet. He can't hurt anyone else. Surely you can tell me what he said. Or tell the police. I don't care."

"It's glorious in Rock Point," Finian said, his voice somewhat choked. "Come for a visit after you clear things up with the police. If this man really was one of your tormentors, the police will understand why you ran."

"I didn't run," Oliver said. "I left. Our conversation is privileged, isn't it? I'm not a parishioner or a Catholic but you're my . . . what? Confessor? Finian . . . what if *I* caused my parents' deaths? Can you absolve me of that? What if I killed Davy Driscoll today?"

"Will you surrender yourself to authorities?"

Oliver realized he'd hit a brick wall. Finian Bracken wasn't talking. "First thing in the morning. Promise."

"I'm sorry, Oliver. I know this is a difficult day for you. Be well."

"Blast it, Finian."

But the Irish priest was gone. Oliver stared at Kitty's phone and sighed.

Well, he'd had to try.

He spotted Kitty in a window in the bar lounge. Dark-haired and attractive, she was laughing, presumably unaware of his presence in her garden. Had she heard about the morning's events in his English village? Did she know he was on the run? Had Detective Garda Murphy warned her to be on the lookout for the thief who'd slipped into her uncle's rambling old house a decade ago and made off with a fortune in art?

Alleged thief.

Oliver went around to the front of the hotel and trotted up the steps into the entry and deposited the phone where he'd found it on the reception desk. A record of his call to Finian would be on it. Kitty might notice, or she might not. If Finian told the FBI about the call — if the FBI had been standing over him, listening in — Oliver could count on gardai arriving at the hotel.

Best not to help himself to an unoccupied room.

He hoisted his small rucksack onto his back and walked into the village, with its brightly colored homes, shops and businesses. It had quite a different feel from his Cotswold village but had changed little in the past ten years, since his first clandestine visit. He came to a red-painted bookshop with a charming display of children's books in the window. With an unexpected pang, he remembered visiting a London bookshop with his mother. He must have been six, no older than that. She'd loved to read.

Had he caused her death?

He pushed aside the thought — it was radical, unthinkable, absurd — and continued on to the headland. He knew this route well. The lane hugged cliffs above the sea and then wound past and through the Murphy farm and eventually out to a church ruin and a trio of Celtic crosses on a hillside at the tip of the headland, as if they were standing sentry above the Irish Sea.

The police would find his car and the texts from Finian Bracken, if they hadn't already.

He'd left Reed Warren's phone and wallet in the Rolls-Royce. He'd seen no point in taking them with him to Ireland, but he'd known his car wasn't inconspicuous and the police would find it rather quickly. He kept an emergency go-bag in the Rolls as a matter of course and had been able to cover his blood-soaked clothes with a jacket and slip into a public toilet near where he'd parked. He'd changed into fresh clothes and binned the bloody ones, but no doubt the police had found them by now, too.

And it *was* Davy Driscoll who'd died in Oliver's arms that morning.

He hadn't gone mad.

"Why, Finian? Why did Davy Driscoll come to you?"

After seeing the texts, Oliver had considered flying to Boston to speak with his friend himself, but he knew he'd have been stopped at US customs. As it was, he'd been lucky to make it to Ireland by air taxi. Then a taxi to Ardmore and a few miles' walk to Declan's Cross. It probably wasn't a wise place for him to come to, but here he was.

He'd left quite the bread-crumb trail for the authorities.

For the FBI, too. No surprise Emma and Colin were in the thick of things. It was their way.

Then there was MI5. Watching him? Protecting him? Planning to kick him into the churning sea? He liked to think such thoughts were drama and hyperbole on his part but he wouldn't put anything past his MI5 handler.

And Henrietta? What wouldn't he put past her?

Oliver didn't dare think about her now. She'd always been there, a part of his life even when they weren't together — a contemporary, a young girl when his parents had died. She'd loved them. He remembered seeing her in the village after the funeral, confused and frightened with her mop of red-brown curls and the spray of freckles across her nose and cheeks. Now . . . well, now she could have dispatched Davy Driscoll herself, no doubt without getting a speck of blood on her. She'd followed in her grandfather's footsteps. She was MI5. No question in Oliver's mind.

He felt no satisfaction at Driscoll's bloody death. It had given him no clarity, no catharsis and no sense of justice. For decades, he'd waited to recognize Davy Driscoll and Bart Norcross on the street, at the butcher shop, having a pint at the local pub. He'd waited for the police to knock on his door and tell him the two killers' remains had been discovered in an unmarked grave or had been plowed up by a construction crew or a farmer.

Never had he imagined one of them would arrive spurting blood, dying, at his door.

Oliver came to the end of the lane, where a small church lay in ruin next to a low stone wall entangled with overgrown trees and shrubs and bursting with June wildflowers — yellow, purple, pink. Henrietta would know their names in her new incarnation as a garden designer. He had no idea what they were called.

Had Henrietta seen the dead man?

Poor Ruthie Burns, horrified at what she'd seen, would have run straight to the dovecote to alert Martin. Once aware of the situation at the house, no way would either Martin or Henrietta have stayed at the dovecote and waited for the police. They'd have charged up to the house to see what they could do to help.

Oliver squeezed past a holly tree and crept into the graveyard by the skeletal remains of the church. His footsteps made little sound on the soft, uneven ground. He squished into a boggy patch but managed not to get his socks wet. He continued through the graves and up the hill to the trio of tall crosses that stood above the sea.

He breathed in the cool ocean air and gazed at the water, quiet and gray under the clouds. He found comfort in the sturdy stone crosses, with their intricate Celtic knots and spirals and their carvings honoring Saint Declan, a fifth-century patron saint of Ireland, founder of its first Christian settlement and a healer and worker of miracles.

"Ah, if only Saint Declan could help me now."

Oliver couldn't manage to smile at his attempt at lightheartedness.

He needed to rest, and to think.

If Finian told Emma or Colin about his call — which he should — or if Kitty or someone else in the village had recognized him, the police would look for him here. It was where he'd hidden twice, once the night after he'd slipped into the O'Byrne house, and then again last November — ten years later — when he'd returned the stolen pieces.

All except one, an unsigned watercolor

171

landscape of these very crosses, painted, he was certain, by Kitty's younger sister, beautiful, talented Aoife O'Byrne. Oliver was quite certain Aoife was in love with his Irish priest friend, Finian. Detective Garda Sean Murphy owned the farm on the headland — it was Sean's sheep Oliver could hear baaing in the distance — and Sean had been the garda who had investigated the deaths of Finian's family. They'd become friends, and that was how Finian met Aoife, before he'd entered seminary.

Life didn't always take the route one expected or intended.

Oliver sat among the crosses. It was early yet. He would return to the ruin and settle into a sheltered spot for the night, where he'd be protected from the worst of the wind off the water. There'd be rain, too. With his luck the warm, dry weather was ending tonight of all nights. He wouldn't die of hypothermia, at least. It had been a nearer thing his first night out here in November ten years ago.

He really wasn't one for sleeping rough but he'd manage.

He watched a seagull wheel above the headland. Its cry mingled with the sounds of the waves crashing on the rocks far below. Was there a lonelier sound than that of a solitary seagull? Where were its mates? He didn't know much about seagulls, or any birds, for that matter.

Henrietta probably would know bird names, too.

He supposed he could yet discover she wasn't and had never been with MI5, but he doubted it. Why had she left? She'd only made vague pronouncements about leaving her dull London office job to pursue her dream job. Of course she missed Posey, too, but ninety-four was a great age. Oliver hadn't brought up MI5 with Henrietta yet. He probably shouldn't, but he was tempted.

What if he was wrong and she wasn't MI5?

"I don't know what's real and what's not."

He spoke aloud, heard the rawness of his voice.

The seagull disappeared back across the headland.

What if he *had* done something all those years ago to cause his parents' deaths? What if he'd pulled the trigger that night and couldn't remember?

Davy, who did this to you?

I did . . . Your mother . . . Deborah . . .

Is anyone else in danger?

Scotland. The Sharpes . . . careful . . . I live in the ruin.

The dying words of a killer. A warning?

An explanation? Delusional nonsense as he lost consciousness? Oliver had tried desperately to save him but he'd lost too much blood. He'd wanted Davy Driscoll alive. He'd wanted him to answer for his crimes — to answer the questions that lingered about that terrible night that had changed so many lives.

Had Driscoll cut himself and arranged to die in Oliver's arms? Had he lain in wait, nicked his own brachial artery and lunged at Oliver when he returned from the dovecote, all part of a calculated, deliberate plan to . . . *what*? Absolve himself? Was that why he'd gone to see Finian Bracken?

Or had he been murdered?

Oliver dug his emergency blanket out of his rucksack and peeled it from its tiny package. He unfurled it and wrapped it around him, wishing he'd had one his first night up here ten years ago. As then, he could see his mother's face when she'd grabbed him, one of her last acts before her death. Her eyes had been bright with fear, her fingers digging into him as she'd desperately tried to pull him to safety.

There had been no safe place that night.

He heard rain spatter onto rocks around him and huddled under his waterproof blanket. He'd have no dinner, but tonight rest was more important.

What if his memory of what had happened thirty years ago was faulty? Finian was right. He'd been a traumatized young boy. What if his mother had grabbed him to silence him — what if he'd been the one who'd alerted the killers that the apartment wasn't empty? What if he'd led them to his parents?

If only he could have gotten Davy Driscoll treatment in time to repair the wound to his artery and ask him questions. Learn the truth about that violent night, about why he'd come to the farm now, after all this time.

Why hadn't Driscoll put pressure on his wound and stopped the bleeding himself? Easier said than done, perhaps. It had been a grievous wound.

Oliver looked up at the crosses, steady and unmoving against the gray sky, holding their spot for more than two hundred years, and he promised himself he would learn the truth.

He felt a fat raindrop plop on his forehead. Right now, he'd love a bottle of good Scotch. He'd even settle for Irish whiskey.

He smiled, thinking of what Finian Bracken would say. Had he inadvertently sent Davy Driscoll to him that morning? To confess, and then turn himself into the police?

Questions. No answers.

A bit longer up here, Oliver decided, and then he'd head down the hill to the ruin and settle in for the night amid the Celtic graves and crosses.

10

The Cotswolds, England

Henrietta sat on a stool at the bar in the village pub. She was in the original sixteenth-century part of the building with its low, beamed ceilings and large, open stone fireplace, unlit on this damp late afternoon. One could imagine rough men giving dark looks in this very spot over the centuries. The pub was bustling but not as crowded as it would be later into the evening. It drew a mix of locals and tourists. The barman and a man at the end of the bar were discussing the death at the York farm. No one seemed particularly concerned about a killer on the loose. Whatever the cause and circumstances of the man's death earlier today, it wasn't unreasonable to think it was confined to eccentric Oliver York and his world and had little, if anything, to do with the village.

Her pint arrived, a local brew that tasted

a bit hoppy to her, but it would do. The police had called on her again to ask about a chisel missing from the stonework studio at the dovecote. They gave no indication they were aware of Oliver's past as an art thief or his work with MI5. She certainly hadn't offered up the information. *Not* her affair. Not any longer. When DI Lowe asked what she knew about the studio, she'd told him, truthfully, Oliver had mentioned he'd taken up stone-cutting as a hobby a while back, but had grown bored with it and decided to move on to other things.

The police didn't find the chisel in their initial search of the house and immediate premises. They were back at it now, presumably. A cut artery was an urgent medical crisis that involved minutes — even mere seconds — before unconsciousness and death. If accidental or self-inflicted, the injured man wouldn't have had time to conceal the implement used to make the cut, whether it had been the missing chisel or something else.

But if a killer had hidden it or taken it?

If a panicked witness had?

Henrietta sipped more of her beer. It really wasn't a stellar choice on her part, but a mediocre brew was the least of her concerns. Annoying she hadn't noticed the missing chisel, but she hadn't been in the studio in days and stone-carving instruments weren't her area of expertise. These days she was preoccupied with flowerpots and color schemes and full sun and partial shade and all the rest of what went into a proper garden. She hadn't noticed anything near the body that could have cut an artery, and certainly not a small, slender chisel.

She dipped into a conversation between a pair of walkers at a table behind her. They were discussing the weather forecast for tonight and tomorrow — rain, then clearing — and she decided to concentrate on her own affairs. She yawned, an involuntary reaction she recognized as an aftereffect of the adrenaline jolt she'd received that morning. A pint might not help that particular consequence of her day, but it would help with everything else.

Was the dead man Davy Driscoll, or had the horror of coming upon a complete stranger bleeding out on his doorstep triggered some kind of post-traumatic stress response in Oliver because of what he'd experienced as a child?

MI5 needed Oliver. That was the whole point of having pressed him into service as an agent in the first place. He'd groomed himself, in a way, to be of help. As the dashing, tragic, wealthy Oliver York and the frumpy, scholarly Oliver Fairbairn — as a secret thief, a Hollywood consultant and a world traveler — he'd operated in a variety of circles, and he'd learned a great deal about the people he'd met. A particular area of expertise useful to MI5 was so-called blood antiquities, the illicit trade and sale of ancient works to fund terrorist activities.

Henrietta sighed and gave up on the hoppy pint. She switched it for a Heineken on tap. As she took her first sip, the FBI agents arrived. They came straight to the bar and greeted her. They looked no worse for the wear but she offered to buy them a pint, anyway. One could enjoy a beer without having discovered a dead body.

"Thank you," Emma said, "but we're checking in to a room here."

"Choose one in the building across the courtyard. They're bigger and you won't have any noise from the pub, as the ones upstairs do. Also the courtyard rooms have tubs. You're on your honeymoon. A bath would be lovely tonight, don't you think?"

Emma smiled, but Colin didn't look amused. "Honeymoon's over," he said.

"Ah, but shouldn't newlyweds say the honeymoon will last forever?"

Still no detectable amusement.

Henrietta sat up straighter on her bar stool and decided to carry on. "You're postponing London, I gather. It's because of the texts from Father Bracken to our dead killer? The police asked me if Oliver has ever mentioned him to me. He hasn't, but I met Father Bracken here. He and Oliver were having whiskey. Oliver introduced us." She pointed to a table by the fireplace. "They sat there. I remember. It was cold enough for a roaring fire."

"You were still with your previous employer then," Colin said.

"Yes, I was." She left it at that and took another gulp of her beer. She set the glass a bit too firmly on the polished, worn wood bar. "I really should get on. I stayed here when my aunt was in her last days and the house wasn't suitable for company. You'll like it."

"I'm sure we will," Emma said.

Henrietta nodded to the barman to put the drink on her tab and eased off the stool. "I'm having dinner with friends and neighbors," she said, addressing both FBI agents. "Why don't you join us? We all could use a good meal and good company after today. Stop by my house first and I'll show you Aunt Posey's flowerbeds. She was a brilliant gardener. I'm up a lane on the right before you get to the York farm. It's on the same stream that runs past the York dovecote."

Emma graciously accepted the invitation. Colin looked less enthusiastic.

"Dinner will be a positive end to a terrible day." Henrietta reached down and grabbed her jacket where she'd dropped it onto the floor. She stood straight. "See you later on."

She left them. No doubt they considered dinner part of their FBI duties, but she had to admit she liked the idea of knowing what they were up to. The sky was an ominous gray but the forecast said any real rain wouldn't occur until nightfall. She tied her jacket around her waist and crossed a small park next to the pub. Children had gathered to watch ducks swimming in a stream that meandered through the heart of the quiet village.

Feeling better for her short time to relax, she took a paved walk that cut behind a row of houses. She noticed a purple clematis in a back garden that needed a good chop, and she jumped when a small dog yapped at her from a porch. She was so preoccupied she barely noticed anything else. Only when a car passed at her toes did she realize she'd come to the street.

What a difference from her MI5 days, when she'd never let her mind wander.

She continued past the tiny post office and the flower shop and chemist before turning onto the lane that would take her to the York farm and her house. Would she follow in Posey's footsteps and die in her nineties, without ever having married, with no children? Posey had enjoyed her life and seemed to have left this earth with few regrets beyond wishing she could have helped her brother, Anthony, who'd died so young. She'd had a half-finished cozy mystery on her bedside table when she'd taken her last breath. She'd have wanted to go out that way, content and yet still with things to do. Who didn't?

Henrietta felt her throat tighten. With all she'd done in her years with Her Majesty's Security Service — the close calls, the daunting responsibilities, the low-life cretins and power-hungry, zealous mass murders she'd encountered — why such emotion now?

But she knew. It was being here, being a Balfour, the thoughts of her lonely childhood and her fears for Oliver. What must it have been like for him to have come face-to-face with Davy Driscoll after all this time? Because of course that was who it was this morning, even if the police wouldn't confirm it to her.

As she reached the turn to her house, Henrietta decided she'd have time to work in the garden before dinner.

While Emma checked in to their room, Colin went out to the courtyard and took a call from Sam Padgett. "I'm in Rock Point having clam chowder with Finian Bracken," Sam said. "He's surveying new whiskeys at the bar at the moment. I've discovered I don't like clams."

"That's not why you're calling."

"Nope. It's not. Where are you?"

"I'm watching a chicken peck in an herb border at the pub where we're staying."

"Uh-huh. I was there in February. Brown feathers or black-and-white feathers?"

"Brown. A hen."

"When you went through the academy, did you ever think you'd be talking chickens with another agent? Don't answer."

Colin smiled, saying nothing. Sam had joined HIT last fall. He'd complained about the cold New England winter into April, unimpressed with the nuances of a New England spring. He and Colin got along.

"Okay," Sam said. "Here's what I have. Father Bracken confirmed the man he saw on Tuesday was Reed Warren, aka Davy Driscoll. He won't say much else. Can't, given the privileged nature of their conversation. The receptionists at Sharpe Fine Art Recovery and at the inn next door both confirm they saw the same man on Monday afternoon and Tuesday morning. He left the inn Tuesday morning. I'll get into more of that in a second. Good so far?"

"Yeah," Colin said. "Good."

Padgett continued. "Driscoll flew from London Heathrow to Boston on Saturday, arriving at four p.m. He rented a car. We don't know where he was between his arrival at Logan and his arrival in Heron's Cove on Monday afternoon. He took a return flight on Tuesday night, arriving in Dublin early Wednesday and then flying on to London Heathrow that afternoon."

"He had time to break into Wendell's place." The hen Colin had been watching joined another hen, also brown-feathered, in a border of herbs in front of a stockade fence. "Passport?"

"In the name Reed Warren. No red flags. He's had that alias for a while is my guess. We also learned he rented a car at Heathrow. Has it turned up?"

"Not that I'm aware of."

"I'm standing at the window that looks out onto Rock Point harbor. Not bad, Donovan, never mind I had to wait until June for a proper summerlike day." He was silent. "Father Bracken was able to tell me that two parishioners saw Driscoll enter the church and might have information. One of them is Franny Maroney. I spoke with her. She's scary but I survived."

Franny. Of course. She was an elderly, spry, opinionated parishioner. Her granddaughter was involved with Colin's younger brother, Andy, a Rock Point lobsterman. He pushed back a sudden urge to be home, having chowder with his brothers — with Sam, grousing about clams.

"The other one?"

"Your mother."

"Hell, Sam. My *mother*?"

"She's a good witness. Franny, too. Tough women up here."

"No argument," Colin said. "What did they have to offer?"

"They said they don't believe Reed Warren, aka Davy Driscoll, was for real. They said he left the church after about twenty minutes. They approached him but he brushed them off. They knew he was up to no good. Said if he made a confession to Father Bracken, it was insincere and he needed to go back and try again, starting with asking forgiveness for being rude to old ladies."

"My mother referred to herself as an old lady?"

"Actually that was Franny Maroney's phrase. Your mother said he was a rude bastard."

That sounded more like Rosemary Donovan.

"Your brothers know I spoke with her. They didn't run me out of town, so I guess it's cool. Your father didn't care."

"He's an all's-well-that-ends-well sort," Colin said.

"Franny and your mother overheard Driscoll say he was in Maine because Bracken, Wendell Sharpe, you and Emma are all friends with Oliver York. That got their attention but Father Bracken shut the door to his office. Your mother wanted to listen at the keyhole but Franny reminded her they can't reveal an overheard sacramental confession or they risk — I don't know what. Bolt of lightning. Something. It doesn't matter."

Colin bit back a groan of frustration. "And they saw Driscoll after he and Fin Bracken were done?"

"Yes," Padgett said without hesitation. "Closed-door conversation lasted no more than ten minutes. Driscoll popped out of the office looking irritated, according to

187

your mother, and upset, according to Franny, and then left. He had a car parked in front of the church. They both were annoyed with themselves for not writing down the plate number. I told them it was okay, we had it."

"That's it?"

"That's it. Your brothers will keep an eye on them. Reed Warren wasn't interested in two parish women, Colin," Padgett said. "He also wasn't interested in confessing his sins."

"Can you put Fin on?"

"Sure thing."

Colin thought he felt a stray drop of rain but the sky didn't open up. The chickens warbled and pecked in the herbs, oblivious to anything but their own simple needs.

"Colin, my friend," Finian said in his amiable Irish accent. "I wish we were speaking under better circumstances."

"I do, too. I spoke with Sam. Come on, Fin, do you really think God will cast you into hell if you betray a dead killer's confession?"

"It's not the point but I'm not going to give you a religious lesson."

"You're playing with fire."

"I have my job. You have yours. Let us each respect the other's role."

Colin sat at a weathered wood table and pulled his gaze from the chickens. A stone fountain gurgled in the center of the courtyard. A stockade fence by the parking lot was covered in pink climbing roses. Finian Bracken was an ordained priest. He couldn't discuss a confession. He had a duty and a right to keep silent. His silence was demanded by his vows but also recognized by US law. As much as he might want to, Colin couldn't force Finian to reveal what Davy Driscoll, aka Reed Warren, had told him.

"What about Oliver? Have you spoken with him?"

Finian was silent.

Colin sat up straight. The chickens had hopped onto a low stone wall. On the other side was the driveway and more chickens, some of them black-and-white as well as brown.

"I saw Oliver last in May, before the wedding," Finian said.

My wedding. Colin felt a sudden ache in the pit of his stomach. It had been a gorgeous day in Maine. He and Emma had lucked out. Their families and friends had gathered in one of her favorite gardens overlooking the sea at the Sisters of the Joyful Heart convent.

Oliver had tried to get himself invited.

"I don't like threading-the-needle answers, Fin," Colin said. "Let me be specific. When was the last time you spoke with Oliver York? He called Emma. The police found Driscoll's phone in Oliver's car. He must have seen the texts between you two."

"Oliver called a little while ago because of the texts. That much I can tell you. I believe the rest was confidential. It's my judgment he was speaking to me not as a friend but as a priest with the reasonable expectation of privacy." Finian paused, and Colin resisted an urge to dive into the silence. "I believe you can trust Oliver to turn himself into the police tomorrow morning."

Colin didn't argue with him. He'd tell Padgett and let him have a crack at Finian. Oliver would have had different escape plans in place should a quick exit become necessary given his larcenous history. He'd put one into operation that morning. He was clever, and he had a labyrinthine mind. He could also have had help from MI5.

"Colin?" There was worry in Finian's voice.

"I'm here. Put Padgett back on."

"It's good to hear your voice, in spite of the circumstances. Be well, my friend. Give my love to Emma."

"Thanks, and I will," Colin said, taking

some of the edge off his tone. He got back on with Sam and told him about Oliver's call with Finian. "Oliver was probably looking for information from Fin because of the texts."

"He didn't get any if my experience with Father Bracken is any indication."

No doubt true.

"Your brother Andy offered to take me out on his antique lobster boat. It's kind of sweet he named it *Julianne* after his girlfriend. I mean, for a Donovan, that's sweet. Better than naming a lobster after her."

"It wasn't that sweet," Colin said. "They've been arguing about that boat forever. Go ahead. Have fun. You and Andy can bond or something."

"I don't bond. It won't sink?"

"It won't sink, Sam."

But they both knew he wasn't going on a boat ride. Sam wouldn't rest until he was satisfied he'd turned over every rock in Maine that might have information about Davy Driscoll.

After they disconnected, Colin pushed back a crawling sense of futility. Then Emma came out of the pub's back entrance and crossed the courtyard to him, and his mood instantly improved. "I waited until you were off the phone," she said. "Do I want to know?"

"No."

"But you'll tell me." She held up a door key. "We're on the ground floor overlooking the stream. Our hosts say it's perfect."

A perfect room it was. Emma cracked a window and listened to birds chirping in the trees crowded on the banks of the shallow stream. She could smell the dampness in the air and felt a drop in temperature. It had been spitting rain but there'd be a downpour before long. She wanted nothing more than to crawl into bed with Colin, pull the covers over them and return to honeymoon mode, but she knew that was not to be, at least not yet.

He set their bags on the floor by the closet. "It feels more like March than June."

Emma shut the window. "Maybe it'll be chilly enough for a fire in the pub."

"A pint by the fire on a damp English night sounds good to me." Colin came to her, put his arms around her. "We enjoyed a few good June fires in Ireland."

She leaned into him. "We did, indeed."

He kissed her softly, his palms coursing over her hips. "Ready to go home, aren't you?"

"With you."

"That's the plan, assuming MI5 doesn't spirit me away." He circled her waist, pulling her closer. "Not funny, I know."

"You have ways of managing when you want to go home and can't."

"I focus on the job."

She kissed him again, felt herself wanting more. "I love you, Colin." But she stood back, eyeing him. "Now, what's on your mind?"

"You know me well."

"Getting there."

She sat on the edge of the bed. The room was decorated in a cheerful, contemporary English country style, with a white duvet, raspberry-colored decorative pillows and a cute stuffed sheep. On a white-painted table were cups and saucers, a kettle, tea bags, packets of instant coffee and cream. And cookies, Emma noticed. Ginger cookies, made locally. She'd peeked into the bathroom. It had a window, also overlooking the stream. She envisioned herself sinking into a hot bath, a cup of hot herb tea at her side as she listened to the birds, smelled the rain and put her worries aside. Colin could join her, or scoop her out of the tub.

She gave herself a mental shake. No hot bath right now. No jumping into bed early with her husband. "I tried to reach Granddad while I was waiting for you to finish your call. He isn't picking up or answering my texts." She was silent a moment. "I worry when he doesn't answer."

"Not because he's in his eighties, either. You worry he's up to something."

She didn't deny it. "Maybe Davy Driscoll was connecting the dots and figuring out Oliver was a thief. He went to a lot of trouble to get information. If he saw the stone crosses in Granddad's study and then sneaked into the dovecote and saw the stone-cutting equipment, he could have concluded the crosses were Oliver's work."

Colin helped himself to a bag of the ginger cookies. "I can think of several reasons Driscoll or someone else could have stolen the chisel that have nothing to do with brachial arteries."

"It hasn't turned up yet. It wasn't in Oliver's car."

"Doesn't mean he didn't throw it out the window." Colin tore open the cookies. "Lucky my MI5 guy didn't have us taken in. He called while we were dealing with texts and chisels. Lectured but he didn't yell."

"As if yelling would have fazed you."

"He says the police want our help, especially with Driscoll having been in the US this week. More likely they want to keep us on a tight leash."

"That's what you would want in their place."

Colin grinned and tapped out the cookies. "Damn straight." He handed Emma a cookie. "You would, too."

"Except for Reed Warren, aka Davy Driscoll, how's Rock Point?"

"Across an ocean. A good thing or I'd probably strangle our friend Father Bracken." Colin took a bite of his cookie and then repeated his conversation with their mutual Irish friend. "Whatever Davy Driscoll told Fin, he's not saying. Any loopholes in repeating a confession?"

Emma shook her head. "The rite of penitence and reconciliation is spelled out in canon law. The seal of a sacramental confession is absolute. The priest can't provide information about a penitent's confession to a third party directly or indirectly. Finian only repeated the nonconfessional interaction between him and Driscoll that was witnessed by others —"

"My mother and Franny," Colin said.

That hadn't been something he'd wanted to hear, obviously. "They can tell you what they overheard provided it's outside a sacramental confession. Otherwise they, too, are bound by confidentiality."

"What happens if Finian talks?"

"Violation of the seal of confession means automatic excommunication. *Latae sententiae.* Even if a sacramental confession is reasonably refused or started and then refused for any reason, a priest is still unable to speak of it."

"What if the guy confessing is insincere?"

"The confessional seal holds with impenitence, too. The penitent wouldn't get absolution but he or she would still be entitled to confidentiality. The priest can also choose to give a blessing instead of absolution."

Colin stretched out on the bed atop the duvet and leaned against the pillows. "Driscoll should have spent the last thirty years in prison. If he confessed to murder, would Fin have encouraged him to turn himself in?"

"Yes, almost certainly. Finian would have urged him to go to the authorities and atone for his past."

"But he couldn't call the police himself," Colin said, not making it a question.

"A priest's role as a confessor is to facilitate a penitent's return to God and an end to the moral disorder caused by his or her sins. Confession isn't a free-for-all. There are conditions that permit a priest to reasonably refuse a confession, but if Davy Driscoll said he was Catholic and dying . . ."

"Finian wouldn't have refused him." Colin finished his cookie and set the empty package on the bedside table. "I never bought the absolute-secrecy thing as a kid. I always figured Father Callaghan would rat me out to my parents if I told him the good stuff. Did you tell your priest all your sins?"

"That's between me and the priest."

"Aha. So you were a bad girl before the nunnery?"

Emma laughed. "You're hopeless."

"Is that a yes? You know I have a reputation as a tough interrogator." But he rolled to his feet and reached for his jacket. "Let's go have dinner with Henrietta and her friends. I'll get your naughty past out of you another time."

She tossed the remains of her cookie in the wastebasket. "I'll try Granddad again on the way."

"He's not going to answer. You know that, right?"

"I can get Lucas and my father to try him."

"He'll ignore them, too. Whatever Wendell's up to, we're in England and can't do much about it. We might as well trust him."

"He's gone to see Oliver. I just know it."

She pulled on her rain jacket. "I swear, though, if Granddad's thrown off an Irish cliff by a crazed art thief, it'll serve him right."

"Never mind getting thrown off a cliff. You need to worry about him getting himself arrested."

"That would serve him right, too."

"It'd be nice if Driscoll confessed to your brother, too, but Lucas would have told you."

"In a heartbeat," Emma said without hesitation.

"If there are any loopholes in Finian's understanding of his obligations with his meeting with Davy Driscoll, Sam will find them."

11

The police found the missing chisel stuck in a pot of coleus by the side entrance where Davy Driscoll had bled to death. Martin confirmed it was, in fact, the chisel missing from Oliver's stone-cutting studio. He recognized the worn handle and the sharp, flat steel blade. Although not sprayed by blood itself, the coleus pot, a stone urn that had occupied that spot for years, was within two meters of the spilled blood. Both the urn and the chisel would be closely examined for forensic evidence.

DI Lowe thanked Martin for his help. "Get some dinner and some rest, Mr. Hambly."

"I will, thank you."

"And lock your doors."

Martin went through the house, hearing only his footsteps in the stone-tiled hall. He said hello to a detective sergeant in the kitchen and left through the back door. He welcomed the cool evening air, its dampness, its feel of impending rain. He decided he wanted a fire tonight, more for atmosphere than heat. He was exhausted and yet his mind was buzzing with worries and questions.

He hadn't said anything to the police, but he suspected it had been both potting soil and blood he'd seen on the chisel blade. It had been stabbed into the soil, not tossed in among the coleus leaves. Martin supposed a flailing, dying man spurting arterial blood theoretically could have flung the instrument of his self-inflicted injury and have it land in the coleus by happenstance, but stabbed into the soil? Unlikely. On the other hand, a calculating killer could have chosen the coleus as a hiding place for the murder weapon, not wanting to risk being caught with it but expecting at least to delay its discovery. Martin had countless questions that he knew the police couldn't or wouldn't answer.

They'd assured him they would keep watch on the property overnight.

Martin put his questions aside and crossed the terrace off the kitchen, one of Henrietta's many upcoming projects. Weeds were popping up through the cracks in the bricks, which were chipped themselves, crumbling, splotched with moss and lichens. Flowerpots helped but it needed a complete redo. Oliver, however, had to be convinced. Martin had tried for years. He'd leave Henrietta to it.

He started across the lawn, past a fenced flower garden in its full June glory. Henrietta approved of its overall design and effect despite its need for an "extreme chop." Oliver had all but paled at that assessment.

"Where *are* you, Oliver?"

Martin knew his words would do no good, even to calm him.

As much as he couldn't envision himself getting any rest, as the detective inspector had suggested, Martin knew it was what he needed, and soon.

After a drink and whatever he could scrounge for supper.

He continued past a Celtic stone sculpture — one of Oliver's early efforts and a sorry one at that — and down a gentle, grassy slope toward his cottage, a stone-and-timber traditional structure that had been built at the same time as the farmhouse.

When he was certain he was out of sight of anyone watching him from the kitchen, he allowed his shoulders to slump and the full impact of the horrid day to show in his stance, his gait, his expression — his entire being. It took all his strength to continue to the cottage he'd called home for nearly forty years instead of sinking into the grass, burying his face in his hands and blocking out the world.

He took comfort in the familiar walk and when he reached his cottage, he went straight in, without hesitation. He seldom locked the doors and hadn't that morning. The police had taken a look inside but hadn't detected anything amiss — at least from what Martin had been able to gather. They hadn't told him. They'd simply emerged from their search without further questions.

He didn't know if police had dismissed him as a suspect in Davy Driscoll's death.

Alfred was asleep on the hearth in front of the cold wood-and-coal-burning stove and barely wagged his tail in greeting, as if the events of the day had left him drained and shaken, too.

Martin had left the door open to the puppy's crate. Given the circumstances, he'd decided to let Alfred have the choice of going in or out. The hearth had won, but he hadn't torn up the place or relieved himself on the floor or the wall, which he'd managed to do early in his training. Oliver had thought that hilarious when Martin had told him. "He's your dog more than mine, Martin, and not because he peed on the wall."

It was true. Martin had pushed Oliver into getting a puppy. He'd believed the farm needed one — that Oliver needed a dog for companionship, to get himself outside his head and into the day-to-day world. Martin was convinced that Alfred's presence had helped lead Oliver to hiring Henrietta, although her curls and warm blue eyes and mad skirts didn't hurt.

What would Alfred have done if he'd come face-to-face with one of the men who'd killed Charles and Deborah York and kidnapped their young son? A wire fox terrier mere months old wouldn't recognize Davy Driscoll and Bart Norcross, of course, but would Alfred have sensed their malevolence? Their capacity for violence?

Martin took a bottle of Lagavulin from his whiskey cabinet. He got a glass and poured a dram of the smoky single malt. It had been a Christmas present from Nicholas York, Oliver's grandfather, shortly before his death. "I worry about Oliver," Nicholas had said, his voice raspy with illness. "A good single malt will come in handy after Priscilla and I are gone and it's just you looking after him."

No truer words were ever spoken, Martin

thought as he sat in his favorite chair and shut his eyes, breathing in the complex scents of his Scotch. Questions overran him. Why had Oliver run? Where was he now? Had Davy Driscoll said anything to him before he died?

Would Oliver's friends in MI5 be able to save him this time?

He was intelligent, clever, solitary and damaged. That much Martin knew and couldn't deny. As much as Oliver claimed to trust him, that trust went only so far. "Some things it's best you don't know, my friend," he would say.

One of them being that Oliver was a master art thief.

Martin sipped the Lagavulin and settled deeper into his chair. An open window would alert him to any commotion outside among the police, and it let in the warm air, fragrant with flowers.

He set his glass on the side table, next to the morning newspaper. He'd meant to finish reading it at lunch. He remembered Henrietta's excitement at having discovered the old flowerpot. MI5 or not, she had a charm about her and her love of gardening seemed genuine. A Balfour trait, she'd called it.

How differently the day had started than

it was ending.

Martin had no appetite. He shut his eyes and listened to birds in the hedges outside the open window. Had the birds witnessed Davy Driscoll's death? Had they seen him sneaking onto the farm and attempted to warn Oliver? Had they followed him in his Rolls-Royce?

Martin sprang to his feet, chiding himself for his wild thinking. Birds. Dear God.

He belatedly took off his shoes and placed them in the copper boot pan by the front door. He'd let his lightweight jacket fall to the floor when he'd taken it off and now hung it on the row of pegs above the boot pan. He welcomed the sense of normalcy he felt. He'd never married. He was tidy, and he had his routines and rituals, relied on them in times of stress.

Alfred stirred, wanting a walk.

Martin hooked the puppy's lead onto his collar and took him behind the cottage. As if sensing the mood of the evening, Alfred got straight down to business and didn't tug on the lead, jump, sniff or dig. He had a white, wiry coat with soft brown markings and excellent terrier features. He would be a handsome dog when fully grown, but Martin had no desire to show him or breed him and he knew Oliver would blanch at

205

the thought.

Although still a puppy, Alfred was also territorial and possessed his breed's strong hunting instincts. No question he'd have yelped furiously at a stranger putting him into the cottage. Ruthie didn't remember seeing Alfred when she'd returned from her errands.

Had Oliver popped Alfred into the cottage before going to the dovecote?

More questions, Martin thought in frustration.

He and Alfred returned to the cottage. The warm hearth for the puppy. A forced bite to eat and more Lagavulin for him.

Henrietta took a walk to burn off her hoppy pint and the discovery of the chisel. She'd heard from the police and then Martin. Nothing, thankfully, from MI5. As she returned to her house, she remembered she'd invited the FBI agents to dinner. They were out front, admiring — or politely pretending to admire — the purple wisteria dripping by the front door and very nearly blocking a window. They greeted her warmly, and she decided to bring them around to the garden rather than through the house.

"We can go through the gate to Cassie and

Eugene's house," she said, leading the way through grass that needed cutting. She'd never had to maintain a house. She didn't know how she'd ever keep up. "Did I tell you we're having dinner at their house? They're wonderful neighbors. They wanted to feed the boys first. You'll want to start getting yourselves back on to East Coast time, I imagine. Five hours earlier there. I loathe jet lag myself."

"Jet lag's no one's favorite," Emma said, glancing around the garden. "The flowers are incredible."

"The garden has good bone structure, doesn't it? It's my great-aunt's doing."

Henrietta paused by a sagging rose trellis. She noticed Colin didn't seem interested. He and Emma didn't seem to mind that she hadn't invited them inside. It was a complete mess. She'd never been tidy. Aunt Posey hadn't objected provided Henrietta contain herself to her room. Any spillover received stern measures. Without her around, Henrietta could indulge herself. *Plus* she had to incorporate her things from London with Posey's things, sort through what she wanted to keep and what needed to go. Oliver had never witnessed her untidy ways and she didn't want the FBI agents reporting back to him. She wasn't sure why.

Otherwise she couldn't have cared less what they thought of her housekeeping skills.

"I've a few things to do in the garden. It's the way, isn't it? The garden designer's garden is the last to be tended. My aunt always said the trick to creating a proper cottage garden is to make it appear accidental when, of course, it's anything but. She had a simple philosophy but she took care to plant flowers where they would grow and then tend them. She's still my inspiration. Makes one wonder about our death today, doesn't it? Perhaps it was meant to appear accidental or at least spontaneous when it was carefully planned."

"It's not for us to say," Emma said.

Oh, right. As if they were here to see the delphiniums.

"Did your aunt grow up in the village?" Colin asked casually.

"No. London. She moved here as a young woman. The Balfours had a country home here. That's where we're headed now. My grandfather inherited it and the Kershaws bought it after his death. Posey had already carved out this lot for herself. I loved visiting her. Freddy — my grandfather — died when I was five. My parents are lovely, but no one would call them doting. They believe in what they like to call healthy neglect."

Henrietta smiled. "I'm in the mood for oxymorons, apparently. The planned garden that appears accidental. Healthy neglect."

"Gets the point across," Colin said.

"Aunt Posey often chided me for my sprinklings of metaphors. She was a concrete sort. I think you two would have got on." Henrietta pinched a faded scented rose. "Deadheading is endless this time of year but worth the effort. Now that's *not* to be taken literally. No lost heads today."

Emma raised her eyebrows but neither she nor Colin commented.

"That's not to be taken as a metaphor, either." Henrietta shrugged. "Sorry."

"No problem," Colin said. "We heard from the police when we got here. They found the missing stone-cutting tool."

"I *was* getting to that in my tortuous MI5 way. That's who I blame, at any rate. Yes, I got word, too. Tucked into the coleus, of all things."

"You didn't put it there?" Colin asked.

"Well. That's direct. No, I didn't. Neither did Martin. We were together the entire time before the police arrived, and we didn't collude. If I'd wanted to get rid of a chisel, I assure you I could have done better than the coleus."

Neither FBI agent commented. Henrietta

felt a kindred spirit with Colin especially, which surprised her, but she supposed it shouldn't have. He reminded her of her early MI5 days, training and then working with operators like him — experienced, observant, skilled and quick to react. They trusted their instincts with good reason. She'd been one of them herself for a time.

She continued past more roses. "The police finally told me it was Davy Driscoll this morning. They asked me to keep it under my hat. They must be looking for evidence Driscoll was in contact with Bart Norcross. I wouldn't be surprised if Driscoll killed him years ago, would you? I've often wondered how Oliver managed to escape that Scottish ruin. Supposedly he seized the moment when Driscoll and Norcross argued. It was a long drive up from London and they must have been on edge."

Emma moved to another rose blossom. "They ended up with relatively little for their night of violence."

Henrietta nodded. "There could have been tension between them and Oliver's escape was the last straw. They had to know he could identify them. They were facing a lifetime on the run or in prison. Driscoll could have cracked under the pressure and killed Norcross after Oliver escaped and then pitched his body off a Scottish cliff, never to be found." She knew she was indulging in wild speculation and the FBI agents would never comment. Part of what drove her, perhaps. She took a deep breath, getting a lungful of sweet garden scents. "How did Driscoll manage to take on his identity as Reed Warren, do you suppose? It would have been easier back then, but still."

"It looks as if he created a new identity rather than stole one," Colin said.

"I've seen Driscoll's wanted photos but they aren't that great and it's been thirty years. I didn't get a good look at his face given the position of the body, but obviously he'd aged. No doubt he did things to change his appearance — if not enough for Oliver not to recognize him. I suppose he could have outright told Oliver who he was." Henrietta felt a rush of energy, fueled by unleashing her brainstorming skills. "Driscoll went decades without being detected or giving himself up. Why come here now? Why not go to London, where he committed his crimes? Why such a dramatic death, whoever is responsible? A stone-cutting tool. It couldn't have been an ordinary kitchen knife."

Colin stepped past her toward the back gate. "All good questions," he said.

"Ruthie Burns did up the coleus pot before I came on scene. They're getting leggy and need a proper chop but they're in partial shade. It's a perfect spot, really." Henrietta swore she heard a rush of rain but she felt nothing. "I've never conducted a death investigation. Straight into MI5 and then gardening. Have either of you?"

"Before the FBI," Colin said.

"Then perhaps you can tell me if what we know so far suggests an accident, homicide, suicide, self-defense or what. I think it's safe to rule out natural causes. I'm not asking you for a definitive answer, just your gut take. I know it's not your call."

Colin shook his head. "Not answering."

Henrietta turned to Emma. "What about you?"

She leaned over and smelled one of the climbing roses. "Beautiful." She stood straight. "What does the evidence you are aware of suggest to you?"

"A quick murder whose perpetrator went unnoticed. I'm keeping an open mind as to whether it was spontaneous or planned, not that what I think about the case matters. Perhaps Driscoll took an unlucky fall. He could have been perched in a tree to spy on Oliver, tumbled off his branch and nicked himself on the chisel when he landed. Or he could have been hiding in the hedges, waiting for Oliver to come out of the house, and tripped and cut himself. Neither scenario explains the chisel in the coleus, but I could come up with something."

Colin frowned at her as if he was trying to gauge how serious she was, or if she'd been into the whiskey cabinet. "Why would a stone-cutting chisel be lying out there in the first place?"

"I don't know, do I? I suppose Oliver could have had it up at the house to do a bit of work on the stones by the door. He's a keen stone-cutting hobbyist. He could have gone inside for a drink of whatever and left the tool where Davy Driscoll landed. Then he panicked and stuck it in the coleus pot."

Colin stared at her. "And you believe that?"

"Awkward, unfortunate falls with catastrophic results happen every day." She was feeling stubborn now. "I've had far-fetched scenarios prove true. We call it thinking outside the box. I suppose you call it wild speculation?"

This time Colin did smile. "I was warned about you."

Henrietta laughed, and she saw a fleeting smile from Emma, who seemed preoccupied with the roses but clearly wasn't. "I see you're both dressed for rain. Excellent. We'll go meet Cassie and Eugene Kershaw. Eugene was a teenager when the York tragedy occurred. He remembers more than I do. I was only five. The murders didn't happen here, but everyone loved Charles and Deborah. Their deaths were a terrible shock."

"I imagine people in the village gave Oliver wide latitude," Emma said.

"Spoiled him rotten according to Aunt Posey. She thought he'd have been better off if everyone had accepted that these things happen and carried on. She was big on bucking up. My grandfather came to live here at the end of his life. They'd have tea in her garden every day until he couldn't walk any longer. They argued but they adored each other. She hated to admit it but she missed him terribly."

Colin pushed upon the rickety gate. "Did they know Davy Driscoll and Bart Norcross?"

Henrietta let Emma go ahead of her and then went through and shut the gate behind her. "We've always been told they were never in the village before or since the murders, but I wonder."

"Did MI5 ever have an interest in the York case?" Colin asked.

"A human interest but the investigation doesn't fall under their mandate. They're a domestic intelligence agency, not law enforcement."

"What about now that Oliver works with MI5?"

Snagged, she thought. Except that was more a feeling than a reality. "I'm not on the job any longer, Colin. I'm a simple garden designer these days."

As they started up a well-worn path, Henrietta received a text from Cassie Kershaw. Can we do dinner at the pub? Eugene says he needs a crowd. Tony offered to stay with the boys.

Henrietta answered without consulting her guests. Meet you there. I'm bringing the two FBI agents.

Cassie's response came almost immediately. The more the merrier and we need merriment tonight.

A typical Cassie attitude. She had no patience with life's dark side.

Henrietta turned to her guests. "Change of plan. We're off to the pub. Rain, gloomy moods, a bloody death — we need multiple pints and someone else doing the cooking and washing up. Sound good?"

"Sounds fine," Emma said. Colin didn't seem to care one way or the other.

"Brilliant," Henrietta said. "We can hop in my car. The clouds are about to burst and you two are testy enough without tramping into the village in a downpour."

12

Despite the varied menu, everyone ordered some version of "pub grub." Colin settled on fish and chips but he knew he wouldn't eat it all — especially with Emma, who'd ordered soup, dipping her fork into his plate. Henrietta had pushed two small tables together in front of the fireplace. A low fire was burning, taking the dampness out of the air more than adding heat. He and Emma sat across from Cassie and Eugene Kershaw, their backs to the fire, with Henrietta holding court at the end of the table.

After an hour, they'd finished their meals, having talked about everything except the death at the York farm and its owner's disappearance. The Kershaws had to get back. "Tony's wonderful, but the boys have him wrapped around their pinkies," Cassie said. "They're five and six."

"Take your time and finish your drink," Eugene said. "I'll see to the boys."

He pointed a finger, indicating he'd hit the men's room first. Colin watched him shuffle off. News that the dead man was Davy Driscoll was still officially being withheld, but it was clear that was what people in the village, including the Kershaws, assumed. It was understandable — inevitable — a violent death would stir up memories of the manhunt for Charles and Deborah York's killers and their son's kidnappers. Eugene had struck Colin as distracted, careful to steer the conversation away from any slide toward the Yorks.

Henrietta yawned and moved to the bar, where she ordered Scotch. It wasn't her first drink of the evening, although Colin wouldn't describe her as inebriated. He glanced at Emma. She gave a slight nod and he got up and joined Henrietta at the bar, easing onto the stool next to her.

"Not the warm English welcome you imagined upon your arrival in our quaint village, was it?" She took her glass from the barman before he could set it down. "Shall I buy you a pint, Colin?"

"Thank you."

"You'll get a drink faster with me here," she added. "My cousin Tony noticed a small leak in the pub kitchen and fixed it before it turned into a massive leak, and the owners were so thrilled that now I can do no wrong, too. He's retired but you'd never know it. He's always busy. Loves to be handy." She waved suddenly. "Eugene! Over here!"

Eugene reddened as he returned from his dash to the restroom.

"I embarrass Eugene," Henrietta said in a low voice, leaning toward Colin. "It's become a game of sorts. He's a great guy but he can be like an old housecoat. Comfy and no bother. A case of opposites attracting, as you see now that you've met Cassie. She's a Yank, did you notice? She's from Boston, as a matter of fact."

"I'm from Hartford," Cassie said, easing between them with a wineglass in hand. She seemed content to stand. "Hartford is decidedly *not* Boston."

"But you went to Harvard," Henrietta said.

"Boston College."

Henrietta grinned at Colin. "Cassie will throw something if I say there's no difference between Harvard and Boston College. You're from New England, Colin. What do you say?"

"I stay out of college rivalries."

"Smart man," Cassie said. "Henrietta's teasing. She visited Boston when I was living there after college. I was working a

dead-end office job in the city. She introduced me to Eugene, as a matter of fact."

"You'll never forgive me."

"Now I *am* going to start a brawl."

Eugene arrived, shaking his head at the
two women as he addressed Colin. "I can
guess what they're on about."

Henrietta's cheeks deepened to a bright
pink, probably from alcohol and heat more
than her attempt to mix it up with her
friend. She grinned, unrepentant. "I broke
the somber mood, at least."

"It's a terrible thing, what happened
today," Eugene said quietly. "I know the
police haven't said, but we all know it wasn't
an accident. We haven't had a murder in the
village since the Yorks. What a shocking
tragedy that was."

"They weren't killed here in the village,"
Cassie said.

Henrietta sipped her Scotch. "We must
remember our Cotswold history isn't all
cute sheep, the Middle Ages wool trade and
the building of twee limestone villages. The
last big battle of the Civil War was fought
up the road in Stow-on-the-Wold. It's said
the streets were soaked in blood from the
dead and wounded." She turned to Colin.
"That was in the seventeenth century, by
the way. It was a nasty war between royalist

and parliamentary forces."

Eugene smiled weakly. "We don't let Henrietta write our tourist brochures. She gets on well with her plants and pots."

She laughed, raising her glass. "Cheers to that, my friend. Are you sure you won't stay? The boys must be asleep by now. Tony's probably reading a book with his feet up."

Colin turned down the Kershaws' offer to pay for his and Emma's dinner. "An FBI rule, is it?" Eugene asked. "We're glad you're here. I know Oliver's a friend —"

"He's not a friend," Henrietta said. "They're FBI agents. They don't have friends."

Eugene winced but attempted a smile. "Henrietta's trying to be funny, a noble gesture tonight, perhaps. We can forgive her. Dinner was a pleasure. If you have a few extra minutes tomorrow, stop by the farm and I'll give you the ten-minute tour."

He said good-night and was noticeably more animated as he started for the exit. Glad to be on his way, Colin thought, not blaming him. Emma joined them at the bar and sat at Henrietta's left. Cassie was still on her feet but looking toward the door. "I should go with Eugene. He won't say so but today's hit him hard. He idolized the Yorks — he was just a teenager when they died."

"That's a difficult age to experience such a violent tragedy," Henrietta said. "I was too young to fully understand what had happened, and I lived in London. Go on, then, Cassie. I'll take care of dinner. Scoot. Catch up with Eugene. I'll see myself back home."

Cassie gave her friend a quick hug. "Today was dreadful for you, too, I know. I hope you can get some sleep tonight."

Henrietta watched Cassie depart, the heavy pub door shutting with a soft thud behind her. "Today's affected all of us," she said finally, more subdued. "We each have our own way of coping. Me, with a trowel and too much drink. Martin's gone to ground with a good Scotch, I've no doubt. He's a rock, of course. He'd have to be working for the Yorks all these years. Ruthie's shattered but Nigel will look after her. Her younger son lives in the area, too. She's worked for the Yorks for nearly as long as Martin. Our dashing bachelor is an interesting sort, isn't he?"

"That's one word for it," Colin said.

She ordered another Scotch. Emma was still nursing her first and only glass of wine. Colin doubted he'd finish his pint. He could hear a rush of rain outside. The fire was dying down, the pub not as crowded as it might have been on a night without the shock of the death that morning, the unspoken certainty it was related to the violence thirty years ago.

An older man in work clothes came into the pub. Henrietta jumped off her bar stool and threw her arms around him, kissing him on the cheek. She introduced him to Emma and Colin as her cousin Tony. "He's my father's first cousin, the son of the middle Balfour, Anthony. My grandfather was the eldest and Posey was the youngest. Tony's named for his dad if you missed that."

Tony looked awkward at the personal attention, but he greeted Emma and Colin politely and then shifted back to Henrietta for what was obviously the business at hand. "I can see to your trellis in the morning. Will that work for you?"

"Perfect," she said. "I had a good look at it last night. It's falling apart, as I suspected. The climbing roses will be crawling roses by July."

Tony's mouth twitched, as if he was holding back a real smile. "Nigel Burns has offered to help. Is that all right with you?"

"Of course. Two strong backs will make quick work of the job. Good of you to mind the boys tonight. Next time you must join us."

"No problem at all."

"Today wasn't the best of days but tomorrow will be better. Did the police speak with you?"

"No, but I was working on the cottage all day. I didn't see Mr. York or any strangers — no one except the Kershaws. I should get on," Tony added quietly. "I don't want to intrude."

"You're not intruding." But he headed out, apparently touching base about her rose trellis his only reason for stopping by. More curls fell in Henrietta's face as she returned to her bar stool. "Tony's divorced, no kids. He met Freddy — my grandfather — once before he died but then we all lost touch. We're like that. Tony was kind to Aunt Posey in her last days. I was 'all work, no play' then. He doesn't remember his father. His mother never got on with the Balfours and went to live with a sister in Connecticut after she was widowed. That's my connection with Cassie."

"Cassie's a Balfour?" Emma asked.

"Sort of. Tony's widowed mother married Cassie's widowed grandfather — he'd lost his first wife to cancer. Cassie's father was already a teenager then." Henrietta screwed up her face. "It's a bit complicated after more than one pint. I can draw you a family tree if you'd like."

Colin smiled. "That's all right. We can follow along."

"Of course you can." There was no detectable edge to her voice. "Cassie likes to lay claim to my grandfather. I can't blame her. He was a legend with MI5, did anyone tell you? An amazing man. Of course, I remember him primarily as my grandfather. I wasn't aware of his hero status until I was older. He and Posey were devoted to each other but she liked to tell me they fought over everything. He disdained cottage gardens."

"No MI5 for her?" Emma asked.

"Oh, no. Never. She loved her life here in her safe, secluded biscuit-tin village."

"You were an operator," Colin said softly.

Her eyes sparked. "You know I can't say."

He nodded, drank some of his beer. "But you were."

She sighed. "For a time," she admitted. "I found it more to my liking than what came next. At least I was more suited to it. You know, if we're going to discuss state secrets, we should at least do it walking in the rain."

Colin saw it now. He'd had hints. After her stint as an operator, Henrietta Balfour had been a senior intelligence officer overseeing domestic operations — responsible not just for the success of the mission but the safety of the MI5 officers, agents and the innocent civilians involved. "A hell of a responsibility," he said.

"Yes. Climbing roses don't plot, although sometimes I wonder when I get at them with the clippers. I swear they fight back."

"Your grandfather must have been something," Emma said.

"I wish I'd had more time with him. My father had no interest in following in his footsteps. He said Freddy wouldn't have been keen on any of his offspring joining up. My dad, encouraging sort that he is, said I shouldn't consider MI5 because I'm an all-in or all-out sort and would never learn to pace myself." She smiled, her warm eyes sparking with humor. "Don't you hate it when your dad's right? Anyway, Freddy Balfour was a legend and a hero, and I happily and eagerly followed his example, at least for a time."

Emma finished her wine and set the glass on the bar. Colin noted he had a few more sips of beer in his glass. "I believe maybe half of what you just said."

Henrietta laughed. "Wonderful. I'm not as rusty as I thought. But you know what — I'm done for. It's been a terrible day, and Tony and Nigel will be in the garden with their crowbars in the morning. There goes the lie-in I had in mind. So. Excuse me, but off I go." She pulled on her rain jacket. "I'll walk."

"We can give you a ride home," Emma said.

"No worries. I'll collect my car in the morning. I've a mad urge to puddle stomp, and there will be loads of puddles tonight."

She said good-night and headed out, cutting quite the eccentric figure. Colin knew that as a former MI5 operator, Henrietta Balfour was well-trained and could take care of herself on her walk home, even with a bit too much to drink.

"I used to love puddle stomping," Emma said, sliding onto Henrietta's vacated stool.

Colin picked up his glass. "As I recall, you still do."

"Oh, yes." She raised her empty wineglass and clinked it against his pint glass. "To puddle stomping and its aftermath."

In the Kerry hills, last week. A puddle that was deeper than she'd realized. His "rescue."

That night had involved one of their June fires.

Colin smiled, ignoring the tension in his gut that Oliver York — of all the people he and Emma knew — was the one who'd launched them out of their honeymoon and back on the job.

He texted Sam Padgett. What do we know about the Balfours?

Sam's response came in seconds. Not enough. I'm on it.

Colin didn't relax but he had confidence in Padgett and the rest of the HIT team. It had taken time to build that trust. He wasn't the team player Emma was.

It was raining hard when they crossed the courtyard to their ground-floor room. Emma switched on lights, peeled off her jacket and shoes and went into the bathroom. In a moment, Colin could hear the tub filling. He took off his own jacket and shoes and pulled the curtains.

He stood in the bathroom doorway. He could feel the steam from the hot water as he watched his wife pull off her shirt. Heavy rain darkened the long June night earlier than usual.

Perfect, he thought, easing into the bathroom and shutting the door behind him.

Henrietta felt a sudden chill as she headed upstairs to bed, in the room she'd always used as a child. She hadn't touched Posey's room. She dreaded going through her aunt's things. She could grab Cassie one quiet, rainy Sunday, buy a couple of bottles of wine and have a treasure hunt. Who knew what Posey had squirreled away in her near century in this life. Maybe they'd find something they could put up on eBay. In exchange for Cassie's help, Henrietta would be delighted to split any profits, but given Posey's habits, they'd be lucky to find anything of enough value to pay for their wine.

Henrietta drew the shades and drapes — frayed, a high priority for replacing — and dug her Swiss Army knife out of a drawer and set it on the bed stand. She didn't own a gun.

Does the killer?

She shook off that thought. She wasn't one to dwell on matters outside her control — fears, the unknowable . . .

But there *was* a killer.

MI5 could help Oliver even now, after bolting this morning. If he got himself killed? Nothing to be done then except bury him in the York family plot in the village cemetery.

Henrietta washed her face, brushed her teeth and fell into bed before she realized she'd forgotten to put on a nightgown. She dragged herself out of bed, slipped into a nightgown and got back in bed, pulling the duvet up to her ears.

For all the wrong reasons, she thought of Oliver. He was suffering, reliving the horror of his boyhood trauma, probably still trying to get all of Davy Driscoll's blood off him — and she was thinking about having him in bed with her. What it'd be like to make love to him. To feel his palms coursing up her skin, lifting her nightgown . . . his tongue following his palms . . .

It was fatigue. Shock. Adrenaline. The emotional connection they'd had since childhood that was now getting all mixed up with everything else.

Not everything else. Sex.

Simple enough and yet oh, so complicated.

She fought hot tears and pulled her duvet down to her waist, but the rush of cool air on her hot skin only made things worse. She ached for him. Feared for him. And she wanted him desperately, more than she'd ever wanted a man before. It had nothing to do with her family or his family or thieving or MI5. It was him.

She could see his irreverent smile, a lock of tawny hair on his forehead, his eyes . . . and his taut abdomen, pants hanging low on his narrow hips. As solitary as he was, she knew he wasn't inexperienced with women. She imagined what his mastery of karate and tai chi would do for him in bed. The control, the hard muscles, the stamina. She longed to fight to keep up with him, to sweat and pant and moan as he thrust into her, taking her to dizzying, orgasmic heights. And she would do the same for him, again and again through nights like this one.

She'd never let herself think this way, with such openness and abandon. She and Oliver weren't lonely children anymore, and it felt good to see him as a man she wanted with her now, in bed, making love.

"Oliver, Oliver," she whispered. "Please get out of this alive."

13

Declan's Cross, Ireland

The rain got worse during the mercifully short night and ended before dawn.

Served him right, Oliver thought, that the long spell of beautiful June weather ended the night he decided to hide on a remote — at least by his standards — Irish headland.

And all was well, really. He'd forgotten how dark it got out here at night, but in addition to a late sunset, June brought an early sunrise.

By the time Oliver made his way to the low stone wall and through two small holly trees, Wendell Sharpe had arrived in his sporty Audi and was waiting on the lane. "I brought you coffee and a scone," he said, handing Oliver a small bag. "I decided against tea. I figured coffee would go down better after a night in the rain, and personally I hate cold tea."

Oliver welcomed the warmth of the coffee

inside the bag. He knew he must look dreadful. "My high-tech emergency blanket worked reasonably well to keep me dry. Didn't help with the rocks and tree roots, unfortunately." He placed his jacket on the stone wall in front of a holly tree, the only spot not covered in dripping moss and foliage. He sat, glancing up at Wendell, who was clad in a waxed-cotton jacket, a cap, khakis and walking shoes. "Thank you."

"Coffee will get cold soon and the scone's leaden."

"I don't mind. I shouldn't be surprised, I suppose, that you managed to find me."

"I know you pretty well."

"Perhaps better than was wise on my part."

Wendell shrugged. "Too late now."

Oliver got his breakfast out of the bag. He'd awakened early, shaking off nightmares. He hadn't escaped getting wet entirely, but he was in relatively decent shape after his long night. He had to admit he appreciated Wendell's company. "Do you want to sit down?"

"I'll stand. Sciatica's acting up. The drive from Dublin feels longer in my old age."

Oliver sipped the coffee and unwrapped the scone. A marginal breakfast, but he was grateful for it. "We've bonded. Inviting you to visit in January sealed our friendship."

Wendell grunted. "I wouldn't go that far but it was a pleasant couple of days. I'd never stayed in an English farmhouse. Amazing you turned into an art thief with all the lousy paintings of dogs on your walls."

Oliver smiled, remembering Wendell sipping Glenfiddich by the fire, the hunter and the hunted ending the chase. "As if you're an art connoisseur."

"I buy what I like."

"Irish artists."

"For the most part," Wendell said, wincing as he rubbed his right hip. But he didn't complain of any pain. "I hear you have a dog of your own now."

"Yes. He's named Alfred, after Batman's manservant. Martin sees to him."

"He must be worried about you. Martin, not the dog."

"I do regret that." Oliver swallowed a chunk of the dry, heavy scone. Wendell hadn't exaggerated its flaws. "Talk to me, Wendell."

He told Oliver about the break-in at his home. "Wasn't you," he said when he finished.

Oliver shook his head. "No, it wasn't."

"That wasn't a question. I know it wasn't

you. I wasn't convinced it had anything to do with you, but turns out this guy who died on your doorstep showed up in Heron's Cove the first of the week, and probably Rock Point, too. It was Davy Driscoll, wasn't it?"

Oliver nodded solemnly but said nothing as he drank the dreadful coffee.

"I haven't spoken to Emma and Colin since I decided to drive down here," Wendell added. "They're in your village. Emma's left messages."

"You don't want to call her back until after you've seen me."

"That's your story. Maybe I haven't called her because I'm getting old and forgetful."

Oliver doubted that. "Everything you do is deliberate, Wendell."

"Used to be, maybe. I'm slipping now that I'm retired."

With the toe of his shoe, Wendell pushed at the muddy edge of a hole in the lane now filled with rainwater. For a man in his early eighties, he did well. He was in excellent shape mentally and physically, especially for a man of his years.

"I wonder," Oliver said, breaking off a piece of scone. "How dangerous might you be if you were cornered?"

"Not very these days, unless I'm armed,

and I'm not."

"I don't mean physically cornered. If you had something to hide and someone was forcing you to face it — threatening your reputation, your relationship with your family, your freedom — what would you do?"

Wendell pulled his foot away from the puddle and stood straight, his green eyes narrowing on Oliver. "What's going on, Oliver?"

He ate the piece of scone and sipped more of the coffee. Bleak, it was. "If you were guilty of something in your past, how far would you go to preserve your reputation and that of the company you built?" He set the coffee next to him on the moss-covered stone. "When was your first contact with my family?"

"Your family?" Wendell was silent a moment. "I've only met you."

"Did you know my parents?"

"No. I was living in Maine when they were killed. I read about their deaths in the paper."

Oliver stretched out his legs, leaning back slightly, the holly's prickly evergreen leaves poking him in the ribs. He kept his gaze on Wendell. "Which paper?"

"I don't remember."

"You traveled frequently for your work

back then. Were you in London?"

Wendell sighed. "I could have been. It doesn't matter. I never knew your parents."

"My grandparents?"

"I didn't know them, either. What, do you think I had something to do with the attack on you and your parents? Is that why you taunted me after each of your thefts?"

"You were in London," Oliver said. "You stayed at Claridge's, just blocks from where my parents were killed. I'm surprised you don't remember where you were."

"I see." Wendell walked over to the wall, to Oliver's right, and brushed his fingertips across a yellow wildflower. "How did you learn that tidbit?"

"We've been doing this dance for a decade."

"Yes, we have. All right. I was at Claridge's. I didn't want to tell you once I realized you were our thief because I knew you'd be tempted to connect dots that don't connect. It was a coincidence, Oliver. I was there on a job unrelated to your family."

"You weren't planning to meet with them?"

Wendell shook his head. "No, I was not."

"I'm trying to make sense of things." Oliver left it at that and picked up his scone again, broke off another chunk. It had come with a small triangle of butter and a plastic knife, but he didn't bother with them and had left them in the bag. "It really is leaden, isn't it? Ruthie Burns makes fresh scones every Friday, enough to last the weekend." He ate the bit of scone. "I'm afraid Ruthie was first on scene yesterday."

"She saw you with Driscoll?"

"Yes."

"That's rough. Did she recognize him?"

"I don't think so. I'm not sure she got a good look at him. I heard her gasp. She didn't scream." Oliver pushed back the images of less than twenty-four hours ago. "I suspect she was in such a state of shock she couldn't get out a proper scream at first. I had to stay focused on Driscoll. He was bleeding out. I did what I could but it was too late. He was unconscious by the time Ruthie came upon us."

Wendell moved back from the yellow wildflowers, sidestepping his puddle. "How long was that after you encountered him?"

"Seconds. He got to me — or I got to him — too late. There's so little time with that sort of injury." He paused. As bad as the scone and coffee were, they were helping to clear his head. The sunshine no doubt helped, too. "I'll go over everything in detail with the police."

Wendell nodded. "You need to turn your-self in to the gardai and let them get you back to England. For your own good."

"I know. I'll do it."

"Was this man murdered, Oliver?"

"Yes. I'm certain, but it's not for me to say."

"Was the cut meant for you instead of him? Did he intervene and save you?"

Oliver got his feet. He noticed raindrops on the waxen holly leaves. "Holly is said to protect against fairies with malevolent intent. Maybe that's what's at work here. Malevolent fairies." He turned to Wendell. "But that's just one traditional belief about holly. Celtic mythology tells us about the holly king who ruled during the dark half of the year. He'd have given way by now to the oak king."

"Oliver."

"I don't believe the cut was meant for me."

"Davy Driscoll didn't come to your farm to kill you and changed his mind and killed himself?"

"By cutting his brachial artery? I could have saved him if I'd gotten to him sooner."

"He could have saved himself," Wendell added.

"Possibly. He might not have known what to do. Whether it was an attack or an elaborate suicide, he's dead and the police are investigating and need to talk to me."

"You didn't kill this man, Oliver. Acting guilty won't help you."

"I'd just been talking about flowerpots when he turned up." Oliver gave a small laugh in disbelief. "If he was in Maine early in the week and at your place in Dublin on Wednesday, he must have taken an overnight flight to Ireland on Tuesday and then continued on to England later Wednesday or early yesterday."

"We shouldn't assume it was Driscoll who broke into my place," Wendell said. "It could have been someone chasing him."

"Fair point." Oliver debated a moment before he continued. "Driscoll mentioned Finian Bracken at the end."

"Did he confess to him?"

"I don't know. Finian can't reveal a sacramental confession. What if Driscoll told him about plans being made?" Oliver felt a rush of blood to his face. Tension, frustration, regret. "Why did Driscoll come to the farm?"

"You're the one who saw him, not me."

"It was a rhetorical question. All this time . . ." He cleared his throat. "I have so many questions."

"What exactly did he say before he died?"

Wendell held up his thin hands. "No, don't tell me. Tell the police."

Oliver was still. His nightmares roared back, quickening his pulse. His breathing was rapid, shallow. But he knew what to do. He'd learned. He listened to the breeze in the trees, concentrated on separating its sough from the sounds of the tide. He picked up his jacket off the wall where he'd used it as a mat. He calmed his breathing as he focused on being fully present in this moment. He was safe. Martin, Ruthie, Henrietta, the farm workers, his neighbors — the police would see to them. They were safe, too.

Finally he turned to Wendell and smiled. "It was a long night."

"I'd have nightmares sleeping in a cemetery even if I wasn't on the run from the police."

"Did you come all this way because you feel sorry for me?"

Wendell zipped his jacket higher against the breeze. "So what if I did? What if someone figured out Reed Warren was Driscoll's alias and was blackmailing him? Did he mention Bart Norcross? We can't rush to answers. We can't assume." The old man winked. "I knew that even before Emma became an FBI agent."

But Oliver saw something — felt it — as Wendell stepped across the puddle to his small Audi, parked at the end of the lane near a trail that would take them up to a cliff overlooking the sea.

"Wendell," Oliver said. "Tell me."

He stopped, shadows deepening the lines in his face. "I've been missing something about you. Your past." He paused, as if to give Oliver a moment to let his words sink in. "I had you on my list of people of interest early on after the Amsterdam heist, but I didn't know you were our bold, cheeky thief. Not until last fall. Oliver . . ." Wendell was silent again. "We're going to figure this out."

"You're not going to do anything of the sort," Oliver said firmly. "You're retired. You're going back to Dublin and doing as Emma and Colin say."

"Yeah, yeah, blah, blah," Wendell sputtered, waving a hand in dismissal. "You get to a certain age and everyone thinks they know better and can order you around."

"This is a police matter. It's not about your age."

He pointed a bony finger at Oliver. "Whatever we missed is haunting you, too, isn't it?"

"A lot haunts me."

"Yeah, I know. What you went through, no child should ever have to go through. Still, though. Ever wished you'd gotten into raising Cotswold sheep to cope instead of thieving?"

Oliver grinned. "I'm glad we've become friends."

"You fled the scene of a death." Wendell softened. "Come on. I'll drop you off —"

Oliver shook his head. "The less you're involved with me, the better."

"A little late for that. In the car, Oliver."

As if Wendell could force him. All Oliver had to do was scoot up the path. It was steep, wet and rugged. As spry as Wendell Sharpe was, Oliver would be able to lose him in seconds. But what was the point?

"Are you heading straight back to Dublin?" he asked.

"Once the gardai send me on my way, which I hope they will. Lucas wants me to stop driving."

"Maybe you should."

"In my own good time." Wendell twisted his mouth to one side, eyeing Oliver, then sighed. "Okay. Walk into the village. I'll let the gardai know you're on your way, but there's no guarantee they'll wait for you."

"I'm not on the run. I bolted. There's a difference."

"You have friends in high places, Oliver. MI5 has your back."

Friend wasn't the word Oliver would use but he smiled at Wendell. "You Sharpes and your imaginations." He looked at the tangle of holly, rushes and wildflowers along the stone wall. "The truth of what happened to my parents, to me . . . I don't trust my memories anymore, Wendell."

"You were eight." As if that explained everything.

"I was the only eyewitness left alive," Oliver said half under his breath.

Wendell stood by the driver's door, his hand on the mirror as he studied Oliver. "Tell the police everything, Oliver. If you don't trust them for any reason, tell Emma and Colin. Tell them, anyway. That's my advice."

"I'm only trouble for my FBI mates."

"They're used to trouble. It's their job."

"Yours, too, isn't it, old man?"

But Wendell remained serious, didn't respond to Oliver's strained teasing. "I don't think of you as trouble, Oliver," he said quietly.

"I suppose you don't have to. You're a Sharpe. Trouble follows you."

"You have a point there." Wendell opened the car door. "These new cars. I like an old-fashioned key."

"How long is Detective Garda Murphy giving me?" Oliver asked.

Wendell sighed at the mention of the senior Irish detective, who had connections to Declan's Cross, to Finian Bracken — to the two sisters whose uncle's home Oliver had broken into more than a decade ago. He and Kitty O'Byrne were engaged. "Sean's waiting at his farmhouse," Wendell said. "I'm meeting him there."

"You're to report our conversation?"

"Every word."

Oliver smiled. "Of course."

"It's for your own good, Oliver."

"You see? We truly are friends."

As Wendell Sharpe started off in his Audi, he managed not to bump into the stone wall but not to avoid the puddle. He tore through it, splashing Oliver with muddy water. A night in the rain without getting drenched but let his elderly art-detective friend get behind the wheel, and here he was, splattered. He laughed and poured the rest of his coffee into the dirt, wrapped the remains of his scone and shoved them into his rucksack.

He took the narrow, winding trail up to the cliff, relishing the rush of wind and sunlight when he reached the top. Waves crashed on the rocks below. Sunlight glistened on the sea. No hint of rain now.

"Glorious," he said. "Absolutely glorious."

He looked back at the trio of tall Celtic crosses on the hill. He wondered if he'd ever see them again. Looking at them now, against the blue sky and green pastures, gave him comfort and solace. He could feel the presence of his mother and father, younger than he was now when he'd lost them. And yet they didn't feel lost to him right now. They felt close.

They'd protected him that night.

Whatever else remained elusive, out of his reach, *that* he knew.

He returned to the lane and set off toward Sean Murphy's farmhouse. For a moment, he pretended it was an ordinary morning. He walked along pastures dotted with grazing sheep and along cliffs above white-crested waves rolling onto the rock-bound coast.

Finally he came to a yellow-painted bungalow. Aoife O'Byrne waved to him from a clothesline with laundry blowing in the breeze. She was a brilliant artist and a beautiful woman. Gleaming black hair, vibrant blue eyes, angular features, tall and slender — and in love with a man she couldn't have. "Not me," Oliver muttered. "More's the pity."

Six months ago, he might have been at least modestly serious. Now . . .

"No."

He could see her with Finian Bracken in Boston last fall. Finian had been in his clerical garb, insisting he was nothing more than a friend. Oliver didn't know the details of their history but there was no question they had one.

Poor Aoife. In love with the forbidden fruit.

And Finian?

Oliver was convinced that his friend loved her, too, if not in the way she loved him. Then again, what did he know of Father Bracken's hopes and dreams on lonely nights on the Maine coast, far from home?

Aoife had told Oliver a few months ago she considered herself free, unbound by her past love for a man who had spurned her for the priesthood.

Not content to wave, she crossed the grass to the lane.

"Paintbrush in hand," he said with a smile. "Appropriate."

Aoife didn't return his smile. "I've been painting nonstop all spring. Kitty will tell you it keeps me out of trouble, although here I am, talking to you. I promised Sean I would stay inside and lock my doors. He wanted me to stay with him and Kitty last night, or at the hotel. I refused. I'm in the zone with a series I'm painting. I can't deal with disruptions. They'll derail me." Her blue eyes steadied on Oliver. "And I'm not afraid of you."

"You've no reason to be afraid of me."

"Sean knows that, too, I think."

"I'm on my way to see him now."

"Good. I'd hate to have to be the one to turn you in." She sighed, shaking her head. "Oliver, my God. It must have been awful yesterday. Did coming here help?"

"In its own way." He nodded to her paintbrush, noted its blue tip. "Sky?"

"Blouse," she said. "It's the wrong blue for the sky."

"Of course. I see that now."

Now she smiled. "Liar." She gestured with the brush to the string of bright-colored clothes hanging on the line. "I'm into clotheslines these days. Normalcy. The routines of daily life."

"When's the last time you washed your own laundry?"

"First thing this morning, I'll have you know."

Oliver pointed to the clothesline. "Those

248

work pants aren't yours."

She crossed her arms on her chest, paintbrush tucked between her fingers, its tip almost hitting her in the jaw. "They belong to Sean's uncle Paddy. They're practically in tatters. Uncle Paddy doesn't believe in buying new until the old is ready for the rubbish. Past ready, in my opinion."

"But they add authenticity to your scene. Your stylish, expensive clothes wouldn't create the look you want on their own."

"Not everything I own is expensive or stylish." The breeze blew dark hair in her face, but she left it, keeping her arms crossed as she scowled at him. "If you keep this up, I'm not going to be a sympathetic witness at your trial."

Oliver grinned, pleased she'd walked over to say hello. He'd met her a few times since fall — in Boston, at a gallery showing her work in London and here in Declan's Cross. She could be starchy and always gave as good as she got, but her vulnerabilities bubbled close to the surface. She'd been inspired to become an artist on visits to Declan's Cross with her childless uncle and aunt, whose home was now the O'Byrne House Hotel. Aoife would steal away to paint local scenes, including the crosses where Oliver had spent last night. Now in her midthirties, she was beloved in Ireland and a highly successful, internationally recognized artist.

She uncrossed her arms and dropped them to her sides, giving the paintbrush a good shake. "I was up early. There's something meditative about pegging out the wash."

"I think Martin made me do it as punishment once."

"For swiping something?"

"Possibly," Oliver said without hesitating. "My grandparents tended to let me get away with misdeeds after I came to live with them. Martin compensated. He can be stern."

Aoife smiled, brushing back the strands of straight hair that had blown into her face. "I'm not surprised, but I like him." Her smile faded. "Why did you come to Declan's Cross, Oliver? Why did you run?"

"It seemed like the thing to do at the time. As I told Wendell Sharpe, I bolted, I didn't run. A distinction without a difference to most, perhaps, but not to me." He nodded to the clothesline. "It's a charming scene but I keep hoping you'll try porpoises again."

"No one shares that hope, I assure you."

He owned one of her few paintings of

porpoises that swam in Ardmore Bay. Legitimately purchased, too. "I'm still trying to decide where to hang my Aoife O'Byrne porpoises. They're in a closet in London at the moment." He studied her. "I spoke with Finian Bracken recently."

"Did you?"

He nodded. He decided not to be too specific. Whatever the police knew or didn't know at this point was irrelevant. He didn't want to involve Aoife in his problems. She was the one who'd initiated this chat, but it was a quick hello, nothing more.

She wiped the sable tip of her paintbrush on her pant leg, as if making sure it was dry. "I debated calling Finian last night," she said, a bit too casually. "I was hoping you'd been in touch with him. I wasn't sure you'd tell me if you had. He's wrestling with something, isn't he?"

"The man who died visited him this week."

Her mouth thinned but she maintained control of herself. "Then he knows something he can't say. He takes his priestly vows seriously."

Oliver felt an unexpected tightening of his throat. Emotion, he thought with a mix of fear and disdain. It was the last thing he needed or dared to indulge at the moment.

But he continued, unable to stop himself. "You and Finian aren't done."

"Oh, we are, Oliver. We are."

"An inscrutable, solitary painter and a tortured, solitary priest. It's the perfect forbidden love. You suit each other's needs even now. You need to paint. He needs to be in Rock Point with his FBI agents and such."

"He's staying on in Rock Point, did you know? He was only supposed to be there a year. Now it's open-ended."

"And you're waiting for him?"

"I'm living my life."

"He's a good excuse for you to be solitary."

Her incisive blue eyes settled on him. "And your excuse?"

"I'm not as solitary these days. I have a dog. A bad-tempered wire fox terrier."

"I bet he's adorable."

Where had Alfred been yesterday morning? Oliver wondered. He went still, the wind feeling cold now. *Did the bloody bastard kill my dog?* He didn't know if he meant Davy Driscoll or whoever had killed him, or what, but it hadn't occurred to him until that moment that Alfred might also have been a victim yesterday. He was a barker. Martin was diligently training him, but

Alfred would have carried on if he'd spotted an intruder.

Or perhaps not. Perhaps he was accustomed now to the comings and goings on a working farm.

"Oliver, are you all right?"

He heard the worry in Aoife's voice and gave her a quick smile. "Yes. Thank you. I'm fine."

"You seem so alone," she said. "You're clever, charming, lonely and an unrepentant thief. You could have been violent but you never were. You weren't yesterday. I know that, Oliver. So does Sean. I'm sure of it."

"But I'll never be Finian Bracken, will I?"

"An Irish priest? No, that's never going to happen. And that was an obvious attempt to change the subject."

He motioned down the lane. "I should go before Sean sends a hostage rescue team."

"That's not funny, Oliver."

"Was I trying to be funny?"

She groaned and threw her arms around him, hugging him fiercely. "Be careful," she whispered. "Be well. Godspeed, my friend."

He hugged her back, a split second of human contact he knew he couldn't let affect him, throw him off his mission — what he had to do. He stood back and smiled. "More porpoises, Aoife. Think about it."

She pointed at his jacket. "I got a spot of blue paint on you."

"It'll be a reminder of your laundry painting when I'm in prison."

She rolled her eyes and said nothing, and he continued along the lane.

Handsome Sean Murphy was waiting outside at his farmhouse, leaning on a muddy tractor at least as old as Uncle Paddy's trousers hanging on Aoife's line. "I was thinking I could have a full Irish breakfast before I turned myself in," Oliver said.

Murphy was unmoved. "Wendell Sharpe brought you breakfast."

"If that's what you want to call it." Oliver could see the Irish detective noting the spot of blue paint on his jacket, guessing how it had gotten there, but he said nothing. Oliver listened to sheep baaing in the distance. He inhaled deeply, taking in the clean air, the scents of farm and sea. "I need to go back to England, Detective Garda Murphy."

"Yes, you do."

14

The Cotswolds, England

Oliver York would be back in the Cotswolds soon. DI Lowe had stopped to let Emma know as she lingered over breakfast in the courtyard. Colin had gone off to meet his MI5 contact, just as well given the detective inspector's information about her grandfather's role in Oliver's return to England. The DI didn't stay long, and once he left, Emma helped herself to more coffee and brought it out to her table. She had the courtyard to herself. Everything was soaked from last night's rain but drying rapidly in the sunshine and warmth. She'd found a reasonably dry chair. She'd like nothing better than to grab Colin for a walk in the English countryside and pretend, even for a few hours, they were still on their honeymoon.

This time when she tried her grandfather, he picked up. *Finally.* "If I could, Granddad," she said after they'd exchanged greetings, "I'd jump through my phone and hurl myself across the water to Ireland. I can't believe you sneaked down to Declan's Cross and met Oliver on the sly. What were you thinking?"

"I was thinking I didn't want to involve you. I complicate your life enough as it is."

"Oh, no — no, Granddad. You're not putting this off on me. This wasn't for my benefit. It was because you didn't want me stopping you."

"I admit I'm used to handling my own affairs without your help." His tone was borderline huffy. "I've had five years to get used to having an FBI agent in the family. I'm not a lawbreaker, but . . . Jesus, Mary and Joseph, Emma, my palms are cold and sweaty talking to you. Is that husband of yours listening in?"

"Did Sean Murphy threaten to arrest you?"

"He all but waved handcuffs in front of my face but we made a deal. He indulged my instincts but I imagine he never will again. I also have the feeling your lot got hold of him."

"My lot?"

"FBI, spies, I don't know. Emma, there's nothing bad here. I brought Oliver coffee and a scone and had a good look at him. I told him to turn himself in and took measures to make sure he did. I have some compassion for the man given what he's gone through. That's all. He'll be back there this afternoon."

"You waited until Oliver was with the gardai before you took my call."

"I wasn't dead or in jail."

"Oh, well. That makes blowing me off all right, then."

"It must be marriage," her grandfather said. "You didn't used to light up this fast. I've always been the hot one in the family. You're the cool milk in the steaming coffee."

She exhaled, aware that her grandfather — renowned art detective, founder of Sharpe Fine Art Recovery — had decades of experience avoiding tight spaces and maneuvering out of them when he couldn't. He wouldn't have lasted sixty years in his profession and earned his reputation by flouting the law and irritating law-enforcement personnel. Everything she'd just heard — the hyperbole, the humor, the long-suffering poke at her FBI status — was all show, either to quiet his nerves or to get her off his back. Most likely both.

"Oliver didn't kill that man," he said.

"So everyone keeps saying. The police will follow the evidence wherever it takes them."

"He's shattered and confused. He came face-to-face with one of the men who murdered his parents in front of him when he was eight years old. I doubt either of us can imagine how difficult that must have been. And he was dying. A killer on the run for thirty years, no trace of him until that moment with his blood spurting —"

"All right, Granddad. What happens with Oliver isn't my call, anyway. Are you sure you've told me everything you two discussed?"

"Next time you want me to record our conversation?"

"There won't be a next time and you didn't answer my question."

"I think Driscoll said something to Oliver. He wouldn't tell me what. Maybe you can get it out of him."

Emma doubted she'd be asked to get anything out of Oliver York, especially given her grandfather's behavior. "What about your visit here to Oliver's farm in January?"

"What about it? We drank excellent Scotch and told stories. His grandparents weren't art collectors. With all the paintings of dogs — anyone's dogs, not necessarily their own — I encouraged Oliver to get a puppy."

"I'm trying to ascertain if your visit here somehow prompted Davy Driscoll to turn up in Heron's Cove and speak with Lucas just days before he died."

Her grandfather sighed. "I know you are."

"Did you see anyone else while you were here in January?" she asked.

"Martin, the housekeeper, a farm worker — old guy, Johnny, I think. Ruthie's son. Nigel. He's a mechanic — he dropped off a bag of groceries for her. Nice kid. Well, he's not a kid, but when you're my age . . . never mind. We said hello. That was it."

"What about Henrietta Balfour? Did you meet her?"

"Not sure. Who is she?"

"A garden designer who grew up with Oliver. Midthirties, unmarried, attractive."

"Right. I remember her. Martin and I went to the pub one night. Oliver stayed home. I ran into a few people there. She was one of them, I believe."

"And Davy Driscoll?" Emma asked. "Did you run into him?"

"Sean Murphy showed me a photo of the murdering bastard. No, I didn't see him on my visit — or in Dublin. If I'd met him on the street, though, I doubt I'd have paid any attention. I was more observant when I visited Oliver in January, given his unusual background."

"That's one word for it."

"The gardai are taking another look at the break-in at my place. I know Driscoll flew to Dublin as Reed Warren but that doesn't mean he's the one who broke in. Could have been someone following him, could have been unrelated altogether. You know it is. You can have a theory of a case but you can't get tunnel vision." Her grandfather was silent a moment. "How are you doing?"

"Being on the sidelines has its challenges."

"Toes everywhere you don't want to step on. What do you think my last couple of days have been like? But I'm used to it. You law-enforcement types don't always appreciate the role of a private interest. Life's full of gray lines. I know it doesn't help that you've got me in the thick of things. I hope I'm not a ball and chain for you, Emma."

"Never," she said without hesitation.

"I bet not stepping on toes is tough for your new husband."

Emma smiled. "Colin's a pro, Granddad."

"Yeah. Well, if it wasn't this mess, it'd be something else. It's what you do."

"Be careful. I wish you'd stay with a friend tonight."

"I missed my bed last night. I stayed in Ardmore. I got up early and walked out to

260

the round tower. I'm walking for as long as I'm able. Don't worry about me, kid. I'll be fine. I've got Sean Murphy breathing down my neck now, too."

"We'll stay in touch. Answer your phone next time I call. Love you, Granddad."

"Love you, kid. And you be careful, too."

After she disconnected with her intractable, unpredictable grandfather, Emma returned to her room. She and Colin had opened a window early, after the rain had stopped, and she could hear the stream and birds. She wondered how many walkers around the Cotswolds were setting off on its network of waymarked trails. She would head to the York farmhouse on her own. She wanted to touch base with the police about the investigation, but she wasn't sure how forthcoming they would be, even with MI5 smoothing the way.

If nothing else, at least it was a beautiful morning for a walk.

"For a recluse, a lot happens around Oliver York."

Colin couldn't disagree with the man striding next to him on the dirt lane that ran along the southern edge of the York farm. He called himself Jeremy Pearson, but that was almost certainly not his real name.

261

They walked toward the barn as if they'd bumped into each other by accident. Pearson was dressed in casual walking attire, a map of the Cotswolds tucked into a plastic ziplock bag hanging from his neck, allowing his hands to stay free.

Jeremy Pearson was anything but an ordinary trail walker.

A humorless, rugged MI5 officer if ever there were one, he was in his late forties, with the sort of amiable good looks that allowed him to blend in to almost any crowd. The lines etched at the corners of his gray-blue eyes and streaks of gray in his dark hair were due, no doubt, to long-term stress and exposure to every manner of bad weather rather than to aging. He had scars on his hands. He would tell people they were from a gardening mishap, but Colin knew they were from Jeremy's days with SAS and then MI6, before he'd joined MI5.

"Davy Driscoll seems to have lived a quiet, uneventful life as Reed Warren for the past thirty years," Pearson said. "He did odd jobs and moved around a fair amount. He got his passport five years ago for a trip to Costa Rica. He didn't use it again until Saturday when he flew to Boston. As you know, he stayed at the inn next to the Sharpe Fine Art Recovery offices and had a brief conversation with Lucas Sharpe. On Tuesday morning, he visited Father Bracken. That evening, he flew to Dublin."

"He arrived in time to break into Wendell Sharpe's place. We want to know what Driscoll did between his arrival in Boston on Saturday and his arrival in Heron's Cove on Monday." Colin paused but decided not to mention Sam Padgett was looing into the Balfour connections in the US. "Maine's a dead end so far. Father Bracken can't reveal the details of his conversation with Driscoll." Colin decided not to mention Franny Maroney and his mother, either. "We'll keep digging."

"It's clear Driscoll was looking into Oliver's relationship with you and with the Sharpes."

Colin didn't argue with Pearson's statement. "We don't know if he figured out Oliver also uses the name Oliver Fairbairn or that he's an art thief."

"Was."

"Just because he's not active doesn't make him less a thief."

Pearson gave Colin a cool look. "Point taken."

Colin noted he had the pasture-and-sheep side of the lane and the MI5 officer had the wooded side. They crossed a small bridge that spanned the stream that also ran behind the dovecote. It was wider here, as it meandered through flatter land. Up ahead, he could see the barn, constructed of the ubiquitous honey-colored limestone. A small tractor was out front, probably the one Nigel Burns had worked on yesterday when he'd seen Oliver sneak off in his Rolls-Royce.

"A working farm can't stop cold for a police investigation," Pearson said, clasping his hands behind him at the small of his back as he walked. "Tractor maintenance could wait, I suppose, but the animals need regular tending. Do you know anything about farming, Special Agent Donovan?"

"I'm from a fishing village," Colin said. "Ask me about boats and lobsters."

Pearson's mouth twitched into something resembling a smile. "I'm a Londoner myself. Oliver draws a modest income from the farm but he reinvests it in improvements. He contracts out any work. He doesn't work the farm himself. Martin Hambly doesn't, either, or, God forbid, Ruthie Burns. Martin oversees staff but he's primarily Oliver's personal assistant. Ruthie's fiefdom is the house."

"Does Henrietta Balfour's role fall under farm improvement?"

"Property improvement."

"MI5 operator to garden designer. I flirt with becoming a tour-boat captain. Ever see a live puffin, Jeremy?"

"No, nor a dead one."

"Stuffed? Cute gift for the grandkids."

Another cool look. "You assume I'm old enough for grandchildren. Also that I'm married and have children. Married, yes. Children, no."

"A grand-dog, then?"

"You haven't changed since we first met," Pearson said. "I thought marrying a Sharpe might civilize you."

Colin grinned. "What says it hasn't?"

"And I haven't said that Henrietta was an operator." Pearson stopped short of the barn. "She blames me for running her out of the intelligence service."

"Did you?"

Not so much as a flicker of irritation. "No. She ran herself out. She used me as an excuse so she didn't have to admit she was burnt out."

"Was she as eccentric when she was with you? The wild hair, the flowered skirts."

"The skirts aren't all flowered," Pearson said drily.

Colin held back a grin. They were deep into Pearson's turf now, discussing a former

MI5 operator he obviously respected, protected and found irritating, troubling and hard to predict. But Colin knew that was just an educated guess on his part. For all he knew, Jeremy Pearson was playing him. But he didn't think that was the case.

"Henrietta's grandfather was Freddy Balfour, a legend in UK intelligence circles and quite the local hero. He was at Cambridge with Kim Philby and helped unmask him and his lot as traitors during the Cold War. Before that, Freddy was involved in counter-espionage during World War II. He participated in the Double-Cross System. Amazing man. Henrietta hardly remembers him but his example inspired her to join MI5. She romanticized the work, but many do at the start."

"Did being Freddy Balfour's granddaughter help or hinder her?"

"Both. People had their ideas about her and perhaps some didn't take her seriously at first, but that wasn't really the problem. The problem was in her own head. That's where most of the help and the hindering occurred." Pearson paused, turned to Colin. "Not unlike your Emma and her grandfather, I imagine."

"Wendell put Emma through her paces

the past twenty-four hours," Colin admitted.

Pearson looked out at an ewe and two lambs grazing next to each other in the pasture, as if they were posing for a postcard. "Freddy loved to garden. It was perhaps the only thing he and Posey had in common, although he didn't approve of her less formal taste. The gardening gene bypassed his son — Henrietta's father — but she makes up for it. Her mother isn't a keen gardener, either. Now there's a couple who wondered why the devil they had a child. Henrietta never fit in. Her parents weren't awful to her, just remote. As I say, I have a dog myself. What about you, Colin? Do you and Emma plan to have children?"

The personal question was payback for Colin's earlier comment. He took it in stride. "We'll see."

"Emma didn't plan on having a husband, did she? Is it true she was a nun?"

"True."

Jeremy sighed. "I'll stop there, then. I've made my point. Oliver won't be charged for running yesterday, but if he killed Driscoll —"

"You can take up dog-walking since you'll be toast as an intelligence officer."

"We could also get Oliver to help us from

267

prison." Pearson glanced sideways at Colin. "That works for you, doesn't it?"

"Oliver's growing on me," Colin said.

"He has that effect. It's a shame someone as extroverted as he is by nature lives such a solitary life. Becoming a Hollywood consultant under a pseudonym gave him a way into the world, but he remained eccentric, private. Imagine if he could simply be the dashing, wealthy Englishman he was meant to be."

"He's been out and about more in recent months. Maybe that's what brought Davy Driscoll here."

Pearson nodded thoughtfully. They stopped short of the barn. Colin expected the MI5 officer to continue on the marked way out to the main road, but instead he turned back toward the dovecote. "We can pretend I'm returning to the village for a pint."

They walked in silence for a few minutes. Colin appreciated the scenery and the warm sunshine, but he and Pearson both had a dozen unanswered questions that hung in the air between them. They had no direct involvement in the death investigation but they both were affected by it.

"Did Henrietta kill Davy Driscoll on your behalf?" Colin asked finally.

Jeremy Pearson didn't break stride. "That's excellent, Colin. You must know I never confirm or deny anything. I prefer having my American friends think I'm capable of having a wanted murderer's brachial sliced open, but Henrietta? She's left the service. The only thing she's killed lately are weeds. For that matter, that's all she's ever killed, not because she didn't face dangers or wasn't good at her job — precisely the opposite."

It was more than Colin might have said in Pearson's place, and certainly more than he deserved in response to his incendiary question. His MI5 counterpart didn't ruffle easily. Not news, but still good to experience for himself.

"Here's our friend now," Pearson said, nodding up a walkway that led to the York house. Oliver and Emma were headed in their direction, Alfred bursting at his leash at Oliver's side. Pearson turned to Colin with an outstretched hand. "Thank you for the directions. Enjoy the rest of your stay."

They shook hands, and the MI5 officer ambled off.

"You're in luck, Colin," Oliver said when he and Emma caught up to him. "Martin's training Alfred to be a well-mannered, respectful dog. Martin's the alpha, by the way. He keeps denying it but it makes sense given my frequent absences and erratic schedule."

"I like dogs." Colin stroked the energetic puppy, who responded by licking his hand. "Did you take him to London with you?"

"Only if Martin joins me. He didn't this last trip."

"And you *were* in London," Colin said.

Oliver ignored him and turned to Emma. "You were more welcoming. Shall I give you a proper tour of my stone-cutting studio? I'd like to see if everything is in order and nothing else is missing. The detectives had me take a look when I arrived home, but I was still reeling at the prospect one of my tools killed a man. At first glance it appeared it's only the one chisel missing."

Without waiting for Emma to respond, Oliver plunged ahead of her, Alfred trotting happily alongside him. Colin eased next to his wife. "You've talked to Wendell?" he asked her.

"I have that look, do I?"

"It's a particular mix of tension, affection, relief and annoyance."

"All at once? Is that even possible?"

He longed to throw an arm around her and walk off into the rolling English countryside, but he settled for smiling at her.

270

"I'll take a picture sometime and you can see for yourself."

When they reached the dovecote, Oliver launched into a detailed explanation of the purpose of a small, pointed chisel, next to the one that was missing. "It's sharp as sin," he said.

"And the one that cut Davy Driscoll?" Colin asked.

"Even more so."

As the chisel lecture wrapped up, Martin Hambly arrived at the dovecote, and Colin seized the moment to get out of there with Emma. They decided to walk back to the inn and stop at Henrietta Balfour's place on the way.

"We can see how the new rose trellis is coming," Colin said, wishing he could make himself sound more amused.

15

Martin Hambly stopped at Henrietta's house on his way back to the farm from the village to let her know Oliver had arrived from Ireland. She couldn't help but notice Martin's improved spirits, although he wouldn't relax, she knew, until the investigation was concluded and the reasons for Davy Driscoll's arrival in the village and the manner of his death were sorted and Oliver was completely in the clear. "We'll get through this," Martin said.

Henrietta smiled, wanting to reassure him. "Of course we will."

After he was on his way again, Henrietta checked her phone but found nothing from MI5 or the FBI agents — or Oliver.

Back to gardening, then.

Tony and Nigel were running late, but they'd called. She didn't mind. She'd had work on the York farm booked today, and with police, FBI agents and an out-of-sort owner about, best she find something else to do.

She knew Oliver. He *would* be out of sorts after his misadventure. Ireland, of all places. Couldn't he have cleared his head in a dark corner of a pub in Stow-on-the-Wold?

She went into the kitchen. She loved her house despite its old-lady quirks and need for updating, Aunt Posey having been both frugal and skeptical of the new. In her later years, she'd found comfort in having her things where they'd always been, and in her familiar routines. Sometimes Henrietta had to remind herself it was okay to put the teapot on a different shelf if she wanted to, never mind make plans to tear the place apart to suit her own taste. She was getting bolder, and she could, indeed, see herself making a proper go of it as a Cotswold garden designer. She could finally put MI5 behind her.

Easier said without Oliver York in her life, across the fields.

Nigel and Tony arrived through the back gate to the Kershaw farm, and Henrietta went outside and met them by the rose trellis in question. They apologized for not getting there sooner. "You'd have woken me up if you'd arrived sooner," she told them cheerfully, although it wasn't true. She'd been awake since dawn, thinking — trying to figure out if she'd missed anything yesterday, any tidbit that could help the police.

"I can stay an hour," Nigel said. "I have to finish work on the tractor at the York farm. I meant to finish yesterday, but . . . well, you know what happened."

Henrietta pinched a sodden, brown rose blossom. Last night's rain had left everything dripping, but the sun was peeking through the last of the clouds, with the promise of renewed pleasant weather. "There's no rush with the trellis. I appreciate the help."

"This won't take long," Tony said, pulling on the old wood.

Henrietta had managed to make tea and pull on fresh clothes — hoody, maxi skirt, Wellies — but with Martin's visit and news of Oliver's quick return from Ireland, she hadn't had anything to eat. "You two will be all right on your own?"

Tony grinned at her. "We can manage tearing down a trellis."

"I've no doubt. It's a job for two people, and I admit I'm glad I'm not one of them. I'll boil some eggs and come back out in a bit. Shout or pop in if you need anything." As she started to the back steps, she glanced at Nigel out of the corner of her eye and saw he was looking awkward, shifting from one foot to the other. She paused, hand on the rail. "Is something on your mind, Nigel?"

He flushed red. For a man in his forties, he'd always struck her as somewhat immature, if a decent sort. "I didn't want to say anything." He chewed on his lower lip. "My mum — she has a suspicious mind. She watches those detective shows. I stayed at her place last night because she couldn't settle down after seeing that man who died."

"It's understandable she was upset," Henrietta said. "Martin and I were, too."

"The police aren't saying much. Mum's got it in her head he was murdered. She doesn't think Mr. York did it, but she doesn't know — I guess no one does. She keeps talking about it."

Tony set his toolbox on a metal chair on the terrace. "Talking about a traumatic event can help. She needs to process what she saw."

"I think she wants to solve it. The murder." Nigel pulled at the wobbly trellis. "Mum says you were calm and cool yesterday, Henrietta. She thinks you're not a real garden designer."

"Well, my father doesn't, either, so I'm

not the least offended. It's a second career for me."

Nigel fastened his gaze on her. "Mum wonders what you're really up to."

"Whoa, Nigel," Tony said. "Watch yourself."

His flush deepened until he was purple to his hair roots. "*I'm* not wondering. It's Mum. I don't want her to make life rough on you, Henrietta. You don't know her. She likes the trains to run on time, y'know? She's set in her routines, and she thinks everyone else should have routines. She doesn't like change, messiness . . ." He stopped himself, blowing out a breath. "Personally I think she's obsessing on you because she's embarrassed she went mental yesterday. She fancies herself having a stiff upper lip. It's good Oliver's back, at least."

"I'm a garden designer, Nigel," Henrietta said, keeping any defensiveness out of her voice. "I work with a variety of clients, including Oliver. Your family's lived in the village a long time. Your mother is aware I've known Oliver since I was a small child."

"She thinks you're with the police," Nigel blurted.

Tony snorted. "Bloody hell. *Henrietta*?"

Nigel put on one of the gloves and nodded. "Maybe MI5 or MI6."

"My, my," Henrietta said mildly. "I never realized what an imagination dear Ruthie has. When did this come up?"

"Just now. Before I came over here. Mum was in a state."

"Maybe she didn't sleep last night," Tony said. "That can scramble your thinking."

Nigel licked his lips, his cheeks a bit less red. "She thinks you're the one who arranged it so the FBI agents could talk to us. *Then* she said maybe you're working with them."

"With the FBI?" Tony snorted. "Your mum needs a quiet day and a good night's sleep."

"I'm hardly an FBI informant." Henrietta did her best to sound amused. Back in her days as an operator, she'd posed as countless different sorts — street walker, drug addict, religious zealot, money launderer. She could pass herself off as a garden designer and neighbor who was shocked but also entertained at the idea of working on the q.t. with American federal law-enforcement officers. Of course, she *was* a garden designer and neighbor. It was precisely this scenario that had helped her see that she'd needed to leave the Security Service. She gave a mock shiver. "I can't imagine, frankly. Special Agents Donovan and Sharpe have a history with Oliver. I don't know the details, but I'm not working with them."

"Mum says it's more like a collaboration between Scotland Yard or MI5 and the Yanks."

"Enough of this, Nigel." Tony grabbed hold of the left side of the trellis and tugged at it hard, loosening it in the muddy ground. "Your mum needs to stick to watching detective shows instead of thinking she's in one. She can't be spreading wild rumors. She'll get herself in trouble."

"That's what I told her," Nigel said, chastened.

Henrietta patted him on the shoulder. "Do I *look* like a secret agent, Nigel? No offense taken, though. Your mum had a shock yesterday. We all did, and we're all trying to make sense of it in our own way."

"She says her only concern is Mr. York."

"I'm sure it is," Henrietta said, gesturing to the back door. "I'll go boil those eggs now."

"Nigel and I will get to work," Tony said, pulling two pairs of work gloves out of his toolbox and handing one pair to Nigel.

Henrietta went into the kitchen. She made short work of the eggs. Too short. The whites were nauseatingly runny, but she averted her eyes and smeared them on heavily buttered toast. No one in the village had suspected she was MI5 when she *was* MI5. Put on a flowered skirt and dig in the dirt, keep from falling to pieces in an emergency, and all of a sudden she was a spy.

She'd have a word with Ruthie, if need be.

She cleaned up the kitchen and brought a fresh cup of tea outside with her and set it on the table. The sun was shining in a blue sky now, not just peeking through scattered clouds. One of the joys of the house was the flow Posey had created between the inside and the outside. Walking from the kitchen to the garden was seamless, as if they were one.

Nigel and Tony had the trellis down and most of the roses pulled out of it, some of the vines intact in the soil, some in a heap for compost. She half expected Nigel to put her gardening knowledge to the test on behalf of Ruthie, but Tony did the talking. "These are beautiful roses," he said. "Posey was proud of them. She'd approve of them getting a good chop and a new trellis."

"She would, indeed," Henrietta said.

"I don't mean to say I knew her as well as you — I just happened to see her one day when she was out here, and she carried on about them."

Henrietta wanted to assure him she wasn't envious of any time he'd spent with his aunt — her great-aunt — but he didn't linger, expecting a response. She returned to her tea and Tony and Nigel cleaned up the trellis debris, grabbing weeds and rose trimmings at the same time and dumping them in the compost.

"Do you have the new trellis yet?" Tony asked when they finished.

"I'm not sure I'm replacing it. I want to see the space without it before I decide."

"Heresy," he said with a grin. "Ring me if you decide to make a change and Aunt Posey haunts you."

Henrietta laughed. "You'll be the first person I phone."

He kissed her on the cheek. "It's good to see you smiling again, love. I'll see you later? I'll be working on the Kershaw cottage."

"I'll probably be in and out. I want to get back to work today myself."

"Good for you." Tony pulled off his work gloves. "Finish your tea and relax first. Work will keep."

Nigel shuffled from one foot to the other. "Forget what I said about Mum, okay?"

Henrietta smiled. "Forgotten."

■ ■ ■ ■

Henrietta finished her tea in the garden, enjoying the weather and contemplating the absent trellis. She hadn't researched its history in Posey's voluminous files on the property, but she supposed she ought to take a look before she made up her mind what to do. What if Freddy Balfour himself had presented it as a gift? She had a vague memory of walking in the garden with him. She must have been only three or four. He'd held her hand. Would he have approved of his only grandchild's first career choice? Or would he have wanted something else for her, if only because he'd understood the life of an intelligence officer?

Aunt Posey had guessed. "You're an operator," she'd said, her voice raspy and slow with age but her eyes piercing, certain. "I can see it in the way you carry yourself. You remind me of Freddy."

She'd been right, of course.

Henrietta wondered if both her great-aunt and grandfather would have approved of her career change. They'd have pretended to, at least, even if they'd secretly wanted her to stay with MI5 — if they'd have been more proud with an intelligence-officer grand-niece and granddaughter.

Her parents, of course, were oblivious. "Garden design?" Her father had looked up from his paper, as if he was supposed to know something and didn't. "Excellent. Fresh air will do you good after working in an office."

Her mother had suggested a professional cleaning service now that her only daughter had a full house to look after.

Henrietta laughed. Clueless but wonderful in their own happy, neglectful way.

Cassie waved frantically from the stone wall that divided their two properties. "Henrietta — Henrietta, I need you. Please. Can you come over?"

Henrietta abandoned her cozy spot on the terrace and crossed the garden, her skirt brushing against dripping rhododendrons the sunshine hadn't yet dried. "I'll be sopping as badly as the rhodies," she said, shaking out her skirt as she greeted Cassie, bits of plant debris sticking to the wet splotches of fabric. "I'll have to change before I go to the York farm. I — Cassie, what's wrong?"

Her friend and neighbor was fighting tears, taking in rapid, shallow breaths, close to hyperventilating. She pointed behind her. "I'm a little freaked out. Can you look at something? I'm here alone. The kids are at school and Eugene's out in the fields." She blew out a breath as if to get herself under control. "I think . . . it looks . . ." She sniffled. "He was here."

"Who was here, Cassie?"

"Maybe I'm overreacting and it was Tony or Eugene or one of the boys. I'll show you."

"Should we ring the police?"

"No — no, not yet. Just come and take a look. Tell me I'm nuts."

Henrietta went through the gate and followed Cassie to the cottage she and Eugene were renovating. Cassie, however, bypassed the cottage's front door and took a path through tall, wet grass to a small attached lean-to, its creaky, half-rotted door ajar. She shoved the door with her shoulder, pushing it open. "I wanted to start clearing out in here. I thought it would help me burn up some nervous energy after yesterday." She drew in another few rapid breaths and then stood back. "And I found this. Take a look."

Henrietta edged past her into the doorway. "Should I brace myself, Cassie?"

"There's no body. At least I don't think so. I didn't see one at any rate, or any blood."

"That's not terribly encouraging."

Henrietta peered into the lean-to, a former wood shed as she recalled. She kept to one side so that sunlight could get into the windowless space and she could see what had sent Cassie into a state of panic and shock. As her eyes adjusted, she could make out a couple of old blankets arranged to create a sleeping mat. A man's change of clothes was heaped next to the bedding — boxer shorts and socks atop trousers and a rugby shirt, all the items neat, folded and clean. Henrietta poked her head farther inside for a closer look. Receipts, coins and a key fob lay at the foot of the bedding, as if the owner had emptied his pockets before setting off for the day.

"The man who died at Oliver York's house must have slept here," Cassie said, sounding calmer. "It was Davy Driscoll, wasn't it, Henrietta? That's not just a wild rumor?"

She stepped backward out of the lean-to and turned to her friend. "We need to call the police at once."

Cassie didn't move. It was as if she'd frozen in place.

"Cassie."

Finally she nodded. "You call. I'm going to be sick."

She backed up in the grass, stumbling on a protruding rock. As she righted herself, she gasped, clutching her chest. Henrietta leaped to her, but Tony got to her first.

"Sorry, love," he said, grabbing Cassie by the elbow, steadying her. "I didn't mean to startle you."

"It's all right." She released her shirt, her hand trembling, but she breathed out, her relief evident. She attempted a smile. "I almost jumped out of my skin."

Tony winced. "Sorry about that. I'm back just now — I went over to the York barn with Nigel after we helped Henrietta with her trellis. I heard you two out here." He stood back, frowning. "Is everything all right?"

"No, it isn't," Henrietta said crisply, pointing at the lean-to. "I'm about to ring the police. Someone decided to bunk in there. It wasn't a friend of yours, was it?"

"A friend —" Tony paled slightly and shook his head. "No."

He swore under his breath and started toward the door but Henrietta grabbed his arm. "We shouldn't touch anything."

Tony turned to her. "You think it was that fellow who died up at the York farm yesterday?"

"That's up to the police to determine. I'm not making any guesses."

"All right, I'll have a look but I won't touch anything." He took a quick peek in the lean-to. "Not quite a B and B, is it? I suppose he didn't want to take a chance someone would see him."

Cassie was noticeably calmer. "It doesn't look as if whoever it was spent much time here."

"He couldn't have," Tony said. "I'm sure I'd have noticed if anyone was back here when I was working. Once I'm asleep, it takes a lot to wake me. I pop awake at six every morning, but I get in a solid eight hours before that."

Henrietta patted her jacket pockets for her phone, but she'd left it with her tea. "Blast. I don't have my phone. Cassie —"

Tony already had his phone in hand. "It's all right. I'll ring the police."

"I really am going to be sick." Cassie put the back of her wrist to her mouth, as if holding back bile, but she rallied. "I should try to call Eugene. He has his phone with him but coverage is spotty."

"I'll ring him when I finish with the police," Tony said. "I have his number."

Cassie nodded. "Thank you."

Rather than sharing Cassie's relief at Tony's take-charge attitude, Henrietta found herself faintly annoyed. Of course, Tony didn't know his younger second cousin was a former MI5 officer who'd confronted far worse than a dead man's sleeping quarters. She might not look capable of handling an emergency at the moment, but she'd done brilliantly yesterday, hadn't she?

She chastised herself for her surly, defensive mood. Tony was only trying to help.

He made short work of the calls. "Police and Eugene are on the way," he said, hanging on to his phone.

Cassie shuddered. "To think this man was here while we were sleeping. If it was one of the men who killed the Yorks — a murderer and a child kidnapper. I don't care if it was decades ago. I don't believe people change, and if he was desperate . . ."

Tony clapped a hand on her shoulder. "Now, now, let's not get ahead of ourselves. There's no good in fretting about what didn't happen. Be glad it didn't, right?"

Cassie smiled weakly. "Right."

Henrietta decided to let Tony be comforter-in-charge without being small about it. Cassie obviously appreciated his manly presence, and Henrietta was able to focus on the matter at hand. At first glance, the attached lean-to had struck her as a risky, unwise choice for Davy Driscoll to have made, especially given the ongoing work on the cottage, but as she surveyed the immediate area, she saw it had its advantages. It abutted woods that could

287

provide cover for someone sneaking on or off the Kershaw property. Through the woods and across the stream and it was a reasonably convenient, mostly off-road route to the York farm.

It was also possible Davy Driscoll had chosen the cottage lean-to at random, his bedding bundled up under an arm as he'd . . . *what*? Wandered through the fields? Crossed the stream? Had he been lost?

As far as Henrietta knew, the police hadn't yet found a vehicle he'd used. Could he have left a car hidden nearby and its location had helped him choose his quarters?

With Tony right there and work going on in the cottage, Driscoll couldn't have stayed in the lean-to for more than a night or two, at most.

A disturbing prospect, nonetheless.

Cassie at least was looking less green. "Eugene wasn't back here yesterday, but he stops at the cottage most days — and always if work's going on. Tony does most of it but Eugene likes to meet contractors, the plumber and electrician and such. We keep the boys away because of the construction. That's something, anyway."

Tony nudged her gently toward the boys' play area, complete with an elaborate climbing structure they were about to outgrow and a table and chairs — adult-size, fortunately. Henrietta, following Cassie and Tony, would have balked at sitting in a child-size chair while waiting for the police. She itched to get her hands on Reed Warren/Davy Driscoll's things. Had he planned to come back here after his visit to the York farm?

The cottage wasn't visible from her house, but still. Henrietta hadn't had a clue the now-deceased had holed up there. She'd always prided herself on her situational awareness during her years conducting surveillance on some very dangerous people.

"I never would have thought to check the lean-to," Tony said. "I've only been in there a time or two."

"It was pure happenstance that I went in," Cassie said. "Maybe it was some kind of sixth sense at work. You don't think the police will be suspicious, do you?"

"Of course not," Tony said without hesitation.

Cassie shifted to Henrietta. "Do you, Henrietta?"

"Let's see if *our* suspicions are right and it's not a game the kids got themselves up to."

Which sounded lame even to her, but she was spared further awkward small talk and reassurances by Eugene's arrival. He was red-faced and sweating profusely, a contrast to Tony's stoic calm, but Cassie, thankfully, embraced her husband and told him she was relieved and glad he was here.

Henrietta seized the moment. "Tell the police I'll be in my garden if they need me."

Henrietta didn't get to her garden. She veered off into the woods behind the Kershaw cottage, descended to the stream and leaped across it to the opposite side. She pushed through more trees. She wanted to test her theory about this being a convenient route to the York farmhouse. She thrashed her way up a short hill and emerged on a seldom-used track that ran along the edge of a field.

For some reason, she wasn't surprised when she saw Emma and Colin down the hill, crossing the stream, following her trail. In another half minute, they intercepted her on the track.

"I was restless," she said before they could say a word. "I'm off on a ramble. I'm only breathing hard because I just crossed a stream. I'm in cracking shape."

"You're used to a team," Colin said.

"Reminding me I'm on my own, without backup?"

"Yes."

"We understand you and Cassie found where Driscoll stayed," Emma said.

"Right under our noses," Henrietta said. Looking around, she observed fresh tire tracks. Then, up ahead, a small black sedan. "I think we've just found Davy Driscoll's car," she said.

She ran ahead of the two FBI agents and peered through the passenger window of the small car. She heard rustling in the trees behind her. She went on immediate alert but relaxed when a rabbit hopped in front of her and disappeared into the thickets. "Startled by a bunny rabbit," she said with a laugh as Emma and Colin fell in next to her.

Henrietta was tempted to try the car door, but she knew she shouldn't touch anything and risk contaminating forensic evidence. Even as she'd lunged toward the car, she'd been careful about corrupting any footprints, although she hadn't seen any in the mud and grass.

She spotted car-hire papers on the passenger seat.

Why hide a hired car here? Why hide it at all? Why even come here?

Interesting questions, but not her problem. Her problem was her rose trellis, her work, her tea. At most she could be supportive of her friends — Cassie, Eugene, Nigel, Ruthie, Tony, Martin. And Oliver, of course. He was home. Safe.

Three fat crows descended to the center of the field, cawing, flapping their black wings. Henrietta shuddered, but she refused to see them as an omen just because she'd spotted them when she'd thought about Oliver.

"We need to get the police here," Emma said.

Henrietta nodded. "Yes, of course. They're already on the way." She quickly explained additional details about Cassie's discovery. "First Davy Driscoll's possessions. Now Davy Driscoll's car. The bastard bedded down within spitting distance of me. If it'd been a warm night, I might have cracked a window and heard him snoring. Well, Tony was right there in the cottage and didn't hear anything, but he's a bit hard of hearing, I think."

"It's possible Driscoll didn't actually sleep there," Emma said.

Colin pointed to the back seat of the car. "Here. Take a look."

Henrietta did so. She caught a glimpse of an amateurish but delightful painting of Edinburgh Castle. It reminded her of the painting of Queen's View Cassie had discovered in the cottage. Henrietta didn't see a signature. There were more canvases underneath it and one on the floor — another scene of Scotland, the Glenfinnan Viaduct of *Harry Potter* fame.

She turned to Emma and Colin. "Cassie found a Scotland painting in the cottage. These paintings must be by the same artist. How did Davy Driscoll end up with them? What interest could he possibly have in amateur paintings of Scotland? He and Norcross took Oliver to the southern Highlands. Maybe he was obsessed with Scotland. Obviously this is his car. It's a quiet spot, but he could pop right out to the road and be in Stow-on-the-Wold, Chipping Norton or Oxford in no time." She tore her gaze from the back seat and turned to the FBI agents with an apologetic smile. "Sorry. I know better than to stand here and waste time speculating."

"Brainstorming can sometimes help," Emma said.

"It has its place, but my only brainstorming these days involves gardens. The police can do their jobs. Oliver's home safe and sound. I can go make tea and deal with the rose-trellis debris."

She had a sudden urge to walk over to the

York farm and see Oliver for herself, but he'd be busy with the police. They'd want him to look at the paintings. Henrietta ignored the rush of emotion she felt. She had to be seriously, irreparably bored, or in a troubled state of arrested MI5 withdrawal. She couldn't possibly be falling for an unrepentant art thief, an expert in folklore, legends and mythology — who *cared*? — and a black belt in this-and-that martial-art discipline. His karate and tai-chi expertise interested her more than his knowledge of ancient gods and goddesses and sacrificial rituals. She found herself picturing Oliver doing katas, sweating as he jumped, leaped, kicked and poked. It was a sexy series of images, but she shoved them aside.

Emma was eyeing her as if she understood such emotional turmoil. Being married to Colin Donovan, Henrietta thought, perhaps she did.

She heard a rustling in the trees, but it wasn't a rabbit this time. Two uniformed police officers were making their way across the stream. She'd answer their questions but Emma and Colin could do most of the talking. Then . . . back to her garden. She needed to stand down and let the professional investigators do their jobs.

16

Emma sat on the stone bench opposite the spot where Davy Driscoll had died. Someone had placed a dark blue tarp over the blood stains. It was held down by stones, but otherwise the scene had been cleared. The police had collected Oliver to take a look at the findings at the Kershaw farm. Emma had returned with him a few minutes ago. Colin was still with DI Lowe at Davy Driscoll's rental car.

"I told the police everything about my Irish overnight, right down to the color of the Atlantic at dawn." Oliver sat next to Emma with a groan of obvious fatigue and frustration. "I couldn't help with the paintings in Driscoll's car. I'd never seen them before. They must be a Balfour or Kershaw thing." He folded his hands on his lap. "You're the art-crimes expert, Emma. Why would a killer and kidnapper be interested in unsigned amateur paintings of Scotland?"

"Best we avoid speculating," she said.

"As the police reminded me and your husband, this isn't your investigation. As if it needs repeating."

Emma smiled. "I don't mind."

Martin Hambly came out of the house. Oliver jumped to his feet and joined him. Emma remained on the bench while Oliver and Martin stood next to the tarp. Now that the detectives had finished interviewing him and he'd avoided arrest, Oliver would understandably want to take his longtime personal assistant and lifelong friend through the moment-by-moment events of the past twenty-four hours, and to hear Martin's story. It could help them both — not just emotionally but it could prod more details from their memories as they processed the trauma they'd experienced.

Alfred had trotted out the open door and stood next to Oliver, who occasionally reached down and patted the puppy, a gesture that seemed to reassure both of them. Oliver and Martin both obviously loved the energetic terrier. Alfred greeted Emma by jumping on her, earning himself a quiet but firm rebuke from Martin.

"Martin spoils him," Oliver said, crossing the driveway to her. "Of course, he denies it."

"He's your dog," Martin said, then went inside.

Oliver sighed. "Yesterday was rough on him. This place has been his sanctuary. That it's now experienced bloodshed . . ." He sank onto the bench next to Emma. "We'll have to do some sort of cleansing ritual."

"You must know some interesting ones."

"I'll go for one that involves flowers and pretty stones rather than some others. I feel terrible that I left him and Henrietta to find the body. At least Ruthie warned them and they knew there was an emergency that likely involved a fatality and a great deal of blood."

"Have you spoken with Ruthie?"

"Not yet. Martin's hoping she's angry enough to quit."

It was an attempt at humor, one of Oliver's ways of coping. "Yesterday wasn't easy on anyone," Emma said.

"I suppose not." Alfred abandoned Emma and nuzzled Oliver's leg. He leaned down and scratched the puppy absently. "Ruthie should have called 999 on her way to the dovecote and Martin and Henrietta should have waited there with her. I left only after I knew Driscoll was dead. I recognized him straight off. I didn't know his adopted identity until I checked his wallet when I arrived in Stow-on-the-Wold."

"You had the presence of mind to take his wallet and phone."

"Yes," he said matter-of-factly. "I had absolutely no doubt who he was. After all these years, having seen him only for a short time as a boy . . ." Oliver waited as Alfred flopped onto the pavement in front of him. "Police say he started living as Reed Warren in the first days after I escaped. It's a new identity, not one he stole from someone else. He wasn't that sophisticated. He must have had help."

"Norcross?"

"He wasn't that sophisticated, either. New identities explain how they disappeared into thin air. I wonder if they had aliases ready and waiting for them when they entered our London home." Oliver paused, rubbing his toe on Alfred's soft abdomen. "Maybe the break-in wasn't as spontaneous and opportunistic as we've always thought."

Emma saw that he'd raised his gaze from the puppy and was staring at the tarp. "Did Driscoll say anything to you before he died, Oliver?"

"He was in bad shape. Bleeding out. I don't know that anything he said would have made sense or been coherent."

"But you told the detectives anything he

did say, no matter how garbled or incoherent," Emma said.

Oliver didn't answer at once.

"Oliver, you need to tell them."

He kept his gaze on the tarp but his eyes narrowed, as if he were concentrating, perhaps reliving the last moments of Davy Driscoll's life. "I asked him who did this to him. He mentioned my mother. He said, 'I did,' and her name. I asked him if anyone else was in danger, and he said, 'Scotland. The Sharpes . . . careful . . . I live in the ruin.' That was it. Then he fell unconscious and died in my arms."

Emma stretched her legs out straight in front of her. "Did any of what he said mean anything to you?"

"He called my mother by her first name, as if she'd been a friend. Scotland was where he and Norcross took me. He must have mentioned the Sharpes because he'd broken into Wendell's house in Dublin. He was fading quickly by then."

"And the ruin?"

"I assume he meant he couldn't escape the reality of what he'd done thirty years ago."

The tarp stirred in a breeze, pushing slightly against the rocks that held it in place. "Why did you go to Declan's Cross?"

He turned to her with a small smile. "It seemed like a good idea at the time."

"It's a place of comfort for you."

"Well, not last night. It wasn't as cold as in November, but the rain was bloody desperate. Terrible. The skies opened up on me. It felt personal, as if God had decided to punish me for leaving poor Martin and Henrietta to find Driscoll and worry about me. Then your grandfather showed up with terrible coffee and a scone that could break a window. More divine punishment."

"Granddad's never been a fussy eater," Emma said.

"He must know the difference between an edible scone and an inedible one. It was decent of him to bring me breakfast. I thought he might be able to help me figure out Driscoll's dying words, that there was something . . ." Oliver groaned and looked up at the stunning blue sky. "The clear weather is supposed to last through the weekend. We had gorgeous weather for days, then we get one night of fierce rain and now more beautiful weather, and guess which night I end up sleeping rough?"

"And all for naught? Granddad couldn't help you?"

"Not all for naught, but Wendell was unusually unhelpful."

"Did you know about the missing chisel, Oliver?"

He shook his head. "No. I didn't take the chisel and I didn't use it on Driscoll. He was already cut and spurting blood when I came out of the house and saw him. I assumed he was a farm worker who'd had an accident, but then I saw those eyes — and I knew who he was. I don't know if he was murdered or he staged an elaborate suicide, but he's gone to God now, as our friend Finian Bracken would say." Oliver patted Emma's knee. "But enough blood and death. Come. Let's find your charming husband."

Henrietta would never in a thousand years have expected to see Jeremy Pearson in her Cotswold kitchen, but here he was. "Is all the furniture here from your aunt?" he asked with a grimace.

"Not all. I brought some from London."

"The chair I'm sitting on?"

"That was Aunt Posey's favorite chair."

"Figures. It has an old-lady feel to it. I swear her skinny arse is imprinted on the seat."

She bit back a smile. "I got rid of all the cabbage-rose chintz."

"My gran loved chintz." Jeremy settled his

steely eyes on her. "If anyone asks, you decided to keep our appointment to discuss the gardens at my Cotswold country home. I spent the morning walking. Love it here."

That was his cover story, then, was it? Henrietta doubted Jeremy knew a geranium from a begonia — or cared — and she knew for a fact that he didn't have a country home. He had a flat in London with his wife and dog. Exercise for him was a job, not recreation.

He raked both hands through his hair and groaned, signaling an end to any friendly banter. "What a cock-up this situation with Oliver York is, Henrietta. Why did Davy Driscoll have to turn up *now*?"

"Because Oliver's not a recluse anymore. That's the short answer." She sat across from Jeremy. Usually he had an unruffled, quiet way about him that somehow made him seem more dangerous. The man was one rough customer, in part because he rarely got riled. "I have a headache. I think it's the damp. It got into the rose trellis. Some days I swear I should move to Portugal. Stress doesn't help. I'm out of practice."

"You're dealing with family, friends and neighbors this time, not strangers. How much did you drink last night?"

"Not as much as your friend Colin Donovan thinks I did."

Jeremy sat back in his chair. "I suppose I don't blame you for that. You've always had a competitive streak, but it probably doesn't hurt to have him think you're more out of control than you are. That's true, isn't it?"

"I've had a rotten couple of days. I'm not out of control." She felt a wave of irritation. "What difference does it make to you if I am out of control? I'm not your problem."

"You will always be a Security Service interest, Henrietta. There's no getting away from that given your years with the service."

"Is that why you're here? To remind me the tethers are still tight on me?"

"Could Oliver have snatched the chisel and used it to kill Davy Driscoll?"

"He never went inside his studio. Even if he slipped in before Martin and I arrived, why would he go to such trouble? He'd have had to know Driscoll was on the property. There must be other sharp implements he could have used at the house."

"Now we have Driscoll's car."

"He was right *there* through the garden."

Jeremy leaned forward, placing both hands on the pinewood table. "What's going on, Henrietta? How bad is this going to get?"

"You're worried I'm going to screw things up for MI5's work with Oliver."

303

"Having a disheveled wannabe garden-designer intelligence officer recommend him was complicated enough."

She smiled. "Wasn't it, though? Are you going back to London tonight?"

"Tomorrow. I'm staying in a B and B down the road. I wanted to see you first." He glanced around the kitchen, sunlight brightening its flaws as well as its virtues. "Are you okay here on your own?"

"Absolutely. No worries. I don't have stone-cutting hisels but I can manage."

"Let's hope you don't have to." Jeremy got to his feet. "We need Oliver."

"More blood antiquities?"

He gave an almost imperceptible nod.

Henrietta resisted pressing him for details, but she admitted to mad curiosity. "That's not my problem, is it, Jeremy?"

He steadied his gaze on her. After a stint with the SAS, Jeremy had worked with MI6 for a decade. They could have him back as far as she was concerned. Now, however, wasn't the time to get cheeky.

He said goodbye and left the kitchen.

"Well, *that* was subtle," Henrietta muttered, hurling herself to her feet.

Jeremy Pearson had just made Oliver her problem.

She followed Jeremy to the front door and

waited until it shut behind him. She peeked out the window. She didn't know if he'd come alone or if he had a colleague waiting for him, but he remained on foot, disappearing down the lane.

He might have told her his plans if she'd asked, and he might not have. Their conversation, she knew, had been entirely within his control. It wouldn't have made any difference if she'd been at the top of her game as an intelligence officer. Jeremy Pearson was the best, a dedicated officer with MI6 and now MI5. At her most confident — at her very best — Henrietta had never thought she could be in his league.

Annoyingly, he'd been right about her from the start.

I don't give a damn you're Freddy Balfour's granddaughter.

I never said you should.

You didn't have to. You have an air of entitlement about you, Henrietta, and if it doesn't get you killed, it'll get someone else killed.

That friendly chat had been ten years ago. Jeremy had been with MI6 then. She'd been an underling on a joint operation, and he'd vowed to make sure she stayed an underling. He'd softened toward her somewhat in the ensuing years, but her *only* regret in quitting the service that winter had been the satisfaction it had given him. She'd been a damn fine intelligence officer but she'd never been as good as Jeremy Pearson had thought she could be — or as good as she'd hoped to be.

Or so he liked her to believe.

"Who was that with you just now?" Cassie asked as she came through the back gate.

"A prospective client," Henrietta said. She'd come straight out to the garden after Jeremy had left and had looked for something to do, settling on staking the delphinium. "I need to get on with my work, but it isn't easy."

"I know. Nothing's easy right now."

Henrietta frowned at her friend. "You look dispirited. We can't let all this get to our core, Cassie. It'll eat us alive."

"Eugene's having a difficult time with the idea this man was on our property. He . . . We both feel so vulnerable." She sniffled, looking back across the gate toward her house. "Sometimes I wonder if I fell for Eugene because of this place. Freddy Balfour's Cotswold farm. My dad loved to tell us about our connection to him."

"Cassie . . ." Henrietta wasn't the best at this sort of conversation. "Please try not to think big thoughts when you're in the midst of a crisis. Everything in its own time."

She nodded, brushing tears with the backs of her hands. "It's silly. I know I love Eugene because he's Eugene. I know that's why I fell for him."

"Of course it is."

"We have so many plans for the farm. We're saving to build stables. We want to get into horses. We have the space, and the boys would love it — it'd be so good for them. We have to watch out that we're not land rich and cash poor, but we're managing. How are you doing with your new career?"

Henrietta abandoned the delphinium. Her emotions were at least as raw as Cassie's but she was more experienced at hiding them. She smiled. "One doesn't like one's clients to be hunted by the police."

Cassie sputtered into laughter. "Oliver, you mean. Obviously. At least he came back, and the police seem to understand what it must have been like for him."

Plus MI5 needed him, which didn't hurt his chances of staying out of jail, but Henrietta kept that thought to herself.

"It's good Tony's here," Cassie said. "He's such a solid presence. Eugene's so remote these days. It'll pass. He worries about the farm. I hate to see Tony leave the village but he reminds me that Stow-on-the-Wold is a stone's throw from us and he'll continue to work in the area."

"His mother hated the Balfours."

"She lost her husband young, to alcohol, and she needed someone to blame," Cassie said.

"It was more than grief, I suspect. Alcoholism can have such devastating ripple effects, and it wasn't as understood then as it is now."

"It can't have been easy for Anthony to be the ne'er-do-well brother even if Freddy had been a normal human being, but he was a superhero. Anthony could never measure up. It wasn't Freddy's fault. It's just the way it was. Tony doesn't remember his dad at all. He just says his mum and dad did the best they could."

"The Balfours don't talk about such things, of course."

"You prune roses," Cassie said with a smile.

"And deadhead. Never forget deadheading."

They both laughed, and Cassie seemed in better spirits when she left.

Henrietta paced. She knew she wouldn't stay and stake the delphinium or fuss with wash or cleaning or making a good dinner.

She'd learned to listen to her instincts, if not always to trust them.

She pivoted and ran into the house, through the kitchen and up the stairs.

She dug Posey's old tapestry weekend bag out of a cupboard. It had to be fifty years old, and it was perfect for what Henrietta wanted to do.

Needed to do, she amended silently, heading to her bedroom to pack.

17

After he pried himself loose from various authorities, Oliver devoured an enormous helping of a steak-and-kidney pie Ruthie had heated for him, having decreed he needed "comfort food." He did appreciate her concern — and her able cooking — but now she was hovering. He stood up from the kitchen table. "Don't fuss," he said, doing his best to keep any irritation out of his tone. "Please, Ruthie. We're all on edge. Go home. I'll manage. Be sure to get proper rest, won't you?"

"Nigel's at the barn. He says he'll stay late to finish work on the tractor. Make up for the lost time yesterday." She reddened to her ears, as if she'd just scalded herself. "I didn't mean . . ."

"It's all right. We all lost time yesterday."

She nodded. "It's good you're back."

"I'm sorry I bolted."

"Your flight home — it went well?"

His flight? Who *cared*? But he smiled. "As well as one can expect with a police escort." His attempt at a lighter note, however, failed miserably. Ruthie didn't come close to smiling. "Go home, Ruthie. I insist. Give my best to Nigel. He saw me leaving yesterday, didn't he?"

"He had to tell the police. He had no choice."

"Of course." *Why* had he brought that up? Oliver gave Ruthie an encouraging smile. "Go on, now. Have a good evening."

She started to the back door but turned to him. "I didn't see that man before yesterday, here, when he died in your arms. I know you were trying to help him. I heard he was in the village overnight — he sneaked into a shed at the Kershaw farm."

"I know about that. The police will investigate. You and I are just witnesses, Ruthie. Nigel, too. We answer the police's questions to the best of our ability and leave the rest to them."

"We're all suspects in his death, though, aren't we?" She didn't wait for an answer. "One has to trust the police to do their jobs, I suppose."

She paused, and Oliver realized she was waiting for him to respond, but what was there to say? "Of course," he mumbled, leaving it at that.

Ruthie said goodbye and left through the kitchen door, out to the terrace. Oliver wondered if she'd ever go through the main entrance again. He'd had a difficult enough time himself, but he'd had Alfred with him and had risen to the occasion. He'd heard his grandmother encouraging him to "keep calm and carry on." Easier to do when one hadn't had a killer bleed to death in one's arms, but that was the point of such words, wasn't it? To help during difficult times, even unimaginable times.

After a moment, Oliver pulled open the back door and went outside. Ruthie was on the far edge of the terrace. "Did you recognize him?" he called to her.

She stopped abruptly and turned, her face ashen, no hint of red now. "No, I didn't." She spoke clearly, her voice steady, and squared her shoulders before she continued. "I never saw him before in my life."

"Did you hear him speak?"

"I couldn't make out anything. It was just mumbling."

Oliver wasn't positive he believed her. Would she have told the police what she'd heard and not him? They would have asked her not to discuss the investigation. "What about Nigel?"

"Best you speak with the police, don't you think? Phone me if you need anything. I'm five minutes away."

She continued on her way, and Oliver returned to the kitchen. He couldn't face more food. He went down the hall to the entry. A police car was idling in the drive, near the bench where he'd chatted with Emma Sharpe. DI Lowe had told him a car would stay through the evening and the night as a precaution. The house didn't have an alarm. Oliver had never seen any point. The cost and aggravation outweighed any benefit. His grandparents were gone, his parents were gone — who was there to protect? *What* was there to protect? The value of the place was in its land and its history, and in the construction of the house itself. It'd be a feat to make off with beams, brick and stone.

And he could take care of himself.

He went into the front room and opened the liquor cabinet by the fireplace. "Now here's something to protect," he said aloud, lifting a bottle of Irish whiskey. It was a fifteen-year-old peated single malt, a limited run from the days when Finian Bracken was at Bracken Distillers with his twin brother. "A bit of fun," he'd told Oliver on one of their visits.

He got out his mobile phone and, after a moment's hesitation, called Finian Bracken in Maine. "I've returned to the farm and I'm not under arrest. I hope you aren't, either."

"I'm not. I'm glad to hear you're well."

"Are you? Good. I'll let others fill you in on the latest developments. I have more questions than ever." His chest felt tight as he envisioned the Scottish scenes the police had shown him. "I honor your rite of penance and reconciliation, Finian."

"Oliver?"

"I'm opening the Bracken 15 — the peated expression."

"It's rare and gorgeous. You have one of the few remaining bottles."

"I'll save the rest for you when you visit next. Come soon."

"I will."

"I've been fighting images since yesterday. Sometimes I can't tell if they're bits and pieces of memories of something that actually happened or of an old dream or nightmare."

"What if you stopped fighting the images?"

Oliver considered his Irish friend's words. "I've always fought them. Is the FBI still on your case about Davy Driscoll's confession?"

"Be well, my friend," he said, ignoring the question.

"You, too."

After Oliver disconnected, he opened the Bracken 15. He could call Emma Sharpe and Colin Donovan to join him, or Jeremy Pearson. He shuddered at the prospect of Pearson joining him for a dram — a *táoscan,* Finian would say, using the Irish word for an imprecise measure. The FBI agents would be better company. So would Martin, and he was no company at all. "You left me to worry and explain your actions to the police," he'd told Oliver. "I promised Nicholas and Priscilla I'd look after you."

"And you did," Oliver had responded. "You dealt with the dead man when I couldn't."

Martin had sniffed, unsatisfied. "I'll see to Alfred," he'd said, and stalked off to his cottage.

MI5 wouldn't be particularly interested in the past thirty years of Davy Driscoll's life or why he'd come to the York farm or even how he'd died, provided the manner of death — including a killer on the loose — didn't interfere and had nothing to do with the assistance Oliver was providing MI5.

Davy's crimes thirty years ago — a double homicide, a child kidnapping — were ancient history to MI5, not relevant to their immediate concerns.

Oliver started to taste the peated Bracken expression when he saw he had a text. He sat up straight, intrigued. It was from Henrietta Balfour. Can I come over?

He smiled, settling onto the sofa as he typed his response. I just poured a good Irish whiskey.

Is that a yes or a no?

Yes.

"Good," she said from the entry. "I'm here. I told the officer out front that I'm invited. He's watching me in case I try to cut your throat with garden clippers."

Oliver set his glass on a side table and went into the entry.

Henrietta pushed the door open wide and waved behind her. "He's here. Have a look." She turned and motioned to Oliver. "Here, smile at the policeman so he doesn't think I'm inviting myself in."

"You are inviting yourself in."

"Semantics," she said dismissively.

Oliver took the door in hand and motioned to the police officer that all was well.

Henrietta stepped past him, and he shut the door.

She raked a hand through her messy curls and managed a half-hearted smile. "Well, then. You're back. Where's that whiskey?"

"In here," he said, leading the way.

She remained on her feet while he poured her a taste of the Bracken 15 and handed her the glass. "It's peated," he said. "The only other peated Irish whiskey I know is Connemara."

"I've been wanting a quiet, leisurely drink since finding that bloodied corpse yesterday. I inhaled a couple of drinks last night and they put me under the table." She nodded to the sofa. "May I sit?"

"Please."

Oliver waited for her to sink into the soft cushions. She truly was an attractive woman, and clearly fit. He remembered playing together as children, before his parents' death — they'd climbed trees and thrown stones in the stream. Unfortunately he wasn't so certain of his memory that he'd mention it to her. It would be terrible if it'd been another little girl. Now that she was here, having a drink in his company, he didn't want to insult her.

"What brings you here?" he asked, sitting

in a chair across from her.

"Mad curiosity."

"Do the police believe you're a garden designer?"

"I *am* a garden designer."

"And I'm a poet," he said with a smile.

"You've seen me with a trowel in hand."

"Handy to split open someone's head, perhaps. Martin? Does he believe you?"

"He did until Ruthie's first blood-curdling scream," Henrietta said, not sounding at all perturbed. "I think he has his doubts now."

"Not easy for you to look shaken by a dead body, was it?"

"I'm ignoring that comment." She looked restless, but she didn't move. "Tell me about Ireland. It's all over the village that's where you went. Off in the Rolls-Royce to Stow, on to an air taxi — or was it a helicopter? And if not Ireland, we can discuss what to do with that ghastly Celtic statue out back."

"I carved that statue myself."

"An early effort, I imagine."

"It is ghastly, but it has sentimental value."

"The bane of the existence of every garden designer." She threw one leg over the other and narrowed her gaze on him. "We aren't going to discuss Ireland, are we? All right, then. I've said why I'm here. Now, why did you let me in?"

"Martin took Alfred with him —"

"I'm substitute for your bloody *dog*?"

"No, no." Oliver grimaced. He really wasn't good with people. "It's been a difficult two days. Let me start again. I'd like company. I'd like your company."

"Much better." She smiled and held up her glass. "Cheers, then."

Oliver returned her smile and held up his glass. "Cheers."

She took a sip of the Bracken 15. "Oh, it is good, isn't it?"

"I think so." He tried his whiskey, then cupped the glass in his palm as he settled back in his chair. "Tell me, Henrietta, does MI5 want you back?"

Her chin shot up. "I beg your pardon?"

"Do you miss intelligence work?"

"I doubt anyone would miss MI5 once they quit. What about you, Oliver? Do you miss art thieving?"

His gaze held hers but she didn't wither in the slightest. "Are you the one who suggested MI5 tap me as an agent? Because you believed I'm a thief and have knowledge and expertise MI5 could exploit?"

She was silent, looking up at a painting of hounds above the mantel. "When you finish refurbishing your gardens, you can start in here. You've hardly touched the place since

319

your grandparents died."

"You'll note I didn't confirm I am an art thief," he said, ignoring her attempt to change the subject.

She tasted more of the Bracken whiskey and shifted back to him. "You're a wily one, Oliver."

"And here we are, in the same village. You with your old flowerpots and your cover as a garden designer. Me with . . ." He thought a moment. "My ways."

"I wonder where you stashed your stolen art."

"I wonder why you left MI5."

"Whatever you think, you can't argue that I'm not a very good garden designer." She set her glass on a small table. "The dead man was Davy Driscoll. We all know that now. Why was he here? Did he tell you? He can't have told you he'd been murdered or *surely* you wouldn't have charged off in your Rolls-Royce and left the rest of us at risk of getting our throats slit with a stone-cutting chisel."

"You'd have dispatched anyone who came at you."

"You have a robust view of my abilities. *Did* you believe he'd been murdered?"

"I did and do, but I believe he was the only target. At least he was the only target yesterday." Oliver set his own glass on a side table. "Things can change. The killer could have new targets. One must stay nimble."

"Nimble. Right." Henrietta stared at him for a few seconds. Then she sighed and shook her head. "I'm not going to try to understand how your mind works. Did Reed Warren, aka Davy Driscoll, mention his cohort thirty years ago? Did he say something that threw you? Is that why you left in such a hurry? He made you question what you and the police believe happened in the incident when you were a boy?"

"Incident?"

"I'm drinking whiskey. Don't parse my words. It seems the police were shocked to discover Driscoll had been living under an assumed name."

"Maybe yesterday wasn't about me." Oliver kept his tone even, speculative — two people discussing a theory about something innocuous, say, the discovery of an old flowerpot. Not death. Not murder. He picked up his drink again. "What if this is about you and MI5? What if you're being played? What if *I'm* being played by MI5?"

"Drink more of your Bracken 15, Oliver. Finish the bottle. Open another. You'll make more sense drunk."

Nothing he said would faze her, obviously.

321

But he kept on. "Someone could have paid to have Driscoll killed."

"You're suggesting it was MI5," she said, her tone mild but also incredulous.

"Why not?"

"I can tick off a half-dozen reasons, starting with murder is illegal and immoral. However, let me try one on you. What if one of your farm workers recognized Reed Warren was Davy Driscoll and had his or her revenge on your behalf? Grabbed the chisel and nicked the bastard's artery. Didn't realize you were back from London and would happen upon your dying kidnapper and killer of your parents." Henrietta tucked her feet up under her on the sofa, making herself comfortable. "Pretty decent theory, don't you think?"

Oliver shrugged. "Not bad." For all he knew, it could even be true. "My parents were killed in London. I was dragged off to Scotland. Davy Driscoll and Bart Norcross were from London. They did odd jobs, including groundskeeping. Did you hope posing as a garden designer would somehow lead MI5 to them?"

"As I keep saying, I am a garden designer."

"You're a liar, Henrietta. An adept liar and an attractive one, and perhaps your lying is for the greater good, but you're still a liar."

She pointed to a stack of novels on the side table near her. "I have a taste for mystery stories. I've been steeping myself in mysteries set in the Cotswolds since I moved here."

"Would you like to borrow a book?"

"Not tonight. Right now I prefer to think of the Cotswolds as a peaceful place free of murder."

"I do, too," Oliver said quietly.

"Blast." She breathed deeply, her warm eyes on him. "Just for a few hours — a moment — I'd like to go back to that summer afternoon when we were children and threw stones in the stream. Do you remember, Oliver?"

His throat tightened. "I remember."

"It was before your parents were killed in front of you. Before I realized my parents could do quite nicely without me. We were lucky, Oliver. We *are* lucky. We had no worries then, that summer day. Not everyone gets that in life."

"Henrietta . . ."

She unfolded her legs, dropped her feet to the floor and jumped up. "That's as maudlin and philosophical as I get. Now, assuming nobody's bugged your house . . ." She paused. "Well, it's entirely possible someone *has* bugged your house. But I don't care.

323

Was Davy Driscoll an artist? A painter? Did he tell you about the paintings before he died? What they mean?"

Oliver stared at her over the rim of his glass, focused on the strong peated scent of the Bracken whiskey. He didn't speak.

Henrietta went on. "Driscoll was a lying, murdering sod and I believe he stole the paintings we found in his car out of the Kershaws' cottage," Henrietta said. "The painting of Queen's View that Cassie found in the cottage itself is an outlier. The rest must have been in the cottage woodshed, or she, Tony, Eugene or Nigel would have found them by now. As far as I know, none of the paintings are signed."

"Every one of them was of an iconic scene in Scotland," Oliver said. "Castles, Celtic crosses, lochs, coastline. Practice studies, I imagine."

"I didn't notice one of the ruin where you were taken. Did you?"

"No."

Oliver managed another sip from his glass. His hands trembled. That *never* happened. He saw that Henrietta noticed. She was calm, centered — a highly trained, experienced intelligence officer, he realized. A member of a clandestine team? A team leader? It didn't matter. He now knew why she was here.

He got to his feet. His hands were no longer trembling. "You want to go to Scotland to see where I was taken."

"I'm already packed. You can throw a few things together since you used your go-bag to sneak off to Ireland." Reddish-brown curls drooping onto her forehead, her long, flowered skirt dusting the floor, she pointed one finger vaguely toward the entry. "We'll take my car."

"I'll let Martin know. You can drive." Oliver gave her a quick smile. "I understand MI5 has the best drivers in the world."

18

The York family plot was located in front of a stone wall at the back of the village cemetery. It was dusk, the long June night slowly giving up its light. On another quiet evening, Emma would have held Colin's hand. Now, though, they stood side by side, not touching, among the headstones, some upright, some placed flat with the ground. They'd spotted Martin Hambly by the church down the lane and joined him.

He stared at the headstone for Oliver's mother, Deborah Summerhill York. "She and Charles were married at the church forty-one years ago. Posey and Freddy Balfour and his wife and their son — Henrietta's father — attended the ceremony. Anthony Balfour had died by then." Martin paused without shifting his gaze from the headstone. "I remember the wedding. It was a happy day." He looked up, turned to Emma and Colin. "Your wedding was a happy day?"

"Very," Emma said.

"The funeral was held at the church here, too. It was Priscilla's decision. She wanted to keep her only son and daughter-in-law close to her. That was one of the saddest days of my life. The Balfours were here then, too. Posey, Freddy, Henrietta's parents. Freddy's wife had died by then. He didn't have long himself. Henrietta was deemed too young to attend."

"Oliver was there?" Colin asked.

Martin nodded. "He'd experienced the brutality of that night himself. He needed to say goodbye." He sniffled, tears shining in his eyes. "Henrietta once asked me to come with her to see the graves. She was about twelve. She was determined to see them but she hadn't wanted to come alone. She said she hadn't asked Posey to go with her. She knew I visited the graves regularly."

"I'm sorry, Martin," Emma said. "The past few days have ripped scabs off old wounds."

"Henrietta and Oliver have gone to Scotland," he said abruptly, standing straight. "Oliver said the police weren't keen on the idea but didn't stop them."

Emma felt Colin tense next to her. "Whose idea was this?" he asked.

"They said it was a mutual decision. They wanted to see the spot where he was taken as a boy. He's never been back. The paintings in Davy Driscoll's car got them stirred up." Martin sighed heavily, his tears vanishing from his eyes. "That's what they told me, at any rate."

Emma could see Martin's distress, his worry. "Did they say anything else?"

"Oh, yes. Oliver apologized for making my life impossible. He believes I could have had a buxom wife and a couple of children but for him. Ridiculous, of course. I made my choices in life. They had little to do with him."

"Is that what you told him?" Colin asked.

"Tonight and many times before tonight. I wasn't destined to marry even before the tragedy. I have women friends and I've had the occasional relationship over the years, but I was never the romantic, marrying sort. One would think Oliver would know that by now."

Colin paused in front of the grave for Oliver's grandfather, bent down and touched a begonia set into the soil in front of the headstone. "You're insulted by his guilt."

"It's patronizing and self-absorbed. It doesn't respect my autonomy. I told him so." Martin sucked in quick breath. "He grinned that cheeky grin of his and *then* he asked me if I'd been in love with his mother. Dear God in heaven. I could have slit his blasted brachial artery myself if I'd had a sharp chisel and could get at him. He'd have flipped me on my arse with one of his karate moves." Martin paused, looked at Emma with a small smile. "I suppose I shouldn't talk like that in front of two FBI agents."

"How did you answer him?" Emma asked. "Do you mind saying?"

"I told him I loved Deborah but I wasn't in love with her. We all loved her." His voice caught, tears welling again. He brushed the corner of an eye with his knuckle and cleared his throat, composing himself. "She would have wanted a different life for Oliver. His is the life that was made impossible by the violence."

Colin stood, flicked mud off the knee of his pants. "I don't know about that, Martin. Oliver made his choices, too. He's had fun with his mythology consulting in Hollywood and a few other things."

"His thieving, you mean."

Martin was definitely in a mood. Emma glanced at Colin and saw that he agreed. "When did you know?" she asked.

"I still don't 'know.' I've drawn a conclusion. I suppose he got to see the world as an art thief. Now he's an agent for MI5."

"Actually," Colin said, "right now he's off to Scotland with a beautiful woman. I don't know that I'd be feeling sorry for him."

"She's MI5, you know," Martin said with certainty.

Colin shrugged. "Then I wouldn't worry about him, either."

"The Balfour plot is over there." Martin gestured across the cemetery to a shaded spot in the opposite back corner. "I always thought Henrietta was more taken with Posey's gardening than Freddy's past with MI5, but apparently I was wrong."

"It's easy to get caught up in speculating when you're under stress," Emma said. She looked again at Deborah York's grave. "Is it possible there was more to the relationship Davy Driscoll and Bart Norcross had with Oliver's parents?"

"What do you mean?" Martin asked.

Emma waited a moment before answering. "Could one of them have been in love with Deborah York?"

Martin gasped. "I can't imagine, no. It's hideous to think so."

"Did you ever see them together?" Emma asked.

"I never did, no, but I worked exclusively

here at the farm then. Driscoll and Nor-cross worked in London."

"Deborah was the one who hired them," Colin said.

"That's what I've always understood. I told the police at the time everything I knew about them. I left out nothing. I've remembered nothing new since then — not even after yesterday."

Emma felt the soft ground under her, smelled flowers, freshly mown grass and, faintly, dirt in the cool air. "And Oliver? He was the only eyewitness police had to what happened."

Martin gaped at her. "What?"

"How reliable a witness was he?" Colin's tone was blunt, direct, but not without compassion. "That's what we're asking, Martin."

He gave a small nod. "It's what Oliver's asking, too, I think. He told me he wonders what he missed thirty years ago. I told him it doesn't matter. It's never mattered. No one expected anything of him. He was a small boy. It was up to the adults in his life to keep him safe. It was and is up to the police to solve the crimes committed against him and his family. It was never up to him. It still isn't."

"What did he say to that?" Emma asked.

"He said he's going to Scotland and we'll discuss his great-grandmother's flowerpot when he returns."

"And you came out here," Colin said.

"I drove. Alfred's in the car." Martin squared his shoulders. "I should go. Come by the cottage for Scotch later if you'd like. I still have some of the single malt Nicholas York gave me before he died."

Emma thanked him, but Colin was studying him. "Did Nicholas and Priscilla York believe their grandson's story about the murders and kidnapping?"

"Davy Driscoll and Bart Norcross are the guilty parties. That's all that matters." Martin nodded toward the lane where he'd parked his car. "I must go before Alfred tears apart the seats. He does well in his crate but otherwise he doesn't like confined spaces."

"Did Oliver return him to the cottage yesterday?"

Martin stopped abruptly, turned to Colin. "No. Alfred wasn't at the house when Oliver returned from the dovecote. At least, Oliver didn't see him, and he would have. Alfred has a way of making his presence known."

"I bet he does," Colin said. "Have a good night, Martin."

"That's not possible but thank you."

Emma eased next to Colin as they watched Martin walk up the main path through the center of the cemetery. "He has a strong sense of duty to the Yorks," she said. "I think he might have been happier if Oliver had confided in him more, especially about his work with MI5."

"Batman's Alfred was in on most of Batman's secrets. I wouldn't be surprised if Martin has known more about what Oliver gets up to than he lets on." Colin nodded to the opposite corner of the bucolic cemetery. "Why don't we take a look at the Balfour graves?"

They walked across the well-maintained grounds to a simple plot in the shade of trees along a stone wall. Freddy Balfour was buried next to his wife, who'd predeceased him. Next to them was Posey Balfour's grave, a rose carved into the stone beneath her name.

There was a fourth stone for Anthony Balfour.

Emma touched the dates under his name. "He was only thirty-five when he died."

"His widow is buried in West Hartford, Connecticut," Colin said.

"Hartford is an easy drive from Heron's Cove." Emma stood straight. "Driscoll could have driven there after he arrived in Boston on Saturday and then driven up to Maine on Monday. He was on a fishing expedition, Colin. His meeting with Finian was a ploy to get information out of him about Oliver and our relationship with him. It wasn't ever a genuine confession or privileged conversation."

"In Finian's mind it was."

"He can change his mind now that he knows the truth."

"But we don't know what they discussed," Colin said.

Emma angled a look at him. "I'm the one arguing for a priest to reveal a sacramental confession and you're the one arguing against it?"

"It's the cemetery effect. Not my favorite place." He gave a mock shudder. "You're not arguing for Finian to break his vows. You're arguing for him to accept that the man who came to see him was a lying murderer, and whatever he was up to got him killed."

"His death wasn't an elaborate suicide or an accident," Emma said.

"No."

"How frustrated is Sam with Finian?"

"Sam doesn't get frustrated. He just stays at it. He's irritated with Fin for calling him dogged, though."

Emma smiled, almost breaking into a laugh. "It'll be good to be home. I want to talk to Finian face-to-face."

"Ex-nun-to-priest?"

"Friend-to-friend," she said. "Would you ever reveal top-secret information to him?"

"Nope."

"Even if it involved something for which you needed absolution?"

Colin shuddered. "Damn, Emma. Bad enough we're in a cemetery." He grinned at her. "Can we go now? A bar stool at the village pub is calling to me."

She laughed, nodding. "Of course."

He eased his arm around her. "Did I ever tell you that Mike almost got arrested for sneaking into a cemetery and scaring the bejesus out of Franny Maroney? Pop would have slapped cuffs on him, but another police officer got to Mike first."

"Did Franny call the cops on him?"

"Without blinking. She was laying a wreath on her mother's grave when Mike pretended to be a ghost. He was eleven and bored."

"Mike doesn't do well bored."

"She ended up not pressing charges. Said she wanted to teach him a lesson. Our folks made him wash her windows. Franny said any of us boys could go ahead and spook her. She'd get her whole house cleaned."

Emma leaned her head on his shoulder for a moment. "Nothing like that happened in Heron's Cove."

"No cemetery antics?"

"No," she said, noticing a spring in Colin's step when they exited the English cemetery. "We have to pass more graves at the church."

"But we're closer to that bar stool."

Emma and Colin skipped drinks and returned to their room to pack. They'd leave for London in the morning, salvage a few meetings and then fly to Boston the next day as planned. They'd stay in touch with Sam Padgett as he followed Davy Driscoll's trail in the US and see him when they were back in New England.

And they'd talk to Finian Bracken themselves, Emma thought as she zipped shut her suitcase. She'd left out clothes for tomorrow. She'd brought a good jacket but most of the clothes she had with her were more appropriate to a woman on her honeymoon.

"I get to see you in that dark gray suit of yours," she said to Colin. "That's worth going home for."

"I wore suits every time I went home to Rock Point." He hung the one suit he'd taken with him on a hanger. "My family still never bought that I worked at a desk in DC."

"What do you most look forward to getting home?"

"A Maine sunrise. The apple pie you left in the freezer." He edged toward her. "Carrying you up the stairs to bed."

"Jet lag might slow you down."

He smiled. "Bet it doesn't."

She returned his smile. "I'm hoping it doesn't."

"I'll touch base with my MI5 contact tomorrow. I doubt he's unhappy we're leaving."

"How far back do you two go?"

"My first undercover assignment. He had intel on our arms traffickers."

"Four years, then. Did you know Henrietta when she was with MI5?"

"No."

Emma sat on the edge of the bed. "There's so much about your undercover life that I don't know and likely never will. We're on the same team — nominally, at least — but I'm not privy to everything about your work. I wonder even if Yank is."

"Not my call." He shut the closet door

and kicked off his shoes. "Imagine all I don't know about art crimes and never will."

"You could find out."

"I don't need to, since Yank has you on his team and trusts you."

"For better or worse," Emma said.

"Still irritated with Wendell?"

"His misdeeds weren't as egregious as I thought but that's not saying much. At least Lucas didn't cross any lines."

"I'm not sure Wendell did, either, but he got his toe right up to a few."

Emma leaned back against the pillows. "We've got Finian to worry about, too."

"He's my problem," Colin said. "Fin's your friend, too, but Yank will hang him around my neck, not yours. Fin would never be in this mess if I hadn't run into him on his first day in Maine."

"He's a good friend, Colin, and he hasn't crossed any lines."

Colin grunted. "Tell Sam Padgett that."

"I don't tell Sam anything," Emma said with a smile. "He's a smart guy — one of the smartest Yank has — and I trust him completely, but he's at his best when he's allowed to sniff his own trails."

"Yank likes independent thinkers."

"Are you saying I'm a lot like Sam?"

Colin sat on the bed, stretching out his

legs so that his thighs brushed against hers. He still had on his khakis and a polo shirt, but he'd pulled off his shoes and socks. "I'm saying you're an independent thinker. You're analytical and a team player, but you wouldn't be on Yank's team if you also weren't able to . . . how did you put it about Sam? Sniff your own trail?"

"It's not the cleverest metaphor. Yank warned me you're independent to a fault, not very analytical or much of a team player. He said it's one of the reasons you do well working long-term deep-cover assignments."

"And you say?"

"I say you do whatever Yank says."

"Ha. That'll be the day."

Emma started to get up, but Colin hooked an arm around her and pulled her next to him. She settled against him, noted his warmth, the strength of his arms, his legs. "The media will be all over the Davy Driscoll story once it gets out," she said. "MI5 might be able to keep it quiet if it suits their purposes, but it's an open secret in the village that Reed Warren was Driscoll's alias."

"We'll be in London or home by the time this breaks. Not sure what we'll do without a breakfast buffet every morning, but we'll manage." He winked at her. "The clock's striking midnight on your warm scones and clotted cream."

"Not going to get up early and make them for me, are you? It's the cut-up fruit I'll miss most. Left to my own devices, I'll grab a banana or apple instead of cutting up a variety of fruit. We won't be having time off for a while."

"We didn't need another Oliver York sideshow."

"Or another Sharpe sideshow. The FBI agents who are friends with Oliver York, the traumatized boy from thirty years ago." Emma snuggled even closer to Colin. "Being married to a Sharpe is already putting pressure on your undercover career."

"I could get promoted to a desk for real." He patted her hip. "It wouldn't be so bad."

"I'd rather it not be my grandfather's friendship with Oliver that pushes you into doing puffin tours, but if you're out, I'll be out, too."

"You can pack the lunches for the puffin tours."

She sat up next to him. He remained stretched out, watching her. "You're serious," she said.

"Absolutely. I even have sample menus. I figure we'd offer gluten-free, shellfish-free, nut-free, sugar-free menus. I'd hate to be allergic to lobster but some people are."

"You've thought it all through?"

"What else am I supposed to do on lonely nights undercover?" He grabbed her by the waist and pulled her down again. "Emma, Emma. Nothing's happened with your family and their contacts that Yank didn't predict and allow for."

"What about you?"

"I didn't predict you to start with. If anyone told me a year ago I'd be married to an ex-nun, lying here in a cute English village worrying about an art thief, I'd have laughed."

"But here we are," Emma said, settling again next to him.

He rolled onto his side, facing her. "We're not about our work, whether it's the FBI or puffin tours." He lowered his mouth to hers. "We're about each other."

Colin awoke to a text from Sam Padgett.

Driscoll visited Cassie Kershaw's father in W. Hartford Sunday as RW, before heading to Maine. Told Kershaw he learned about Balfours while looking for place to retire in Cotswolds. No details. Dad didn't know RW/DD dead.

How'd he take it?

Not well. I didn't tell him RW was DD.

Colin knew Padgett would inform the British investigators. Before he could respond, another text popped up on his screen.

What are you doing up? Don't answer. I'm going back to Maine. Try again with FB.

Finian Bracken. Colin gritted his teeth. Good luck.

Excuse to have Hurley's donuts. Later.

Colin thanked him and slid his phone back on the bedside table. Emma stirred, placing a palm on his chest. "That was Sam." He told her about the texts. "What are the odds Sam can get Fin to talk?"

"If Davy Driscoll genuinely confessed to him? It won't happen. Finian won't talk."

He placed his hand over hers. She snuggled closer to him, and he could see them in Maine, laughing with Fin Bracken over whiskey, clam chowder and wild blueberry pie. "Do you think this confession will ruin our friendship with Fin?" he asked, staring up into the dark room.

"Not if we respect his vows as a priest. He respects what we can and can't say as federal law-enforcement agents."

"I could tell him things in confession but I don't."

"You're friends," she said, as if that settled it, explained it.

"I wish to hell Davy Driscoll had chosen another priest."

"But he didn't." She rose up, her hair hanging within inches of his face. "He didn't because it wasn't a confession, Colin. Finian wasn't in his role as a priest hearing a conversation between a penitent and God. He wasn't in his role as a pastoral counselor. He was in his role as your friend, my friend and Oliver's friend. That's why Davy chose him."

"Fin will see that?"

"I think so, yes. It's not up to us. Only he knows what was said."

Colin curved an arm around her. "You've been thinking about this, haven't you?"

He saw her smile in the moonlight. "I'm always thinking," she said.

He pulled her closer. "Not always."

She lowered her mouth to his. "So true."

19

Southern Highlands, Scotland

"If one's going to do a mad, all-night drive to Scotland, best to do it in June," Henrietta said, stifling a yawn. "It's light already, isn't it?"

Oliver shrugged next to her. "I'm not sure it ever got dark."

He was driving. He'd taken over the wheel before they'd reached Edinburgh. She'd dozed off. *Really* rusty, she thought, if she couldn't stay awake with a possible murderer in the car with her. Which she knew was absurd, but still.

Now they were cruising on the A9 motorway north of the city. Henrietta was positive Oliver hadn't slept at all on their interminable drive. She hadn't even caught him in a yawn, but he didn't strike her as particularly fatigued.

She forced herself to sit up straight. Easier to shake off sleep that way. "Were you tempted to invite your FBI friends to join us?"

Her out-of-the-blue question didn't seem to throw him. "I wouldn't want to put them in a difficult position." He glanced at her, and she was struck by how good-looking he was, how alert with his black-lashed, deep green eyes focused on her for that brief few seconds before he turned back to his driving. "What about you? Did you ring Jeremy Pearson and tell him you and I were on the way to Scotland?"

"I didn't tell anyone, actually. I don't know if that's an act of trust or stupidity. You have a lot of stone-carving tools. You could have tucked one in a cup holder when I wasn't looking."

"But you did a search," he said calmly.

"You know what they say. Trust but verify. And don't think I'm intimidated by your martial-arts skills," she added. "You black-belt types never count on us non-black-belt types being able to defend ourselves."

"Aunt Posey's tapestry bag would fell me."

Henrietta grinned, amazed how comfortable she felt with him — for reasons she couldn't fathom, either. "I should never have told you it was her bag. I only packed a change of clothes and toiletries. I'm not spending a week in Scotland with you. I can't leave clients in the lurch."

"I'm your major client at the moment."

"I have to make plans. If you want to stay on in Scotland longer than I'm able to, I can take the train back."

"Decent of you, but you didn't answer my question. Jeremy Pearson vetted you for MI5, didn't he? And you put him onto me."

"For what?"

He kept his hands at a proper ten and two on the wheel. "I won't insist you drop this garden-designer act but I won't pretend you're not MI5, either. Martin knows. I'm sure of it."

"Martin knows everything. You shouldn't feel guilty about him, by the way. He's old-school. He'll view guilt as belittling. He's not the sort to waste time on regrets. You should follow his example." She stared out her window, the Scottish scenery coming into view as dawn took hold. "Of course, if you weren't the mopey type, I wouldn't have had this long trip north with you."

"You snored."

She laughed, turning to him. "I hope so."

"Did you want to be a garden designer before you decided on MI5?"

"Garden design is my dream job."

"Another of your parsed answers," he said. "Posey never coddled me as a boy after my parents' murder. She told me not to dwell on it because life would hand me more setbacks."

"When you were *eight*?"

"Around then. It wasn't long after I was orphaned."

"This from a woman with a trust fund, a home in a beautiful and safe part of the world —" Henrietta broke off. "I'm sorry, Oliver. You deserved only kindness and understanding."

He was silent a moment. "I might argue that Posey was being kind and understanding. She was right, you know. She could have phrased her advice a bit differently, I suppose."

"A bit?"

"She meant well."

"I adored her, but she wasn't one to beat about the bush."

"It was refreshing," Oliver said. "Even now, most people don't know what to say to me given my history."

Henrietta stretched her lower back. They'd stopped three times, never for more than a few minutes. She'd let herself get carried away with a sense of urgency that didn't exist. "Frankly, Oliver, I think that's in your head. Most people don't think about you at all. Sorry, but it's the truth. And if they are awkward, it could be because you don't like being around people and spend your time studying things like ancient Celtic death rituals. I wouldn't be surprised if you have a bog body tucked in a back room."

His mouth twitched but he didn't turn to her. They were off the A9 now — she'd barely noticed — and were driving through the tourist village of Pitlochry, dead quiet so early in the morning. "Have you ever seen a bog body, Henrietta?" Oliver asked.

"On BBC. As close as I care to come to one. Have you?"

"I have, although I don't make a point of studying death rituals."

"Saint Declan of Ireland is your type," she said.

"He was a healer."

She put her feet up on the dash. She'd have hung them out of the window if she could have managed, but there wasn't enough room. "I'm glad you didn't boot me out of the car and leave me in the dark."

"You'd have managed. I've no doubts whatsoever."

He sounded distracted, and she noticed the tension in his forearms as he clutched the wheel. She put her feet back on the floor and sat up straight. "Are we getting closer?"

He nodded but grew quiet as they pushed

north. "Do you know Scottish history?" he asked.

"Some."

Without warning, he pulled into a small picnic area just past a caravan park. "This is where the Battle of Killiecrankie took place. It was part of the Jacobite uprising meant to restore the Stuarts to the throne. That didn't work, of course. Blair Castle isn't far. Balmoral Castle, summer home to the royal family, is a bit farther up the road."

"We could chuck seeing the ruin where you were taken and tour castles instead."

"Have you spent much time in Scotland?"

"The occasional weekend holiday since I left home." Henrietta decided not to mention her visit with her churl of an ex-boyfriend. "My parents and I never visited when I was growing up. My parents tended to go on holiday without me. They thought I would be bored."

"That's why you spent so much time with your aunt. Was she good company?"

"She practiced what she liked to call healthy neglect. She didn't hover. I was able to roam about and do as I pleased for the most part. She didn't own a television or a computer. I found that stifling or liberating, depending on my mood."

"I wish I'd known her better. My grandparents and Martin always spoke well of her."

"She'd have liked that," Henrietta said.

It was clearly difficult for him to speak. He took a breath and turned to her with a smile. "A short walk to welcome the new day?"

"All right." She pointed to the back seat where she'd set a small rucksack. "And breakfast."

"You have food?" His smile broadened to a grin. "Brilliant. MI5 thinks of everything."

"An accomplished international art thief who's never been caught must think of food."

"I often forget food," he said without, she noted, admitting he was a thief.

She reached for her rucksack. "Not me. I never forget food."

They ate while sitting across from each other at a roadside picnic table. Henrietta set out a thermos of tea, cups, apples and bacon sandwiches. Two of everything. "I have protein bars if you're still hungry," she said. "I didn't unpack them."

"Let's walk down to the river."

They took a well-traveled trail that wound through the trees, down a steep hill to a river. Their trail ended at another, wider trail that ran parallel to the river, wide, shallow and slow-moving here.

"We're not far from Soldier's Leap," Oliver said. "It's the spot where a Jacobite soldier is said to have jumped across the river, a near superhuman feat. He was being chased by hostile forces, so he was highly motivated."

"It's one of the scenes in Davy Driscoll's car."

"Yes."

"The police showed the paintings to you."

It was a statement, but he nodded without looking at her. He stared at the river in the milky light.

"I didn't get a good look at all of them," Henrietta added. "You're the art thief. Are they any good? Did our anonymous painter of Scottish scenes go on to become a famous artist?"

Oliver continued to stare at the river, as if its steady, relentless flow soothed him.

"Oliver?"

Still he said nothing.

Henrietta swore under her breath. "You recognized the paintings? Did Davy Driscoll do them? Then how did the one of Queen's View get into the Kershaw cottage? Oliver." She took a breath. "Whose work are they?"

He turned to her, his breathing ragged.

She touched his shoulder. "Please don't make me guess. Just tell me."

"They're my mother's work."

Henrietta lowered her hand from his shoulder. As far as she knew, none of the paintings in the car had a signature. The one of Queen's View certainly didn't. The truth was, she had no idea if Oliver was being straight with her. She hadn't seen the detectives at his house, or coming or going, when she'd returned with her car for this mad trip to Scotland.

"If you're making this up, I'm going to throw you in the river," she said.

"I'm remembering."

"What does *that* mean?"

He gave her a faint smile. "I love that you don't coddle me."

"I only coddle hybrid roses and clematis. Oliver, anyone could have put the paintings in the cottage, assuming that's where Driscoll got the ones in his car. It seems likely. Could he have painted them?"

"They're not his work."

"Why do you think they're your mother's work? What are you trying to remember?"

"I'm trying to clear the fog," he said. "It's like thinking you heard Santa Claus in the parlor and then trying to figure out what it was and how you could have been so wrong."

"Because you were eight. You experienced a violent, traumatic event and your mind locked onto images that you don't know now were real." Henrietta stared at the river now, too. "Santa Claus is a bad analogy, by the way. Seriously. You think back on footsteps in the parlor and know it was your dad. You're thinking back on . . . what?"

"Hiding in the library."

"Before your parents were killed," she said softly.

He nodded. Henrietta didn't know what else to say. What did Jeremy Pearson know about the paintings? Had he told her everything? She rubbed the back of her neck, feeling the strain of their hours on the road. She listened to a red squirrel chattering high in an evergreen on the edge of the picnic area and, beneath the chattering, down the steep hillside, she could make out the soothing sounds of the river flowing downstream. The beautiful setting was a disconcerting backdrop to the raw intensity of the man next to her.

"What else, Oliver?" she asked finally.

He turned away from her and peered up at the evergreen, as if trying to spot the chattering squirrel. "Since yesterday . . ."

He paused, lowering his gaze again to the river. "I'm missing something. I've been missing it all these years. It's as if old and new images are jumbled together and I can't make sense of any of them."

"Don't try. Just let them be. Accept them."

He glanced at her, his eyes lost in the early-morning shadows. "Do you think that will help?"

"Yes."

"Always so confident."

"It's training, Oliver. Experience. Force can make things worse. What do you see?"

"I see us walking on the farm by the dovecote. My mother, my father and me. We're holding hands. It's not a memory. I think it must be an image I held in my head to keep me calm."

"Even if it's not a memory, it's real. You're the type of family that would hold hands and walk on the farm together."

"Yes. We were."

"Are there other images, Oliver?"

He shut his eyes, opened them quickly. "I see my mother with a paintbrush in hand. She puts a finger to her lips and tells me not to tell anyone." He paused, his gaze again fixed on the evergreen. "The paintings in Driscoll's car — the one Cassie found — are my mother's work, Henrietta.

They're hers. I know it."

"This image of her with a paintbrush — where was she?"

"London. The library. That's what I see but it can't be true. No paintings or painting supplies were found there."

"Was she alone?"

"I don't remember. I've tried. I don't. I can't." He blew out a breath. "Blast it."

"Why would Davy Driscoll take them? I refuse to believe he was blackmailing her because she had a secret passion for painting Scottish scenery. Upper-class women of your mother's generation sketched and painted. It's hardly scandalous. Why didn't she want anyone to know?"

Oliver didn't respond.

"Was she having an affair?"

He turned to her. "Do you blurt out everything that pops into your head?"

"No, but I'm not afraid to ask a question. Was she? Upper-class women do that, too, you know. Have secret affairs. She didn't have one with Driscoll, did she? He wasn't terribly good-looking, but I only saw him after he was dead."

"Henrietta."

"What? I'm sorry. I'm a hound on a fox trail. You were just a boy. You could have misread the situation. Well, we'll get to the bottom of it — the police will, I should say. Are you hoping the ruin where you were held will help jog your memory?" He nodded, and Henrietta noticed he looked less strangled. She motioned toward the trail. "Then let's go."

"Henrietta," Oliver said again.

"I didn't let you answer, did I? It's caffeine and lack of sleep, and these images of yours. When did you remember about the painting?"

"I've always remembered. I just didn't think about it."

"That makes sense on a certain level, I guess. But what were you trying to say before I interrupted?"

"I'm falling in love with you."

She gaped at him. "You're falling in love with me. I could murder you right now myself. We're here in the wilds of Scotland and you've had no sleep and we're discussing your mother's secrets, and *now* you decide to tell me?"

"I should have waited?"

"It was going to be a brick dropped on my head whenever you told me. Didn't you ask me to marry you when I was five?"

"No."

"You should have. I'd have said yes."

"And now?"

She smiled suddenly, even as unexpected tears sprang to her eyes. "We're train wrecks, Oliver, the pair of us. You're in far worse shape, of course." She tilted her head back and looked up at the sky, giving way to dawn. Then she shifted back to him. He wasn't looking sheepish or embarrassed or showing any sign he'd regretted his admission. She laughed, pleased, and took his hand. "We need to change *falling* to *fallen,* don't you think?"

He squeezed her hand, pulling her toward him. "It's happening," he whispered, and his mouth found hers. It was a tender kiss, brief, a brushing of lips, a promise of more. He stood back with one of his enigmatic smiles. "Jeremy Pearson told me you're falling in love with me."

"He's manipulating you."

"Probably."

"And he has his nerve," Henrietta added, truly irritated.

"But is he right?" Oliver asked.

She heard the emotion in his voice, felt it in herself. What did Jeremy Pearson matter now, at this moment?

She smiled. "You must know by now a senior MI5 officer is always right."

20

Rock Point, Maine

Finian Bracken sat with a pot of tea in the rectory kitchen. It was very early. He was keeping lobsterman hours these days — or he was on Irish time. He shrugged off that thought and opened his breviary. He preferred the traditional black-bound paper breviary to a digital edition. He was to keep it with him at all times and pray the Liturgy of the Hours throughout the day, but he'd neglected that duty since Tuesday. Never since he'd become a priest had he done so. The Liturgy of the Hours framed his day, provided the bones upon which he built his schedule . . . lived his life. He'd let his ambivalence about Reed Warren and his worries about his friends drive him away from his breviary when the opposite should have happened.

And now, he thought, he was paying the price. He stared at the familiar words of

Psalm 50 but didn't read them. Never since he'd left Bracken Distillers and entered seminary and the priesthood had his vocation put him in conflict the way this week had done.

"I did a terrible thing in my youth, Father Bracken. A terrible thing."

Some lines in his work were bright, clean and clear. Sacramental confession was one of them. But what was that mess on Tuesday morning?

He thought again of the nondescript man who'd arrived in his office, asking to speak with the parish priest. He'd pleaded with Finian to hear his confession. He'd said he was dying and wanted to confront the grave sins he had committed.

But what he'd wanted was information about Finian's friends.

He heard footsteps on the small porch through the open screen door. Early for a visitor. He rose from the table as Sam Padgett rapped his knuckles on the door frame. "Mind if I come in, Father?"

"Not at all. Please. Welcome."

The FBI agent pulled open the door. "I know it's the crack of dawn but I figured you'd be up."

Would it have mattered if he hadn't been? Padgett was professional and uncompromising, but Finian was getting used to that sort given his life in Rock Point. He gestured to the table. "Please, take a seat, Special Agent Padgett. I was just having tea. Can I offer you some?"

"No, thanks."

"I thought you'd gone back to Boston."

"Connecticut. I drove up again last night and stayed at an inn in Heron's Cove." Padgett pulled out a chair across from Finian's tea and breviary. He hesitated, then sat. "I'm interrupting your prayers. The Liturgy of the Hours, right?"

Finian nodded, returning to his seat.

"I'm not Catholic," Padgett said. "I had a case early in my career that involved a priest. I learned a few things."

"It's early, Special Agent Padgett. Are you returning to Boston?"

"Soon. Have you spoken with anyone this morning?"

"I haven't."

"Oliver York is back in England. He spent Thursday night in Ireland."

"In Declan's Cross," Finian said half to himself.

"That's right."

"He called me last night. We discussed Irish whiskey."

Padgett settled back in his seat, taking in

the small kitchen. Finian had added a few items to personalize the space and suit his needs — an electric kettle, a coffee press, a calendar of Irish coastal scenes. The rectory was located next to the church, both buildings over a century old and in need of remodeling but sturdy and comfortable, suitable for a small-town priest and parish.

"Did you speak with Reed Warren — Davy Driscoll — in here or in the church?" Padgett asked.

Finian frowned. "Is that relevant to the investigation into his death?"

"It's just a question, Father."

Nothing was just a question with an FBI agent in the midst of an inquiry, Finian had learned. He added hot tea to the lukewarm tea in his cup. He doubted much about Sam Padgett's actions since he'd arrived in Rock Point yesterday hadn't been thought out, deliberate and part of his investigative role.

Finian decided he could answer Padgett's question. "We spoke in my office at the church."

"We're up with the lobstermen but it looks as if it's going to be another beautiful day in Maine," Padgett said. "I like June in New England a lot better than February. What about you?"

This was small talk that wasn't small talk.

"June is glorious but I appreciated experiencing Maine in February."

"The ice, the snow, the frigid temperatures. Skiers love February. I'm not a skier. I tried once in college. A group of us took off for Aspen. My girlfriend broke her leg. She blamed me. I blamed me." Padgett paused. "Ever blame yourself for something that wasn't your fault?"

"Most of us have, Special Agent Padgett. That's one thing I've learned as a priest."

"I do what I can to see to it people aren't prosecuted for crimes they didn't commit. I like to be thorough and careful. I don't take a confession at face value, for instance. I'm not talking about a sacramental confession, of course. Different thing. Different rules."

Finian drank some of his tea without comment.

"Father, Davy Driscoll spent the last thirty years of his life on the run for killing Oliver York's parents and kidnapping him. I'm not here to try to drag his confession out of you. It's not up to me to decide if it was a proper confession under canon law. Instead I'd like to hear about your visit to Oliver York's farm in the English Cotswolds."

"My visit isn't a secret. I joined my brother Declan in London and ran into Oliver at an art gallery."

362

"You were both at Aoife O'Byrne's London show."

"That's right." Finian kept his tone even but he glanced at his breviary. He could feel its absence in his life. He shifted back to the FBI agent. "I accepted Oliver's invitation to visit his farm. Then I returned to Maine and my duties here in Rock Point."

"Who else did you see while you were in the Cotswolds?"

"I met Martin Hambly, Oliver's assistant, and Ruthie Burns, the housekeeper. I met a few farm workers but I don't recall any names."

"What about Henrietta Balfour?"

Finian thought a moment. "Yes. We ran into her at the pub. Attractive, reddish-brown curly hair, blue eyes. She and Oliver grew up together. Nothing's happened to her, has it?"

"No, she's fine," Padgett said. "What about Cassie and Eugene Kershaw? Did you meet them?"

"I don't think so. I could have. I didn't pay close attention, I'm afraid."

"I'm not going to ask if Oliver York made a confession to you then or the other times he's spoken with you."

"You just did," Finian said with a small smile.

"If you can't say someone made a sacramental confession, can you say if someone didn't?"

"Once again, Special Agent Padgett, I don't discuss confessions."

"Fair enough." Nothing in Padgett's tone suggested he was insincere. "Wendell Sharpe visited Oliver York in the Cotswolds in January. Know anything about that, Father Bracken?"

"Both Wendell and Oliver mentioned their visit to me in passing, nothing more." Finian set his cup in its saucer. "Please don't read anything into my inability to reveal details of my conversations with people."

"I gather evidence, Father. I let it show me where it's pointing. I don't shape it. I imagine it's much the same with you and a confession. People tell you their sins. You don't tell them their sins."

Finian considered Padgett's words. "The priest isn't to hold what's said in confession," he said. "He doesn't make an effort to remember because he's not really supposed to hear it. It's a conversation between the penitent and God."

"If it's a true confession," Padgett said. "If it's phony, I bet you remember."

Finian said nothing.

Padgett rose, buttoned his suit jacket.

Although he and Finian were about the same height, the FBI agent seemed taller. But that was the idea, Finian thought. Sam Padgett in his dark suit and polished shoes, standing straight, was meant to intimidate, or at least assert himself as a federal agent who had a duty to uphold the laws of the United States. Finian had seen Colin and Emma adopt much the same demeanor — although *adopt* perhaps wasn't the right word.

"You're one of the last people Davy Driscoll saw before his death," Padgett said. "If you knew he posed a danger to others, what would you do?"

"A priest can warn authorities without revealing their sources or the facts or details of a confession."

"You can say, 'So-and-so might be killed tonight. Don't ask me how I know.' "

Finian shrugged. "Something like that."

"Then I take it because you didn't warn anyone, Davy Driscoll didn't make any specific threats in your presence."

Finian got to his feet. "Have a safe trip to Boston, Special Agent Padgett."

"I understand you can't reveal a confession but you wouldn't lie about one. Am I right about that, Father Bracken?"

"You truly are dogged, aren't you?"

Padgett managed a smile. "That word again. I prefer *persistent* to *dogged.* The texts between you and Davy Driscoll — my read? He wasn't a penitent seeking reassurance you'd uphold the seal of confession. He was a killer manipulating you into silence. You were factual just like you are now with me. You didn't assure him he'd made a proper confession to you."

"It was a single short text from me," Finian said, struggling to keep his tone neutral.

"It's okay. I get it. Anything else you want to tell me?"

"I hope the investigation into this man's death continues to progress and you get the answers you seek."

"Do any of us ever get the answers we seek? Thanks for your time, Father. You have my card. Call if you think of anything else you can tell me." He nodded to Finian's laptop, open off to one side of the kitchen table. "Ireland?"

"Scotland."

"Where in Scotland?"

As annoyed as he was, Finian considered his next comment carefully. "It's a church ruin in the southern Highlands. I looked it up online. It's where Oliver York was taken as a boy after his parents were killed. I left it open on my screen last night."

"Interesting choice of image. When did you look it up?"

"Shortly before you arrived."

"Why?"

"I was curious."

"Because of something Davy Driscoll told you?"

"The church ruin Oliver was taken to isn't a secret."

"No, it's not, but that doesn't answer my question, does it?" Padgett's gaze narrowed on Finian. "The FBI respects your sacramental responsibilities. That doesn't mean I do on a personal level. Davy Driscoll showed up at the home of the boy he tormented thirty years ago — the boy whose parents he and his partner in crime murdered in front of him. Driscoll bled to death in Oliver's arms. Whoever was responsible, it was a hell of a nerve to show up at the York farm, don't you think?"

Finian glanced at the photograph of a roofless church ruin, Celtic crosses and gravestones against the orange glow of a Scottish sunset. They reminded him of Declan's Cross, and yet they were different, too. There was an air of mystery about them, a remoteness, a deep, searing loneliness. Perhaps he was reading too much into it, given what he knew had happened there — given his own mood.

Finian turned back to Sam Padgett. "Best of luck gathering your evidence."

Padgett nodded again to the screen image. "What do you think those two men had in mind when they took an eight-year-old boy to a remote Scottish ruin? Think they'd have turned him over to his grandparents after they ransomed him? Come on, Father Bracken. You're not that naive. Would you violate the seal of confession to stop a child molester?"

"That's a hypothetical question."

"Is it?"

Sam Padgett was an experienced interrogator and no doubt would recognize Finian's expression for what it was — irritation, avoidance, fear. He went to the sink, aware the FBI agent was watching him. His head throbbed. He knew his duty but he didn't have the words to express it.

"All right, Father," the FBI agent said. "I respect your vows but I don't believe one syllable this man uttered to you was on the level. You don't owe him your silence. In fact, I'd argue the opposite. Whether or not you gave Davy Driscoll absolution — however you two ended things on Tuesday — I don't believe Saint Peter welcomed him at the pearly gates yesterday morning." Padgett started toward the screen door, stopped and turned again to Finian. "Thanks for your time. I'm going to stop at Hurley's for breakfast and then head out of town."

"You might run into Donovans," Finian said.

Padgett grinned. "I have one brother. Lives in Austin. You?"

"A twin brother and three younger sisters. All live in Ireland."

"They're not Donovans, though. See you, Father."

Finian didn't finish his morning prayers. Instead, he jumped into his BMW and followed Sam Padgett to Hurley's, a popular, rustic restaurant on Rock Point harbor. He found the FBI agent at a table by the back windows, in a section of the building that jutted out over the water, a silvery blue in the morning sun. The tide was rising, and it felt almost as if they were on a boat.

"Coffee, Father?" Padgett asked.

Finian shook his head. He sat down, placing his breviary on the table with its red-and-white checked oilcloth. "You're right. The man who came to see me on Tuesday did so with the sole purpose of manipulating me into giving him information about my friends." Finian inhaled, noticing the sky was brightening, as if to reassure him that he'd come down on the right side of his dilemma. "By the time he died, I hope he'd asked God for forgiveness. I hope he was in a place where he was willing to face his past and atone for his sins. That isn't where he was on Tuesday."

"He was working an angle," Padgett said.

Finian nodded. "I've struggled with that question and my responsibilities. When I found out his true identity . . ." He opened the breviary and took out a faded color photograph of four people standing in front of a honey-stone cottage. An older man, an older woman, a younger man and a curly-haired little girl. Finian placed the photograph faceup on the table and slid it across to the FBI agent. "There's a note on the back. It just says *the Balfours.*"

"I was with the stepson of Anthony Balfour's widow yesterday." Padgett scrutinized the photo. "The older man and woman must be the other two Balfour siblings, Freddy and Posey. The girl must be Henrietta Balfour. The younger man — her father, maybe." He sighed, looking up. "When and where did you get this photograph?"

"I found it in my breviary this morning,"

Finian said. "It was tucked in the back. I haven't been as diligent about my daily prayers since Davy Driscoll's visit. I've been . . . I can't explain."

"Conflicted is my guess. He put the photo in your breviary?"

"Yes. He must have slipped it in when I stood up to shut my office door. We didn't discuss this photograph, Special Agent Padgett."

"Why did he leave it with you?"

"He included a note for me with the photo." Finian unfolded the note, written on stationery from the inn in Heron's Cove where Reed Warren — Davy Driscoll — had stayed and slid it to Sam Padgett. "It makes clear his intentions. He tells me if he doesn't do the right thing, he knows I will. He acknowledges he lied to me and he was looking for information. I believe he was fighting temptation, Special Agent Padgett."

"Leaving the photo with you was a way for him to try to keep his darker angels at bay?"

"Perhaps. It could be more manipulation. The man I knew as Reed Warren never admitted to being Davy Driscoll or to killing the Yorks, and he didn't tell me his plans. He said he was Catholic and dying, and he asked me to hear his confession. I agreed, with reservations, but I soon realized he was insincere and broke it off with a blessing. He wasn't pleased, and I've been wrestling with what to do ever since he left my office." Finian was silent a moment. "It's been a long few days."

Padgett studied him. "Go on, Father."

"He said he knew something — a secret that tortured him — and he'd done a terrible thing in his youth. He asked about Oliver York and his relationship with Colin Donovan and the Sharpes, Emma and Wendell in particular."

"What did you tell him?"

"Nothing."

Padgett gave a curt nod. "That I can believe."

"I encouraged him to go to the authorities. I'm not a law-enforcement officer." Finian was silent a moment. "We now know his death was imminent, and perhaps he knew that, too — but he wasn't dying, was he? He didn't have a terminal illness."

"Doesn't look that way."

"It makes no difference. Our conversation was a lie."

"Why did you look up the ruin where Oliver was taken?"

"Because this man mentioned Scotland. He said he lived there."

"At the ruin? Why?"

"He said he went to the ruin with his family as a child and had good memories of it."

"He said that, huh?" Padgett sat forward. "That's not the story police have gone by for the past thirty years. They have Davy Driscoll and Bart Norcross choosing the ruin where they took Oliver at random — happening on it while they were on the run after their robbery in London went wrong. It's long been assumed Driscoll and Norcross didn't realize the Yorks were home when they broke into their apartment. They panicked after Deborah York recognized them and shot her and her husband and took their son."

"They could have decided to head to the ruin at the last minute, at Driscoll's suggestion," Finian said.

"Maybe." Padgett frowned at the photograph and note in front of him on the table. "What does a photograph of the Balfours have to do with that night?"

"I don't know."

"The murders, the kidnapping, Scotland. It's starting to look as if they were planned in advance." Padgett peered more closely at the photograph. "Something about this photo tells us what Davy Driscoll had on his mind when he left your office and headed to Dublin and then to England. Why break into Wendell Sharpe's home?"

"Information," Finian said without hesitation. "The same reason Driscoll came to Maine. He didn't tell me his plans but it makes sense. I told him not to wait and go straight to the authorities. I offered to go with him to the Rock Point police."

"What did he say?"

"He said he'd consider it and then asked me if Oliver had ever been back to the ruin."

Padgett blew out a breath. "Yeah. Back to the ruin."

"This was a conflicted, angry, bitter man, Special Agent Padgett. He mentioned his mother died last year. He couldn't attend her funeral. The police would have been watching. Even after all this time, the York murders are still an open case. He knew he ruined his life and the fault lay with him, but he blamed others."

Padgett picked up his coffee mug and looked out at the harbor for a few seconds before shifting back to Finian. "You must deal with tortured souls and a lack of remorse in your line of work."

"I'm revealing my conversation with this man just because it was filled with lies. I wouldn't reveal mere lies. This was never a confession."

"A difficult spot to be in."

Finian sat back. "I'm satisfied I did the right thing."

"I am, too. Thanks for coming down here." Padgett nodded toward the restaurant entrance. "We weren't fast enough. Here come a few Donovans." He leaned back, more relaxed. "Time for doughnuts."

21

The Cotswolds, England

When Emma and Colin arrived at the Kershaw farm, they had their bags in the trunk and had checked out of their room — and they'd spoken with Sam Padgett and Finian Bracken about Davy Driscoll's "confession."

And then Cassie Kershaw had called and asked them to meet her at the Kershaw farm. They drove out there and she met them in the front yard. She was dressed for the day but her hair was in tangles, old mascara or liner smudged under her eyes, clothes mismatched, as if she'd grabbed whatever was heaped on a chair or by the bed and thrown it on.

"Thank you for coming," she said. "I didn't know what else to do. I thought you might be able to tell me what's going on. The FBI paid my father a visit yesterday."

Colin nodded. "That's right, Mrs. Kershaw."

"You know already? I should have guessed." She pointed vaguely. "Let's go round back. Eugene's here somewhere. The boys are with Eugene's sister. I'm — I'm freaking out. Tea in the garden, don't you think, and you talk and I listen?"

She shot forward without waiting for an answer. Emma exchanged a glance with Colin, but they said nothing and followed Cassie around to the back of the house, an elegant, postcard-perfect two-story in the ubiquitous Cotswold yellow limestone.

Cassie pushed hair behind an ear as she stopped at a table and chairs. She didn't sit down. "Dad emailed me last night. He didn't want to call because it was late here. I got the email when I woke up. I don't understand. Why would this man who died visit my father in the US and ask him about our connection to the Balfours?"

"Have a seat, Mrs. Kershaw," Colin said.

She shook her head. "I'm too agitated to sit. You two feel free. You look calm, cool and collected. Easy, isn't it, when it's not your family under the microscope by both the FBI *and* a killer? That's who this Reed Warren was, isn't it? Davy Driscoll. A killer. A kidnapper of little boys."

Emma placed a hand on the back of a chair but remained on her feet. "We know he visited your father as Reed Warren last Sunday. Did he ever come round here asking about the Balfours, the history of the farm?"

"No. I never saw him before. I told the police. We had *no* idea he sneaked onto our property. He never did work for us. Henrietta gets Tony and Nigel to do things for her from time to time. I don't think she's had anyone else there to do work since she inherited the house. Posey might have spoken with him. I didn't keep track."

"What about when Freddy Balfour was still alive?" Colin asked. "That goes back thirty years, but could Driscoll have done work for the Balfours back then?"

"I suppose he could have, but I don't know. I wouldn't. I was in first grade in West Hartford." Cassie yanked out a chair and plopped into it. "My dad believed this man." She groaned, throwing up her hands. *"Idiot."*

"This man evaded authorities and lived under an assumed name for thirty years," Emma said. "He fooled a lot of people, Cassie."

She went still, the last of the color draining from her face. "He could have killed

378

Dad, couldn't he? Poor Dad. He and my mother are looking forward to selling the house and retiring here. They'll start out spending half the year — they're finalizing all the paperwork. It's a safe village. Charming. Storybook." She bit down on her lower lip, then gave a laugh that didn't come close to sounding genuine. "I suppose I should have remembered that storybooks have their evildoers."

Emma ran her palm over the back of the chair, warmed by the morning sun. She noticed the Kershaws had a large urn of annuals on the terrace but few other flowers, relying instead on flowering trees, shade trees and a large, lush lawn. Children's toys and equipment were scattered on the terrace and a play area. It was the home of a young family, Emma thought. Henrietta Balfour's home with its climbing roses and "accidental" cottage garden didn't have that feel, at least not yet.

"Do you remember your stepgrandmother?" Emma asked.

Cassie shook her head. "She died before I was born. She and my grandfather found each other later in life. She'd moved to the US after she was widowed but they didn't meet until Tony had graduated high school. My grandfather lost his first wife when my dad and his sister were still in high school. I think he and Tony's mom had a happy marriage. They were each other's companion until she died. He died a short time later." She threw one leg over the other, foot shaking with nervous energy. "What do the Balfours have to do with Davy Driscoll?"

"The detectives investigating his death are going to meet us here," Colin said. "Is Tony Balfour here?"

"I don't know. I've been pacing and obsessing. Eugene might be with him. I'll go see."

She leaped up and burst across the yard toward the cottage. Emma and Colin fell in behind her. As they came to the cottage, Emma heard a noise — a groan — from around back. Cassie shot forward, but Emma grabbed her as Colin eased past them and disappeared around the back of the cottage.

"Stay back," Emma said firmly.

Cassie pulled against Emma's grip. "Why, what — is it Eugene?"

Before Emma could respond, Colin came around the corner of the cottage. "It's Nigel Burns. He needs an ambulance."

Emma let Cassie break free and run toward Colin. Emma got out her phone and hit the number of DI Lowe's mobile phone as she followed Colin and Cassie behind the cottage. Nigel was on his side in the grass and mud by the attached woodshed. He was conscious, swearing and moaning as he struggled to sit up.

"He was hit on the back of the head," Colin said. "He's been out here all night."

"I'm okay." Nigel grimaced, holding his neck as he sat up. More swearing. "Sorry."

Emma reached the detective inspector and gave him a quick rundown of what was going on. "On the way," the DI said, disconnecting.

Cassie wrung her hands together. "Where's Eugene? Have you seen him? And Tony — is he here?"

"It's just me," Nigel said, then snorted. "Whoever clocked me is probably long gone."

Colin stayed close to him. "Did you see who it was?"

Nigel shook his head, winced. "No."

"Why did you come here?" Colin asked.

"You don't have to answer, Nigel," Cassie said. "They're FBI agents but they're American. The police will be here soon."

"It's all right. No point now . . ." He leaned back against the cottage's back wall. "I saw that man here in January. The one who died. He said he was looking for

Cotswold scenery to paint — you know, a painting that goes on the wall, not painting the wall. It was when Wendell Sharpe was visiting Mr. York. I'm sure of it. I saw him at the dovecote — lots of the walkers take pictures of it — and I saw him here."

"On our farm?" Cassie asked.

"Right here. This spot."

She groaned, her skin a greenish color. "Who else saw him? Who did he see? My God, Nigel, why didn't you say something?"

"I didn't think anything of it," Nigel said with a shrug. "Not until he turned up dead."

"Did he speak with Wendell Sharpe?" Colin asked.

"I don't know. I never saw them together."

Colin narrowed his eyes. "What else, Nigel?"

"You don't have to worry about Bart Norcross turning up," Nigel said. "He's dead."

"How do you know?"

"I didn't kill him. I saw his grave. I know that now. It's not what I thought at the time."

"When?"

"Back then. I was thirteen. Scared. I blocked it out. I was back here sneaking a smoke and came on disturbed ground. I got it in my head it could be buried treasure. I don't know — I wanted to see what it was.

Never thought . . ." He looked ill. "I saw it was a man's clothes and I didn't want to see more. I put the dirt back on them and that was that. Let someone else find them. I wasn't going to take the blame. I really thought it was just clothes. One of the killers changed clothes here and buried them. They fit the description police gave of the clothes Bart Norcross was wearing the night he and Davy Driscoll killed the Yorks. I figured he changed and buried them here."

Cassie snorted. "You moron, Nigel. You withheld a key clue that could have aided the manhunt."

"You eventually realized it wasn't just clothes," Colin said quietly. "Didn't you, Nigel?"

He nodded grimly. "Guessed. Didn't know. I never checked. I figured anyone in the village could have hit him on the head with a shovel or something. Everyone was upset about the Yorks. Whatever happened, the bastard had it coming. I just blocked it out."

"Good God, Nigel," Cassie whispered.

"I didn't tell anyone. Not even my mum. I came back here last night to see if my mind had played tricks on me, if the clothes . . ." He shut his eyes, his face ashen. "It wasn't just clothes." He vomited into the grass, then leaped to his feet in a burst of panic. "I can't stay here."

Colin clamped an arm on him. "Easy, Nigel. You need medical attention."

"No worries. My mum's good with injuries. I'll go see her."

Colin didn't respond, just eased Nigel back onto the ground.

"The police are on the way," Emma said. "They know we need an ambulance."

Cassie was trembling next to Emma. "I have to find Eugene."

As she spoke, Eugene staggered around from the front of the cottage, tears streaming down his cheeks. "Nigel's all right, then?" He stood still, sniffled. "I didn't know . . . I was so afraid." He gulped in a breath. "I'm sorry. I left him there. I thought he was going to attack me. I panicked and hid in the cottage. Tony's not there. I haven't seen him since last night."

"When did you hide in the cottage?" Emma asked.

He lifted his gaze to her but seemed to have trouble focusing. "What?" He held up a hand. "Just before you and Cassie and Agent Donovan got here. I've never . . ." He looked down at Nigel. "How are you?"

"I'll be okay, I think," Nigel said.

Cassie stood next to her husband. "You're

384

a wreck. What's going on, Eugene? Tell me."

"Henrietta's gone to Scotland with Oliver. They must know by now . . ." He didn't make eye contact with his wife. "I've known Henrietta since she was born, and Posey — she was a constant in my life, a good neighbor. I remember Freddy Balfour. He was a character. I've met Henrietta's parents, but they're city people. They remind me of my parents, but mine will tolerate an occasional weekend in the country — they're just in Oxford, not too far. Henrietta's parents break into a cold sweat whenever they're here, I swear."

"Eugene . . ." Cassie said, her voice a croak. "You're not making any sense."

"No, no, it's all right, Cassie. I need to . . ." He sniffled again, but he seemed stronger. "Tony didn't come round for years — I think he was here once before Freddy died. He worked in the States in his twenties. He visited when Posey got sick, at the end. I overheard a few unkind remarks in the village suggesting he was ingratiating himself to get something out of her when she died, but I never saw any evidence of that. He was always quite kind to her. He decided to stay in the area in retirement. He and Henrietta seem to get on well."

"Tony was never really a part of my family," Cassie said.

"Davy Driscoll left a photograph with a priest in the US," Colin said. "We believe he stole it when he visited your father last Sunday. The police will show it to you. It was taken here when Freddy Balfour was alive. Do you know anything about this photo, Eugene?"

He squeezed his eyes shut, but fresh tears oozed down his cheeks. He shook his head. "I saw it on a visit to Cassie's family in the US. I didn't pay any attention. It was taken a long time ago . . . before the Yorks were killed."

Cassie had gone silent. "Eugene . . . the paintings. You've been acting weird ever since I found the one of Queen's View. What haven't you told me all this time? Damn it, you're hiding something. Just like Nigel." She balled a hand into a fist. "*You* didn't kill Bart Norcross, did you? Davy Driscoll — please, Eugene. Tell me you didn't kill anyone."

He threw back his head and moaned. "I haven't killed anyone." He stood straight. "Freddy Balfour let Deborah York use the cottage to paint, in secret. She was self-taught. She practiced by copying scenes of Scotland. She used photographs. She had some of her own, and I gave her some, too.

386

I ripped some out of magazines. I looked for anything she might like. Painting was her creative secret, she called it. No one knew."

"But you knew," Cassie said. "Freddy knew."

"I meant her family. I don't think Posey or my family knew, either. I caught her in here one day, by accident. She was painting to her heart's content. She was embarrassed. It wasn't that painting was a forbidden pastime, but she'd made such a secret of it — she thought she should have been using her time and energy for more productive pursuits and painting was self-indulgent. When she died . . ." He shut his eyes, more tears leaking out. He opened his eyes again and pushed his palm over his balding head. "I hid the paintings after she was killed. Any that were here. Deborah didn't want anyone to know and I couldn't let —" He gulped, as if he were a tortured teenager again. "I needed to keep her secret. I thought that's what she'd have wanted. I tucked the paintings in the woodshed. They were mixed in with all sorts of dusty, worthless relics from Freddy. I put them out of my mind."

"Until your wife discovered one during renovations and then Henrietta discovered the rest in Davy Driscoll's rental car," Colin said.

"That's right." Eugene cleared his throat. "Scotland . . . I knew Oliver was taken to a Scottish ruin. I knew a ransom demand was made to his grandparents but he escaped before it could be paid. I didn't want there to be any scandal that would harm Deborah's memory."

"Dear God, Eugene," Cassie breathed. "You were just a kid."

"It's all right, Cassie. It's an emotional memory, one I've kept to myself for far too long. I'll tell the police everything."

"Where were you when the Yorks were killed?" Colin asked.

Eugene's relief at the direct question was almost palpable. "Everyone assumed I was at home in Oxford, but I was here. I'd biked. I did work for Freddy. He was so sick then. I wanted to help, and . . ." He didn't finish.

"And you were hoping to see Deborah York," Cassie said. "You were in love with her."

He looked up at his wife. "I was fifteen, Cassie." His voice was calmer, more controlled. "I had an enormous crush on her. I suspect most of the boys around here did."

"I did," Nigel mumbled.

"Deborah was a lovely, generous woman," Eugene said. "She was also devoted to her husband and son, just as I'm devoted to my wife and boys now. We were all devastated by her and Charles's murders, but our sense of loss didn't compare to what Oliver must have felt. It's easy when you're hurting yourself to lose sight of someone who is hurting more."

"I'm not sure what I feel," Cassie said. "I'm numb. Too many emotions all at once."

"I didn't kill anyone. I didn't destroy the paintings. I didn't know Davy Driscoll was here, searching for them. I don't know why he wanted them. Deborah York loved her family. I love my family." Some of the starch went out of him. "I never hurt her, but I can't shake the notion that I did something to cause her death."

Martin was having difficulty coping with his irritation with Oliver and Henrietta for what he was convinced was their impulsive, reckless decision to drive to Scotland overnight. He hadn't heard a peep from either of them since their departure. He'd come to the house with Alfred hoping no one jumped out of the bushes and slit his brachial artery. He no longer tried to convince himself Davy Driscoll had died in an elaborate suicide attempt. It was fanciful, a way of avoiding the truth, whatever it was.

He hadn't wanted to find Ruthie in the kitchen, attacking an imaginary spot on the cooker.

"You're clever, Ruthie," Martin said. "You could nick an artery."

She didn't look up from her work. "I could, but I didn't. I haven't killed anyone, ever, even to protect my sons."

"I was teasing, Ruthie. Are you all right? What's got in to you?"

Her shoulders slumped but she kept at the cooker. "Nigel's been hurt. Paramedics checked him over. He's with the police. They let him call me. I told him to tell them everything he knows," Ruthie said, as if Nigel he were still thirteen. "I never knew. He could have told me. Dear God. He could have told me."

Martin went still. "Told you what, Ruthie?"

"Nigel knew Bart Norcross has been dead all these years. He saw his grave on the Kershaw farm a week after Deborah and Charles were killed. He thought . . . he was just a boy, Martin. He thought it was clothes buried there."

Martin couldn't speak at first. All he could think to do was to go to Ruthie. "Dear

Ruthie. Oh, love." He took her by the elbows and turned her to him, embraced her. "Nigel was just a boy. He's a man now, a good man. He'll get through this. We all will."

"I never knew. He never told me." She fought back sobs. "He was thirteen, Martin. Thirteen."

"We didn't take into consideration the impact of the tragedy thirty years ago on the young people in the village," Martin whispered.

"I just wanted to protect my boys."

"I know, Ruthie. There were different levels and kinds of loss and trauma, but everyone here was forever changed."

She nodded, returned to her cleaning.

A few minutes later, Emma and Colin arrived with DI Lowe. The DI reported that Cassie's father in the US had identified the people in a photograph Driscoll had stolen from him and left with Finian Bracken.

DI Lowe nodded to Colin, who continued. "Cassie's father identified Freddy Balfour, Posey, their nephew Tony and Freddy's young granddaughter, Henrietta. It's been years since the photograph was taken," Colin added, "but that Tony Balfour isn't the Tony Balfour who's been living in the Kershaws' cottage on the old Balfour farm."

Martin could hardly breathe. "Then it's not Bart Norcross in the grave."

22

Southern Highlands, Scotland

The stunning Scottish landscape was awash in sunlight, a contrast to Oliver's last visit to this quiet spot in the Highlands above Pitlochry. He drove in silence on a narrow, winding road, descending to a loch, its still waters glistening on the late spring morning. Henrietta had insisted he sleep. He hadn't wanted to, but she was inflexible when she was certain she was right. "You don't want to see this place ragged," she'd said. "Tilt your seat back and close your eyes. You'll thank me later."

He hadn't thanked her, not because he wasn't grateful but because he was preoccupied. For the past few miles, he'd had to stop himself from reliving his escape along this very road. He'd run until his sides had ached and he'd been panting so hard he thought he would die, and then he'd dipped among the trees on the side of the road. He'd been terrified his captors would find him by his shadow.

"Are you sure we're on the right road?" Henrietta asked. "I don't remember hearing about a golf course."

"What?"

"Look there, Oliver." She pointed up ahead. "That's a tee."

"There was no golf course here thirty years ago. This road's been improved considerably since then, too."

"I saw a sign for a castle hotel up ahead."

"The castle was abandoned then. An American with Scottish ancestry bought it ten years ago and invested millions to turn it into a five-star hotel. I read about it. I knew it was in the area, but I didn't think it was this close."

"This must be its golf course."

Oliver glanced at her. She had her back to him as she looked out her window. He noticed snarls in her hair. He doubted she'd slept during his nap, but she'd dozed on the drive up from the Cotswolds. He trusted so little about himself right now but he trusted that he couldn't imagine life without her. She'd always been there, rambling through the village on her visits with her aunt. Whether five or thirty-five, Henrietta Balfour had been a constant in his life. She was smart, funny, coping with her own ambitions, demons and secrets.

And pretty, he thought. He'd noticed that about her before, many times, but not in the same way he did now.

The road narrowed as it curved past the sparkling loch, the golf course sprawling above its banks. His grip tightened on the wheel, involuntarily, in reaction, he knew, to being here, remembering.

"It's not a surprise the area's changed in thirty years," Henrietta said. "But a castle hotel resort does make your escape from mad killers a bit more difficult to imagine."

He smiled. "Are you minimizing my ordeal?"

"Not at all. Just imagining what it was like here before the eighteenth hole was put in."

"I was allowed to look out the window when we got to this road." He slowed the car, nodded to the loch. "It was dark but I saw stars reflected on the water. I thought they were actual stars shining in the lake, shining up through the water. I thought they were a message from my parents in heaven."

"I'm sorry, Oliver."

No irony in her tone now. He shrugged. "Of course there were no stars in the lake. It was just starlight. It helps to be here. The lake is real. The road. The hills. Different, yes, but I didn't make them up."

"Where did the priest find you after your escape?"

"Somewhere near what's now the ninth hole, I imagine. He's since died. He was elderly then. I was suffering from mild hypothermia. I'd have died if not for his morning walk."

"I'm glad you didn't die." Henrietta was silent for a moment as they passed another sign pointed to the castle hotel. "Takes an edge of drama off the story of an eight-year-old boy left in a remote Scottish ruin, doesn't it?"

"If I'd been kidnapped today, instead of trudging in the bleak, cold rain, I could have slipped into the hotel and had tea and kippers."

"I can't believe you've never returned until now."

Oliver frowned at her as if she'd gone mad. "Why would I have returned?"

She considered his question. "Out of sight, out of mind, was it?"

"Never out of mind," he said. "Maybe that's what I hoped would happen if I didn't come back."

He didn't continue, concentrating as the road curved away from the loch. Remembering. He could hear his rapid breathing and whimpers as a boy. Running, grief-stricken, terrified, exhausted, freezing and utterly determined. He'd wanted to get to the police. He remembered that now. His parents had told him to get to the police in an emergency.

"You think you missed something that night, or forgot something due to the physical and emotional trauma you experienced." Henrietta turned to stare out her window again. "It's difficult to interview small children after a violent event even with proper training."

"You've done it?"

"Yes."

It was a whisper, perhaps not meant for him to hear.

He pulled into a dirt parking area on the side of the road. The golf course had veered off on the opposite side of the road, up toward the castle hotel. Here tall trees shaded both sides of the road. Oliver turned off the engine and got out of the car. Henrietta followed, silent, and met him by a footpath on the edge of the parking area.

He pointed to a small sign with an arrow pointing up the path. "Directions nowadays." He could hear the hollowness in his voice, memory bleeding through his resolve. He looked down at his feet as if he expected to see the shoes he'd been wearing that night. Little-boy trainers. He forced himself to turn to Henrietta. "We can pretend we're tramping through Scottish ruins on a romantic getaway."

"Only the weather and scenery are romantic, Oliver. Nothing else about this is."

He slipped his hand into hers. "I've taken you for granted all these years. Never again."

"I'm not going to hold you to that under the circumstances." She squeezed his hand and let it go, smiled, and then nodded to the path. "Shall we?"

They took the path to the ruin, uphill through dense trees. It ended in a clearing where the skeletal remains of a small church stood among graves marked by carved headstones. Three Celtic crosses stood on the edge of the clearing, at the crest of the hill. The ground was uneven, the grass tended if tall now in the June morning sun. A low stone wall lined with trees bordered the clearing on three sides.

"It must be popular for visitors to the hotel," Henrietta said. "Have a wander to a proper Scottish ruin after breakfast. I wonder if it was part of the castle grounds at one time. I suppose it must have been."

Oliver walked across the churchyard, imagining the faithful coming here hundreds of years ago — imagining himself arriving with Davy Driscoll and Bart Norcross. "We didn't come up a path," he said. "Driscoll dragged me out of the back of the car. No. It was a van. He didn't carry me. He shoved me through trees. The other man . . ." He paused, shutting his eyes, then opening them again, needing the sunlight, the green trees and grass, the wildflowers poking up among the graves. "I didn't have as much to do with Bart Norcross. I remember he threatened to kill me if I didn't do as they said."

"Awful memories for anyone never mind an eight-year-old." Henrietta nodded toward the trees on the opposite side of the clearing. "There's another road. It must come round from farther up the road where we turned." She touched Oliver's elbow. "We have company."

He could see a small white caravan parked through the trees. "Before he died, Driscoll said he lived at the ruin. I thought he was speaking metaphorically."

"Most people don't speak metaphorically, Oliver."

He supposed she had a point.

A path of pounded grass went through a small opening in the wall to the narrow road. He could feel Henrietta wanting to shoot past him and go first, but he took the lead. This was the route his kidnappers had taken that night. They'd parked where the caravan was now.

It was an old caravan — crooked, dinged and rusted. Henrietta peered into the cab. "Just a lot of rubbish," she said, standing back.

Oliver edged to the main door at the back of the caravan. He expected to have to use his skills to break in, or suggest Henrietta use hers, but he saw that it was ajar.

Tony Balfour burst out of the caravan. "Don't come near me." He leveled a pistol at Oliver. "I'll shoot. I'll defend myself. You've both lost your bloody minds."

Henrietta eased in closer. "Tony? What's going on?"

"He killed that man, Henrietta. He wants to blame me. Don't let him fool you. Don't believe his lies."

"What are you doing here?" Oliver asked him.

"Reed Warren told me he was Davy Driscoll. He told me if anything happened to him, I was to come up here. I'd find answers. He said you killed your mum and dad that night. He was going to see you and tell you — so you could make peace with yourself." Tony steadied the pistol. "He was

400

afraid you'd kill him when he told you the truth, and you did."

"Davy Driscoll was a liar and a manipulator, Tony," Henrietta said. "Here. Give me the gun and we'll sort this calmly."

"There's no sorting this. I'm getting out of here. I tried. I did right by Posey, and you, and the Kershaws, but you'll never let me be a real Balfour. I'll retire somewhere else. Maybe go back to America."

"Is that the weapon you used to kill my parents?" Oliver asked.

"It's the weapon you used to kill your parents. I didn't kill anyone. I wasn't anywhere near London that night. Or here. I was just in the wrong place at the wrong time for that fellow's confession. I didn't know what to do."

"I'm sure you didn't," Henrietta said. "Go on, then. Leave me here with a killer."

"Sorry, love," Tony said, taking a backward step. "I thought you'd beat me here."

She sighed. "We shouldn't have rested, Oliver. Tony got ahead of us. You did tell me you didn't need to sleep."

"It's not your fault," Oliver said.

"I know that. I was right. You did need sleep."

"She's something, isn't she?" Tony grinned, but his gun didn't waver and there was no amusement or affection in his eyes. "A true Balfour."

"Unlike you," she said.

"I won't shoot unless I have to. I'll have a head start and disappear. That's all I want."

"Who are you going to pretend to be this time?" Oliver asked.

"Don't follow me. I'll shoot you if you do."

Henrietta leaped at him without warning, and Oliver pounced, kicking the gun from Tony Balfour's hand. It dropped to the road, slid on the dirt and rock. Tony was tall and fit, but he lacked Henrietta's MI5 experience and training and Oliver's black belt in karate. They overpowered him, twisted his arms behind him.

Oliver scooped up the pistol and pointed it at Tony. "There must be something in the caravan we can use to tie him until we get the police here," he said to Henrietta.

"Don't leave me alone with him," Tony said. "He'll kill me."

She looked up at Oliver. "We don't need to tie him. We can keep the gun on him until the police arrive. I'll call them now. Don't move, Tony. I'm not in the mood to tackle you again, and I really don't want Oliver to have to shoot you."

She stepped away from him. He glared at

her. "I don't want to end up like that man, bleeding to death in the grass."

"You won't. You'll be shot, not cut." Henrietta got out her phone. "Oh. How convenient. The police are on the way. The FBI agents were worried about us and called on friends in high places. Perfect." She put her hand out toward Oliver. "Best I have the gun when the police get here."

Oliver hesitated.

"Oliver," she said. "I've got him."

"You're certain?"

"Yes. He's not going anywhere. I promise."

"No worries, then." He handed Henrietta the gun. "He's not your cousin."

She nodded. "I know."

Oliver turned to the other man. "You're Bart Norcross," he said. "You've done your best to change your appearance, play a somewhat older man . . . but it's you. I wouldn't have recognized you even without changes as readily as I did Davy, but I see it now. You aren't Tony Balfour. You're one of the men who murdered my parents and kidnapped me."

"You're wrong, Oliver." Tony — Bart — spoke with absolute conviction. "I'm Tony Balfour. I'm Freddy Balfour's only nephew. My father was Anthony Balfour, Freddy and Posey's brother. I didn't know them growing up because my father died young and my mother moved to the US with me. I grew up there. She separated me from my only family except for her. I moved back to the UK thirty years ago."

"That's what the real Tony did," Henrietta said. "You killed him and took over his identity. No wonder you're able to haul trellises and swing hammers like a man ten years younger. You *are* ten years younger. Bastard."

Oliver paced in front of Norcross, who sat in the grass by the side of the road, sullen, still convinced from the look of him that he had a way out of his predicament. "You killed Davy," Oliver said. "You know my farm well enough. You've been around. People know you, but you took care not to be seen, just in case. Did you intend to nick his brachial artery or was that a happy accident? An artery cut was a good choice for the chisel you used."

"I haven't killed anyone. I thought it was you. Maybe I got that wrong." He sounded reasonable, apologetic. "Maybe Eugene did. He hasn't told the truth about your parents. You'll see."

"Why come up here?" Henrietta asked. "Why grab the gun?"

"I don't know who is friend or foe. Reed

404

— Davy — told me things I didn't want to know. You know what he said? He said you two would have had dull, ordinary lives without the deaths of the Yorks. Those were his words. Dull and ordinary. Imagine that."

"You two provided motivation, did you?" Oliver asked coolly.

"Not me. I'm an innocent bystander. I admit I could have handled myself better but I'm just a guy and Davy Driscoll's death scared the hell out of me. I was afraid I was being framed. Still am. Driscoll did a lot of damage before his untimely end."

Henrietta remained still as a breeze stirred. "When did you kill the real Tony Balfour?"

He raised his eyes to her. The breeze blew his thin, graying hair, but Oliver could see now that he wasn't as old as he was pretending. "You don't want to hear the truth, either of you. Trust me."

"I don't trust you," she said coolly, "but I do want to hear the truth."

"When I returned to England thirty years ago, I wanted to meet my father's family. I came to see Uncle Freddy and Aunt Posey in their quaint Cotswold village. I ran into Davy Driscoll and Bart Norcross at the pub. Everyone thought they never made it out to the twee Cotswolds, but they did. It was before they started work for the Yorks in London. I figure now they were gauging how wealthy the Yorks were and starting to make their plans to rob them. They just seemed like a couple of regular guys to me. I went on to see my only cousin — your dad, Henrietta — in London, but we never got on."

"What rubbish," she said.

"What did you expect to find here?" Oliver asked casually. "Were you looking for evidence that would show you're not the real Tony Balfour? You knew Henrietta and I would find Davy's caravan up here. The police would have found it eventually. Did you come up here to make sure any evidence of your true identity was destroyed?"

"If there's any so-called evidence, it's fake."

Sticking to his story, he was. Oliver ignored him. "I'll guess Driscoll didn't know you were pretending to be Tony Balfour until he saw you in the village. That must have been a moment. Was he blackmailing you with what he knew about you? Was he afraid you'd kill him because he recognized you? You enjoy being a Balfour. Posey left you money."

"Davy told me his buddy Bart had an affair with your mother."

"Don't listen to him, Oliver," Henrietta said.

Tony smirked. "The two of them got it on at the Kershaws' cottage. Her painting hobby was cover for screwing the help."

Henrietta rolled her eyes. "I hope you're enjoying your stories. It's good practice. You can tell them to your cellmates in prison."

"I can't help what I know," he said, all innocence, his focus on Oliver not wavering. "Driscoll was in love with your mother himself, but not in that way. He didn't want to screw her. He idolized her. She was the classy, beautiful upper-class woman he put on a pedestal. She painted photographs of Scotland, places she'd gone and loved before she was saddled with a husband and child. Other places she wanted to go but couldn't, not then. He believed her little cottage studio was all about the painting. Never occurred to him she was an unfaithful wife."

"You can't rile me," Oliver said. "I've had thirty years to imagine meeting you face-to-face."

"He wasn't the only one who adored your mother, you know. She had a way about her, and she was unhappy and needy. The bored, rich housewife. Classic. I saw right through her but I never said anything. Then she was

407

killed. I'd left the village by then. I worked, lived my life, but I couldn't erase what I knew. Why do you think I stopped coming around?"

"Because you're Bart Norcross," Henrietta said calmly. "The real Tony Balfour was dead and you'd taken over his life and couldn't risk you'd left any loose ends — people who might recognize you, ask a question you couldn't answer. After Posey's death, you grew more confident no one was left who could spoil your life as a Balfour. You must have killed the real Tony when he visited Freddy shortly before his death — before you killed the Yorks, I think."

"You're the one talking rubbish, Henrietta."

"Where did you bury my real cousin Tony?"

"I *am* your cousin."

"No, you're not. You killed him. The poor man."

Oliver turned to Henrietta and saw her mouth had thinned but her hand remained steady on the gun. "Do you want me to take over the gun?" he asked her.

She shook her head. "The police will be here in minutes." She held up her phone in her other hand. "I've a text to that effect."

Not a ploy, Oliver saw.

The fake Tony looked less confident. "Eugene killed Bart Norcross." His voice held an edge of defiance. "I see that now and so will the police when it's all done and said. Young Eugene was besotted with Deborah York. She wasn't sure what to do about him. She didn't want to hurt his feelings. I suspect she introduced Eugene . . . you know, to the pleasures of the flesh."

Henrietta sighed. "You can stop this nonsense anytime."

"She wouldn't be the first older woman to have her way with a teenage boy. I was the fly on the wall — the eccentric cousin from America no one paid attention to. No one even remembers I was around thirty years ago. I didn't want to sully her reputation. Who would I tell, anyway? It'd be shoot-the-messenger time. Then she and her husband were murdered and awkward little Oliver was kidnapped . . ." He shook his head. "Awful. I admit I got away from there. I didn't want to get into the middle of that mess."

"Why come back, then?" Oliver asked.

"Because Posey left him money," Henrietta said. "He likes being a Balfour. Don't you, Bart?"

"You're mistaken, love," he said. "You'll see that soon. I don't blame you. You were traumatized by the York tragedy, too. I only saw Bart and Davy that one time, but my guess is they didn't plan to hurt anyone that night. They wanted profit, sure, but they weren't violent. Didn't have it in them."

Henrietta shook her head. "Amazing. Keep going, Bart."

He shrugged. "As you wish. These two lowlifes figured they'd grab cash and valuables and be done and gone, no one the wiser it was them. They'd melt back into their lives doing odd jobs, until the next opportunity. Only the Yorks were at home in London with their kid. You, Oliver. Driscoll wasn't lying. You killed them, didn't you? Will the police discover that's your dad's gun? No one will blame you. You were scared. Did you cry? Were your mum and dad trying to keep you quiet? Damn. What that must be like to have on your conscience."

Henrietta inhaled sharply. "You're a thorough but unconvincing liar."

"I'm not lying," he said with a hint of anger. "I'm sorry you don't want to hear the truth. I've been doing my damnedest to spare you and Oliver both."

"I was there." Again Oliver heard the hollowness in his own voice. "What you describe isn't what happened."

"He wants you agitated, Oliver," Henrietta said. "Don't let him get to you."

"I'm not," he assured her.

Tony — Bart Norcross — settled his gaze on Oliver. "Your memory of that night is unreliable. Everyone will understand your emotions got the better of you the other day when you recognized Davy Driscoll and killed him. He had a hell of a nerve showing up on your doorstep and threatening you."

"He didn't threaten me. He tried to warn me. In the end, I believe Davy Driscoll wanted to stop hiding, stop running. He wasn't a good man, but I wanted him to tell his story to police. He didn't get that chance because you killed him." Oliver paused, noting that his voice sounded more normal as he absorbed the truth, the reality that Bart Norcross was here in front of him and soon would be in police custody. "You will spend the rest of your life in prison for killing three people and kidnapping and planning to kill a boy. You intended to kill me no matter if you received a ransom, didn't you?"

"I'm not Bart Norcross. I am Tony Balfour." He swallowed, faltering, and then smiled at Henrietta. "You always have believed you were Posey's favorite. She was desperate for family at the end. Her brothers were gone, and she had no children. Your father never had much to do with her — with you, either. And then you neglected her. Too busy with your work in London. I was there for her. She liked me. She was disappointed in you after all she'd done for you. I talked her out of cutting you out of her will."

"He's baiting you," Oliver said.

"Yes, I'm aware of that."

He heard the police arrive. Henrietta had given them a description of the situation. Tony Balfour — Bart Norcross — was arrested without further incident, and Henrietta handed the police the gun. She turned to Oliver with a smile. "My knees are a bit wobbly."

He hooked an arm around her waist. "Liar. You're as steady as a rock."

She put her arm around him and pulled him close. "And you, Oliver. Not a word he said about your mother was true, or about you."

"No."

"Bloody fool doesn't realize forensics have advanced in thirty years. It'll take no time to prove he's Bart Norcross." She was silent. "You remember something from that night, don't you?"

He nodded, feeling her warmth. "A painting. They stole my mother's painting."

The police presence was, indeed, thanks to Emma Sharpe and Colin Donovan, but also to Jeremy Pearson, who, of course, would make certain his name — his identity as an MI5 officer — wasn't involved. Henrietta couldn't wait to get away from Bart Norcross and was only too happy when he disappeared inside a police car. He'd killed Oliver's parents and he'd killed her cousin, a man she'd never had the opportunity to know. Davy Driscoll hadn't been an innocent bystander in the York murders — he'd been a willing accomplice — but he hadn't pulled the trigger that night.

Police discovered Deborah York's painting in the caravan. It was an unframed canvas mounted on board. They carried it out for Oliver to identify. He stared at it, transfixed at the image of three figures — a man, a woman and a small child — walking hand-in-hand on a lane, past a pasture and a small honey-stone building. It took a moment, but Henrietta recognized the dovecote on the farm, flowerpots and potting equipment arranged by the door. Her eyes filled with tears when she realized it was the image Oliver had been trying to understand.

"My mother was devoted to her family,"

he said. "She did none of those things Norcross described."

Henrietta nodded. "You can see her love for her family in the painting."

"He and Driscoll took it that night. I remember now. I had never seen it. She had it in the library, and she showed it to me to help me to stay calm. It was her first attempt to paint a scene on the farm. She said everything else she painted were scenes in Scotland."

"Driscoll would have known it wasn't valuable."

"Norcross didn't."

"It's one reason he came here," Henrietta said. "It's not the only one, or even the main one. He was looking for the photograph Davy had threatened him with of the real Tony Balfour, only it was never here. It never left the US. And poor Nigel . . . Norcross left him for dead. He wouldn't give up. He knew his life as Tony Balfour was unraveling but he thought with Davy dead, if he got here before the police found the caravan . . . there was a chance."

"Eugene, Nigel, you, me." Oliver's eyes were shining with tears. "We were all so young, Henrietta."

"Yes, we were. The police have no more questions for us for the moment. Now we

414

have to drive home." She made a face, hoping to cut through Oliver's somber mood. "We should have flown up here."

He made a decent attempt at a smile. "Leave the car. We'll fly home and come back for it when we're ready."

"We can stay in the castle and have breakfast in bed and play golf and take falconry lessons, is that it?"

But her humor fell flat, and she saw him glance back toward the ruin, its Celtic crosses and headstones visible through the trees. "I remember everything," he whispered. He turned to her with a genuine smile and touched her hair. "It frizzes up in any humidity, did you know?"

"I'll never get used to it."

A text interrupted their hair discussion. It was from Jeremy Pearson. He'd made travel arrangements for them. An MI5 officer would drive her car back to the Cotswolds. She and Oliver would fly. *Pronto.*

23

The Cotswolds, England

Henrietta and Oliver were back at the York farm well before the June sunset. Colin had almost nixed joining them at Oliver's farmhouse, and he knew Emma had had her doubts, too. But here they were, in the York sitting room. Henrietta and Oliver sat next to each other on the couch. They looked as if they wanted to hold hands. Colin couldn't pinpoint what it was, but something about the way they were with each other suggested the easy familiarity of adults who'd known each other since childhood yet were surprised to discover they were falling for each other.

The turn to romance between them was impossible to miss, and Colin doubted it was just the result of their whirlwind trip to Scotland and their encounter with Bart Norcross. Whether it would last was anyone's guess. Colin would bet it would. He'd bet on him and Emma, and they'd been a less certain match. She sat on the floor, legs stretched out in front of her, as if she was visiting friends.

It'd been a long, intense day. They hadn't made it to London. In the hours since they'd arrived at the Kershaw farmhouse, Sam Padgett had been all over Tony Balfour's history in the US. School records, friends, neighbors, his mother's records — if he thought it could be relevant and it existed, he had it. There was no question the man in custody in Scotland wasn't Tony Balfour. He was Bart Norcross, and the remains the police unearthed in the Kershaw garden would no doubt prove to be the real Tony Balfour.

"Norcross fed us such lines," Henrietta said. "I almost didn't want to stop him, just to see what he'd come up with next. He didn't want to give up being Tony Balfour."

Colin appreciated that Jeremy Pearson had briefed him and Emma on what had transpired in Scotland. Driscoll hadn't been the one with expertise in faking identities. That was Norcross. He'd created Driscoll's Reed Warren alias. The difference was, Davy didn't take over a real person's identity as Reed Warren.

"Police didn't have good photos of either

Driscoll or Norcross," Colin said. "Norcross had no real family. He had an early failed marriage as Tony Balfour. Driscoll had a mother and a sister. He never married or settled down as Reed Warren. He went from job to job and lived a nomadic life in his caravan, painting."

"He never made any money at his painting," Emma said. "He probably didn't dare try, but the police found art supplies and a stash of sketches and watercolors in his caravan."

"I spoke with Finian Bracken on the way down here." Oliver's voice was quiet, none of his natural cheekiness in evidence since he'd arrived at his farmhouse. "Driscoll told him it had been hard on him not to see his mother especially."

Henrietta snorted. "I'm not shedding a single tear for him. I never had a clue he wasn't Tony." She paused. "Sociopathic bastard."

A faint smile from Oliver. Colin doubted either of them would spend any time berating themselves for not having figured out it wasn't the real Tony Balfour retiring to the Cotswolds. "Davy never fully confessed to Finian or told him his plans," Oliver said. "He didn't tell him the man we knew as Tony Balfour was in fact Bart Norcross."

It was clear now Bart Norcross had meant to kill Deborah and Charles York and kidnap Oliver from the start. Davy Driscoll hadn't, but he'd realized the truth at the end, if not its full ramifications until Bart slashed him with the stone-cutting chisel.

The choice of Scotland and the ruin thirty years ago had been Driscoll's idea. He'd believed they would hide there while the hunt cooled.

He hadn't realized Bart had other plans.

Colin saw now the ripple effects of the past thirty years of questions, erroneous assumptions, uncertainties, trauma and loss. And memories, he thought. Oliver's in particular, of a mother, a father, the boy he'd been.

Oliver was into filling in any blanks now. "It wasn't a confession, but Davy's visit with Finian did have an impact on him," he said. "Ultimately Davy wanted to tell the truth, if only because he wanted revenge against Bart for ruining his life. As if he played no part in that night."

Henrietta nodded. "Liars and manipulators. Davy and Bart both."

Colin said nothing. Neither did Emma. They both understood that Oliver and Henrietta had been through a deeply personal ordeal that reached back into their early childhoods. They needed to go through it.

"Davy recognized Bart in January but he was more interested in why Oliver was hanging out with Wendell Sharpe, FBI agents and an Irish priest. He went back to Scotland but started putting the pieces together."

"It became a mission for him," Colin said. "Fin Bracken says he was obsessed."

Oliver didn't respond at once. "Davy knew my mother had painted in secret in the cottage on what had then been the Balfour farm. It was a toehold for him. He wanted to know more and came back down from Scotland. By then Cassie had found one of my mother's paintings. Tony — Bart — was living in the cottage."

"Davy was looking for a way to profit from what he knew," Henrietta said. "Must have annoyed him when he realized his partner in crime had a better life than he did."

"Money, a good name." Oliver seemed transfixed by the details that had eluded him for so long. "Bart couldn't risk exposure. Davy must have told him about his caravan. Bart needed to get there before the police did. I've been remembering things." He paused, his eyes distant. "I escaped when Driscoll and Norcross argued. Driscoll thought they would just grab a few things. Norcross had bigger plans. The weapon used that night was never recovered."

"Until the bastard almost shot us with it," Henrietta said.

"They stole the gun from another client they did odd jobs for," Oliver said. "Police always believed the gun was opportunistic — part of the spontaneity of the night rather than a vital part of a developed plan to kill the Yorks. Bart did the killing. Driscoll kept the gun, obviously. I imagine he made sure he never left any fingerprints of his own on it. He knew he would face murder charges despite not pulling the trigger himself, but he still thought it was a hold over his violent friend should their paths cross again. At least Davy knew he had a weapon if Bart ever showed up."

"They knew you were home that night," Henrietta pronounced.

Oliver nodded grimly. "Norcross knew. I always believed we surprised them, but he knew. I never got a particularly good look at him. I was mostly with Davy. My mother recognized him." Oliver paused, splaying his fingers on his thighs. "I understand now the sense of betrayal I heard in her voice. It wasn't just that two contract workers would steal from her. She'd seen Davy as a kindred soul, an artist like herself."

Colin could only imagine. Jeremy Pearson had told him about a notation on the back of the canvas police had discovered in Davy Driscoll's caravan. Deborah York had painted the scene as a gift to her husband to celebrate their tenth wedding anniversary.

To Charles and to many more decades together, with all my love, Deborah

Apparently she'd brought the painting to London from her secret studio in the Cotswolds to give to her husband. But they never got the chance to celebrate that or any other anniversary.

Police discovered photographs in Davy's caravan of Scotland that he, like young Eugene, had given to Deborah to paint. There was also a sketchy painting Deborah had done of the ruin where, weeks later, Davy Driscoll and Bart Norcross had almost killed her son.

That had always been part of their plan.

"She knew," Oliver said, his voice ghostly quiet. "After Davy died in my arms, I kept hearing the horror in her voice. The sense of betrayal. I couldn't shake that it was directed at me. But it wasn't. It was directed at him. He had to live with that for thirty years. It's a small consolation."

"Bart followed Davy here and stole the chisel with the intention to kill him," Colin said. "He wasn't going to trust Davy not to tell everything once police got hold of him. He wasn't going to trust that Davy didn't have anything damning stashed in his caravan."

"Davy wanted to see me first. If he'd gone to the police instead . . ." Oliver didn't finish. "Bart must have put Alfred back in Martin's cottage to keep him from barking. He could have killed Alfred, too, and he would have, I've no doubt, if it hadn't been convenient not to. Then he intercepted Davy, cut his artery and walked away. I arrived back from the dovecote and found Davy bleeding out. Bart Norcross wanted to remain a Balfour. He wanted to *be* Tony Balfour."

"Stealing Tony's identity was part of Bart's plan from the get-go," Henrietta said. "He just never told Davy. He helped Davy pull together a new identity as Reed Warren and then figured they'd never see each other again."

"Davy might have had regrets in the end," Oliver said, "but he was a killer."

"He and Bart were both killers and kidnappers." Henrietta patted Oliver's knee.

"It's a bit late in the day, but we've got the bastards."

Oliver invited Emma and Colin to stay in one of his guest rooms, but, as usual, they refused. "I'm sending an Irish landscape to Wendell Sharpe as a gift, a token of gratitude, you might call it, for his years of dedicated service to the art world. He'll know what to do with it. It's of the church ruin on the headland above the village of Declan's Cross. I believe the painting's an early work by Aoife O'Byrne. I don't remember how I came by it."

"You ripped it off on a dark and stormy Irish night," Colin said.

Oliver ignored him. "Aoife's heart belongs to Finian Bracken."

Emma hadn't touched the Bracken 15 he'd poured. "Do you have a better understanding now of why you became fascinated with all things Celtic?"

"The workings of an eight-year-old mind. The shadows of unreliable memories. The love of parents who would sacrifice themselves to save their only child. The crosses I saw the night I was taken for ransom. The closeness I felt to death and the afterlife. Celtic myths, legends and folklore in particular resonated with me. I visited the Skelligs — I was drawn to asceticism for a time, but it was Saint Declan who hooked me. I couldn't tell you why. I loved Ardmore. I was there several times before I discovered Declan's Cross."

"Did you case John O'Byrne's house or sneak in one night on the spur of the moment?"

"Spur-of-the-moment has its place but so does planning. I'd sit among the crosses on the headland. Loss, loneliness, confusion built up inside me. I wanted to heal and protect." He shrugged. "But one can only do so much. You know that from your own work, but I'd had that lesson taught to me in a horrible way I couldn't process or accept, not bit by bit, over time, as most children do."

"You started helping MI5 before you were discovered," Emma said. "You'd send them tidbits anonymously."

"Do you think so? That sounds rather daring."

"You saved lives through what you know and learned as a thief and a scholar."

"Plus there's insufficient evidence against you," Colin said, "as well as issues with jurisdiction, prosecutorial priorities and statutes of limitations."

Oliver smiled. "I know nothing of that."

■ ■ ■ ■

Henrietta sat across from Jeremy Pearson at the pub. It was a warm night. The fireplace was unlit, and she had on a tank top with her jacket draped on the back of her chair. "You look as if you've been up for twenty-four hours straight," the MI5 officer said to her.

"At least I don't look as if I took on a mad killer and lost."

A twitch of a smile.

But the levity didn't last. "Poor Tony. I wonder if he'd lived if we'd have come to know each other. I'll have him properly buried in the Balfour plot, next to his father. MI5 interviewed my family when you did a background check on me. Did you interview Tony? He'd have been Bart then. Did you miss that?"

Jeremy was nursing a pint. "You don't think I will ever tell you, do you?"

"Of course not. I wasn't thinking."

"You're still MI5, Henrietta," he said, matter-of-fact.

"In my heart, perhaps. I can't argue."

"Not just in your heart. We never put your papers through."

"What?"

426

"You are, have been and no doubt will for some time be an officer of Her Majesty's Security Service."

"You faked everything. You cheeky bastard. This calls for Scotch. An expensive one. On you."

"It does, but not tonight. Go on. Be with Oliver. We'll have to sort you two but in due course. First things first." He settled back. "Our FBI friends are joining me for a drink."

Henrietta left him alone at his table. The long June night hadn't given up its light, but her energy was giving up. If indeed she was still MI5, she had to up her game. She smiled at the thought. Jeremy Pearson was truly one sneaky bastard. She had no idea if anything he told her was strictly on the level, but it didn't matter. He was the best and he wanted her back on his team, whatever that meant. He usually got what he wanted.

She kept walking and ended up again at Oliver's house.

Martin Hambly welcomed her and let her to the sitting room. Oliver had showered, and Alfred was asleep in front of the liquor cabinet. "I'll leave Alfred with you two," Martin said, then withdrew.

"I've told Jeremy if I'm to continue to

work with MI5, he needs to include Martin."

"And he said?"

"He said it was a brilliant idea. He has enormous respect for Martin and knows he's discreet. I think I might be jealous."

Henrietta laughed. Oliver handed her a glass of Bracken Distillers 15-year-old peated single malt. "It was rare when it was opened. Now it's almost gone. All of it, not just this bottle. I wonder how Finian feels about that, since it was put into casks when he was still a whiskey man — and a father and husband."

"He seems to have made a place for himself in Maine."

"For now," Oliver said.

They sat together on the couch, and she saw that he'd placed his mother's painting on the mantel. The police had let Oliver take it home with him. She could sense his emotion as he gazed at it. "I want to donate it to the pub in the village. It would be difficult to have it here. It wasn't until I saw it in Davy Driscoll's caravan that I remembered . . ." He cleared his throat. "Norcross thought it might be valuable. Davy knew better."

"It's a wonderful painting, Oliver. It'll be fantastic at the pub. People will love it."

"It's a way to celebrate her memory and the village she so loved. It arrived a little while ago with your car."

"It's good MI5 didn't drive my car off a cliff just for sport. I stopped at the Kershaws before I went to the pub. They're coping, as we all must do. Nigel's doing well. I realize now they were only thirteen and fifteen thirty years ago. They seemed so grown-up when I was five."

"To think they tortured themselves all these years," Oliver said quietly. "They never believed what they knew amounted to anything in terms of the investigation."

"Eugene was terrified his affection for your mother would be misconstrued."

"He was protecting her reputation as well as his own against gossip."

"It's all so terribly sad," Henrietta said. "I know that's inadequate to say but I can't find the words."

Oliver eased an arm over her shoulders and brushed his lips on her hair. "You just did, Henrietta." He sat back slightly. "Did you have a crush on an older man at fifteen?"

"At twelve on a fifteen-year-old."

"In London?"

"Here. Dolt. You were my brooding Heathcliff."

His smile was there and then gone again. "Posey didn't die alone. She had friends here. She was proud of you, Henrietta. I think she knew you were MI5."

"She always had an imagination. You can see it in her gardens."

"Is Jeremy Pearson in trouble for not figuring out Tony sooner? Must have interviewed him when did background on you."

"Jeremy lives for trouble, I do believe."

"Will you continue to live here, or will you have to go back to London?"

"I'd like to see your London apartment. We can have a drink at Claridge's. You're a regular there, from what I hear. Or am I getting ahead of myself?"

He looked at her with open affection. "Where would I be if you didn't get ahead of yourself?"

"In prison, I imagine." She snuggled next to him. "Bart Norcross pretended to be my father's only first cousin not just for a few months but for decades. No wonder he never came round until Posey was at the end. It's awkward, isn't it?"

Oliver laughed softly. "I'd say *awkward* is an understatement. What do you want now, Henrietta?"

"This moment, Oliver. Just this moment here with you."

He clinked her glass with his. "To this moment, then."

"I remember when your parents were killed. I was here visiting my aunt, and I saw you. We were small children."

"We're not small children anymore."

"Go back in time and tell the frightened little boy you were that he will be okay."

He kissed her softly. "It's the truth. I wasn't okay for a long time, but I am now."

She smiled, content.

"I think Davy Driscoll was truly remorseful as he was bleeding to death," Oliver said.

"You'll have to ask your Irish priest friend if that counts."

"I will do so."

"I'm sorry Driscoll died here, and you went through that," Henrietta said.

"It was unpleasant." He shifted to her, his eyes a dark green in the dim light. "I'm sorry, Henrietta. I left you and Martin . . ."

"We managed." She pointed her glass at the painting. "That's your great-grandmother's flowerpot in front of the dovecote. See it? I think it's planted with dahlias. We have time to plant dahlias in it this season."

Oliver shook his head. "I don't think it's the same flowerpot."

"It is. It's lovely. Your mother made up in

heart what she lacked in technique, though, didn't she? Technique would have come with practice, I'm sure." Henrietta squinted at the simple painting. "I like the black sheep that's out of the fence trotting after you and your parents on the lane. It's a clever touch. Sweet."

"That's a dog, Henrietta."

"Oh. Well, then." She smiled. "I like the dog."

He laughed and kissed her. "I love you, Henrietta," he said, then smiled and kissed her again. "We're going to have fun together."

24

Sam Padgett stopped at Finian's office late on Saturday. "I'm heading back to Boston. I know the past few days have been difficult for you," the FBI agent said. "For what it's worth, thank you for your assistance."

"You're welcome," Finian said.

Padgett nodded to Finian's breviary. "They have that online now."

"I like having it with me. An e-reader wouldn't be the same somehow."

"You keep the photos of your family close to you. Is that wise, Father?"

Finian got up from his desk, picked up his breviary. "I took them out. I'll frame them and put them in the dining room with several others I treasure. I only . . ." He hesitated, uncertain whether to finish. He rubbed a thumb on the worn cover of the breviary. "I put the photographs in there a few weeks ago. I wanted to keep Sally and the girls close during my daily prayers."

"You have doubts about your vocation, Father."

"I miss my family, Special Agent Padgett."

He nodded. "I know. The novelty of seminary and now Maine has worn off and the hurt is still there. Good luck sorting things out. Anything else I can do for you?"

"The priest you mentioned. Was he the villain?"

The FBI agent's eyes darkened. "Was and is. We'll get him one day."

"I know you will," Finian said.

"See you around, Father. Thanks again."

After the FBI agent left, Finian returned to the rectory. He saw he had an email from his sister, Mary, in Ireland.

I'm in Declan's Cross, on my way to Dublin on distillery business. Aoife O'Byrne is painting porpoises again. She says it's Oliver York's influence. She insists they're not whimsical, though. She says she thinks of you when she pours her Bracken 15.

Mary had attached a picture of a painting Aoife had given to her for the distillery. She refused any payment, saying the publicity of having one of her paintings at Bracken

434

Distillers was enough profit given the increasing popularity of their whiskey tours.

The simple life in the painting depicted one he wasn't leading and Aoife wasn't leading. Even on his laptop screen, Finian could feel the longing in the painting for something that was out of reach.

That was the effect of Aoife's work, its union with the viewer.

As he took in the colors and light of the south Irish coast, he could see Sally turning to him from the line at their cottage in the Kerry hills, with their girls' clothes drying in the summer breeze.

The memory faded, and as he looked at the image, he could hear the sounds of the sea and sheep, as if they were calling to him with the promise of home.

He shut off his laptop. Finian glanced at his breviary on the table next to him. Tonight he would give thanks for the safety of his friends, and he would start again tomorrow, a priest in a small Maine village far from home.

He was where he meant to be and so was Aoife.

Emma and Colin drove to London on Sunday, conducted their meetings on Monday and were on a flight to Boston later that day. They arrived at the HIT offices in time to meet with Matt Yankowski and Sam Padgett first thing and review the past few days.

"Oliver's growing on me," Colin said. "Still wouldn't call him a friend."

He noticed Emma smile, even if Yank and Sam didn't.

Back to work, Colin thought.

By Friday, he and Emma were in Maine. They entered Hurley's on a beautiful June evening. Colin wasn't surprised to find Finian Bracken at his favorite table in back, in front of the windows overlooking the harbor.

Finian rose, kissed Emma on the cheek and shook hands with Colin. "More Donovans will be joining us," Finian said. "I've a new Bracken expression for us to try."

"Excellent," Emma said, taking a seat.

Colin sat between her and Finian. "Hell of a week, Fin. You and Sam Padgett at loggerheads. My mother getting interviewed by the FBI. Worked out. I think she's got a crush on Sam. Pop does, too. Gets a kick out of it. She admit anything in confession?"

"Your parents are never bored," Finian said, neutral.

"Has Mike tried to get you to find out which one of us stole his baseball glove when we were kids? What if I told you it was me?"

"This isn't a confessional, Colin."

"Can't wipe the slate clean?"

"I'm not sensing contrition, regardless."

"I never said it was me."

Colin grinned as Finian opened the Bracken Distillers pot-still and splashed some into three glasses. The mystery of the stolen baseball glove would keep for now.

Finian handed Emma and Colin each a glass and then raised his glass to them. *"Sláinte."*

They raised their glasses. *"Sláinte,"* they said in unison.

In another moment, Mike, Andy and Kevin Donovan joined the gathering. Colin slid closer to Emma to make room. He slung his arm over her shoulders, everything right in his world.

It was late when Emma followed Colin into the small home they now shared above the harbor. They had a quiet weekend planned. Then it was back to Boston on Sunday and to work again on Monday. Matt Yankowski had called a full HIT meeting for ten o'clock.

"We complicate Yank's life but we get things done," Colin said. "He'd be the first to say so, but if it stops working — we have a good life, Emma."

"Yes, we do."

"A six-pack in the fridge and an apple pie in the freezer."

"Oliver's sheepskins on the floor."

Colin grinned. "I wouldn't go that far."

"That reminds me. I promised to let him know when we were back in Maine."

"It's late in England."

"Who says he's in England?"

She grabbed her phone and texted him. Colin and I are home.

His response came within seconds. Excellent. Henrietta and I have garden tips.

Meaning info the FBI could use. Or not. They could, in fact, have gardening tips. Emma typed a quick response. We welcome any and all garden tips.

She hit Send and set her phone on the counter.

Colin didn't ask about the texts. "Even jet-lagged," he said, "I bet I can carry you upstairs."

"I've no doubts whatsoever."

He swept her into his arms in a single, smooth movement. Emma laughed, and he had her up the stairs in no time. He laid her in their bed, and his mouth found hers as he settled on top of her.

"Let the honeymoon continue," she whispered, a familiar warmth spreading through her.

"I love you, Emma."

She hooked her fingers into his. "The two of us, Colin. Always and forever."

AUTHOR NOTE

Sometimes writing and life mix in unexpected ways, and that was the case with *Thief's Mark*. We welcomed a baby girl, saw my mother through life-threatening surgery and said goodbye to a beloved uncle, and through it all, I got to dive into Emma and Colin's world, with a cheeky art thief, a spy with a penchant for gardening, an Irish priest tested by a murderer's secrets and an octogenarian art detective who doesn't mind breaking a few rules. I hope *Thief's Mark* has been a pleasant diversion for you as much as it was for me.

I'm immensely grateful to my editor, Nicole Brebner, for her patience — let's just say with all that was going on, this book didn't come in early — and her "fresh eyes" on the story, and to my agent, Jodi Reamer, for being absolutely the best. A huge thank-you to the entire team at MIRA Books for their creativity and unwavering dedication to readers everywhere.

For help with canon law, whiskey and all things Irish, many thanks, once again, to my good friend John Moriarty. Not only does he answer or find the answers to all my questions, one evening over whiskey he produced a breviary that I was able to flip through, a first for me. Joe and I both are forever grateful that he encouraged us to visit Ardmore and Saint Declan's monastic ruins. Incredible — and that's where I had my first strawberry meringue; you can find the recipe on my website!

Joe and I visited Scotland for fun and research. Of course we want to go back, but I'm grateful for the amazing amount of literature I gobbled up there and online on iconic sights and Scottish history. I learned so much just chatting with a woman at the Soldier's Leap visitor center.

While I've always been a gardener (one of my earliest memories is pulling weeds with my Dutch-born father), English cottage gardens are very special. We saw many gorgeous ones while wandering the Cotswolds. Many thanks to my cousin Christine, whose lovely garden in the Netherlands was inspired by her five years living in England and in turn helped me create Aunt Posey's garden.

Most of all, I want to thank my 82-year-old mother, M. Florine Harrell Neggers, whose strength and grace through a difficult season in her life humbles and amazes me. I love you, Mom.

Now it's on to the next Sharpe & Donovan adventure. Thank you, and please feel free to get in touch with me anytime. I love to hear from readers.

Take care, and happy reading!

Carla.

CarlaNeggers.com.